W9-ANV-889

# BEND SINISTER

Books by Vladimir Nabokov

*Bend Sinister*, a novel
*The Defense*, a novel
*Despair*, a novel
*Eugene Onegin*, by Alexander Pushkin,
translated from the Russian
*Ada*, a novel
with a Commentary
*The Eye*, a novel
*The Gift*, a novel
*Glory*, a novel
*Invitation to a Beheading*, a novel
*King, Queen, Knave*, a novel
*Laughter in the Dark or Camera Obscura*,
a novel
*Lolita*, a novel
*Mary*, a novel
*Nabokov's Dozen*, a collection of short stories
*Nabokov's Quartet*, a collection of short stories
*Nikolai Gogol*, a critical biography
*Pale Fire*, a novel
*Pnin*, a novel
*Poems and Problems*
*The Real Life of Sebastian Knight*, a novel
*A Russian Beauty and Other Stories*, a collection
of short stories
*The Song of Igor's Campaign*, Anon.,
translated from Old Russian
*Speak, Memory or Conclusive Evidence*,
a memoir
*Three Russian Poets*, verse translation
from the Russian
*Transparent Things*, a novel
*The Waltz Invention*, a drama

# BEND SINISTER

by
Vladimir Nabokov

**McGraw-Hill Book Company**
New York • St. Louis • San Francisco • Düsseldorf • Mexico • Montreal
Panama • Paris • São Paulo • Tokyo • Toronto

First McGraw-Hill Paperback Edition, 1974

3456789 FGRFGR 79

Library of Congress Cataloging in Publication Data

Nabokov, Vladimir Vladimirovich, 1899–
Bend sinister.

I. Title.
PZ3.N121Be6 [PS3527.A15] 813'.5'4 73-5990
ISBN 0-07-045710-7

# INTRODUCTION

BEND SINISTER was the first novel I wrote in America, and that was half a dozen years after she and I had adopted each other. The greater part of the book was composed in the winter and spring of 1945–1946, at a particularly cloudless and vigorous period of life. My health was excellent. My daily consumption of cigarettes had reached the four-package mark. I slept at least four or five hours, the rest of the night walking pencil in hand about the dingy little flat in Craigie Circle, Cambridge, Massachusetts, where I lodged under an old lady with feet of stone and above a young woman with hypersensitive hearing. Every day including Sundays, I would spend up to 10 hours studying the structure of certain butterflies in the laboratorial paradise of the Harvard Museum of Comparative Zoology; but three times a week I stayed there only till noon and then tore myself away from microscope and camera lucida to travel to Wellesley (by tram and bus, or subway and railway), where I taught college girls Russian grammar and literature.

The book was finished on a warm rainy night, more or less as described at the end of Chapter Eighteen. A kind friend, Edmund Wilson, read the typescript and recommended the book to Allen Tate, who had Holt publish it in 1947. I was deeply immersed in other labors but nonetheless managed to discern the dull thud it made. Praises, as far as I can recall, rang out only in two weeklies—TIME and *The New Yorker*, I think.

The term "bend sinister" means a heraldic bar or band drawn from the left side (and popularly, but incorrectly, supposed to denote bastardy). This choice of title was an attempt to suggest an outline broken by refraction, a distortion in the mirror of being, a wrong turn taken by life, a sinistral and sinister world. The title's drawback is that a solemn reader looking for "general ideas" or "human interest" (which is much the same thing) in a novel may be led to look for them in this one.

There exist few things more tedious than a discussion of general ideas inflicted by author or reader upon a work of fiction. The purpose of this foreword is not to show that *Bend Sinister* belongs or does not belong to "serious literature" (which is a euphemism for the hollow profundity and the ever-welcome commonplace). I have never been interested in what is called the literature of social comment (in journalistic and commercial parlance: "great books"). I am not "sincere," I am not "provocative," I am not "satirical." I am neither a didacticist nor an allegorizer. Politics and economics, atomic bombs, primitive and abstract art forms, the entire Orient, symptoms of "thaw" in Soviet Russia, the Future of Mankind, and so on, leave me supremely indifferent. As in the case of my *Invitation to a Beheading*—with which this book has obvious affinities—automatic comparisons between *Bend Sinister* and Kafka's creations or Orwell's clichés would go merely to prove that the automaton could not have read either the great German writer or the mediocre English one.

Similarly, the influence of my epoch on my present book

is as negligible as the influence of my books, or at least of this book, on my epoch. There can be distinguished, no doubt, certain reflections in the glass directly caused by the idiotic and despicable regimes that we all know and that have brushed against me in the course of my life: worlds of tyranny and torture, of Fascists and Bolshevists, of Philistine thinkers and jack-booted baboons. No doubt, too, without those infamous models before me I could not have interlarded this fantasy with bits of Lenin's speeches, and a chunk of the Soviet constitution, and gobs of Nazist pseudo-efficiency.

While the system of holding people in hostage is as old as the oldest war, a fresher note is introduced when a tyrannic state is at war with its own subjects and may hold any citizen in hostage with no law to restrain it. An even more recent improvement is the subtle use of what I shall term "the lever of love"—the diabolical method (applied so successfully by the Soviets) of tying a rebel to his wretched country by his own twisted heartstrings. It is noteworthy, however, that in *Bend Sinister* Paduk's still young police state—where a certain dull-wittedness is a national trait of the people (augmenting thereby the possibilities of muddling and bungling so typical, thank God, of all tyrannies)—lags behind actual regimes in successfully working this lever of love, for which at first it rather haphazardly gropes, losing time on the needless persecution of Krug's friends, and only by chance realizing (in Chapter Fifteen) that by grabbing his little child one would force him to do whatever one wished.

The story in *Bend Sinister* is not really about life and death in a grotesque police state. My characters are not "types," not carriers of this or that "idea." Paduk, the abject dictator and Krug's former schoolmate (regularly tormented by the boys, regularly caressed by the school janitor); Doctor Alexander, the government's agent; the ineffable Hustav; icy Crystalsen and hapless Kolokololiteishchikov; the three Bachofen sisters; the farcical policeman Mac; the brutal and imbecile soldiers—all of them are only absurd mirages, illusions oppressive to Krug during his brief spell of being, but harmlessly fading away when I dismiss the cast.

The main theme of *Bend Sinister*, then, is the beating of Krug's loving heart, the torture an intense tenderness is subjected to—and it is for the sake of the pages about David and his father that the book was written and should be read. Two other themes accompany the main one: the theme of dim-brained brutality which thwarts its own purpose by destroying the right child and keeping the wrong one; and the theme of Krug's blessed madness when he suddenly perceives the simple reality of things and knows but cannot express in the words of his world that he and his son and his wife and everybody else are merely my whims and megrims.

Is there any judgment on my part carried out, any sentence pronounced, any satisfaction given to the moral sense? If imbeciles and brutes can punish other brutes and imbeciles, and if crime still retains an objective meaning in the meaningless world of Paduk (all of which is doubtful), we may affirm that crime *is* punished at the end of the book when the uniformed waxworks are really hurt, and the dummies are at last in quite dreadful pain, and pretty Mariette gently bleeds, staked and torn by the lust of forty soldiers.

The plot starts to breed in the bright broth of a rain puddle. The puddle is observed by Krug from a window of the hospital where his wife is dying. The oblong pool, shaped like a cell that is about to divide, reappears subthematically throughout the novel, as an ink blot in Chapter

Four, an inkstain in Chapter Five, spilled milk in Chapter Eleven, the infusoria-like image of ciliated thought in Chapter Twelve, the footprint of a phosphorescent islander in Chapter Eighteen, and the imprint a soul leaves in the intimate texture of space in the closing paragraph. The puddle thus kindled and rekindled in Krug's mind remains linked up with the image of his wife not only because he had contemplated the inset sunset from her death-bedside, but also because this little puddle vaguely evokes in him my link with him: a rent in his world leading to another world of tenderness, brightness and beauty.

And a companion image even more eloquently speaking of Olga is the vision of her divesting herself of herself, of her jewels, of the necklace and tiara of earthly life, in front of a brilliant mirror. It is this picture that appears six times in the course of a dream, among the liquid, dream-refracted memories of Krug's boyhood (Chapter Five).

Paronomasia is a kind of verbal plague, a contagious sickness in the world of words; no wonder they are monstrously and ineptly distorted in Padukgrad, where everybody is merely an anagram of everybody else. The book teems with stylistic distortions, such as puns crossed with anagrams (in Chapter Two, the Russian circumference, *krug*, turns into a Teutonic cucumber, *gurk*, with an additional allusion to Krug's reversing his journey across the bridge): suggestive neologisms (the *amorandola*—a local guitar); parodies of narrative clichés ("who had overheard the last words" and "who seemed to be the leader of the group," Chapter Two); spoonerisms ("silence" and "science" playing leapfrog in Chapter Seventeen); and of course the hybridization of tongues.

The language of the country, as spoken in Padukgrad and Omigod, as well as in the Kur valley, the Sakra mountains and the region of Lake Malheur, is a mongrel blend of Slavic and Germanic with a strong strain of ancient Kuranian running through it (and especially prominent in ejaculations of woe); but colloquial Russian and German are also used by representatives of all groups, from the vulgar Elkwilist soldier to the discriminating intellectual. Ember, for instance, in Chapter Seven, gives his friend a sample of the three first lines of Hamlet's soliloquy (Act III, Scene I) translated into the vernacular (with a pseudo-scholarly interpretation of the first phrase taken to refer to the contemplated killing of Claudius, i.e., "is the murder to be or not to be?"). He follows this up with a Russian version of part of the Queen's speech in Act IV, Scene VII (also not without a built-in scholium) and a splendid Russian rendering of the prose passage in Act III, Scene II, beginning, "Would not this, Sir, and a forest of feathers. . . ." Problems of translation, fluid transitions from one tongue to another, semantic transparencies yielding layers of receding or welling sense are as characteristic of Sinisterbad as are the monetary problems of more habitual tyrannies.

In this crazy-mirror of terror and art a pseudo-quotation made up of obscure Shakespeareanisms (Chapter Three) somehow produces, despite its lack of literal meaning, the blurred diminutive image of the acrobatic performance that so gloriously supplies the bravura ending for the next chapter. A chance selection of iambic incidents culled from the prose of *Moby Dick* appears in the guise of "a famous American poem" (Chapter Twelve). If the "admiral" and his "fleet" in a trite official speech (Chapter Four) are at first mis-heard by the widower as "animal" and its "feet," this is because the chance reference, coming just before, to a man losing his wife dims and distorts the next sentence. When in Chapter Three Ember recalls four best-selling novels, the alert commuter cannot fail to notice that the titles of three of them form, roughly, the lavatorial injunction not to Flush the Toilet when the Train Passes through Towns and Villages, while the fourth alludes to Werfel's trashy *Song of Bernadette*, half altar bread and half bonbon. Similarly, at the beginning of Chapter Six, where some other popular romances of the day are mentioned, a slight shift in the spectrum of meaning replaces the title *Gone with the Wind* (filched from Dowson's *Cynara*) with that of *Flung Roses* (filched from the same poem), and a fusion between two cheap novels (by Remarque and Sholokhov) produces the neat *All Quiet on the Don.*

Stéphane Mallarmé has left three or four immortal bagatelles, and among these is *L'Après-Midi d'un Faune* (first drafted in 1865). Krug is haunted by a passage from this voluptuous eclogue where the faun accuses the nymph of disengaging herself from his embrace "*sans pitié du sanglot dont j'étais encore ivre*" ("spurning the spasm with which I still was drunk"). Fractured parts of this line re-echo through the book, cropping up for instance in the *malarma ne donje* of Dr. Azureus' wail of rue (Chapter Four) and in the *donje te zankoriv* of apologetic Krug when he interrupts the kiss of the university student and his little Carmen (foreshadowing Mariette) in the same chapter. Death, too, is a ruthless interruption; the widower's heavy sensuality seeks a pathetic outlet in Mariette, but as he avidly clasps the haunches of the chance nymph he is about to enjoy, a deafening din at the door breaks the throbbing rhythm forever.

It may be asked if it is really worth an author's while to devise and distribute these delicate markers whose very nature requires that they be not too conspicuous. Who will bother to notice that Pankrat Tzikutin, the shabby old pogromystic (Chapter Thirteen) is Socrates Hemlocker; that "the child is bold" in the allusion to immigration (Chapter Eighteen) is a stock phrase used to test a would-be American citizen's reading ability; that Linda did not steal the porcelain owlet after all (beginning of Chapter Ten); that the urchins in the yard (Chapter Seven) have been drawn by Saul Steinberg; that the "other rivermaid's father" (Chapter Seven) is James Joyce who wrote *Winnipeg Lake* (ibid.); and that the last word of the book is *not* a misprint (as assumed in the past by at least one proofreader)? Most people will not even mind having missed all this; well-wishers will bring their own symbols and mobiles, and portable radios, to my little party; ironists will point out the fatal fatuity of my explications in this foreword and advise me to have footnotes next time (footnotes always seem comic to a certain type of mind). In the long run, however, it is only the author's private satisfaction that counts. I reread my books rarely, and then only for the utilitarian purpose of controlling a translation or checking a new edition; but when I do go through them again, what pleases me most is the wayside murmur of this or that hidden theme.

Thus, in the second paragraph of Chapter Five comes the first intimation that "someone is in the know"—a mysterious intruder who takes advantage of Krug's dream to convey his own peculiar code message. The intruder is not the Viennese Quack (all my books should be stamped Freudians, Keep Out), but an anthropomorphic deity impersonated by me. In the last chapter of the book this deity experiences a pang of pity for his creature and hastens to take over. Krug, in a sudden moonburst of madness, understands that he is in good hands: nothing on earth really matters, there is nothing to fear, and death is but a question of style, a mere literary device, a musical resolution. And as Olga's rosy soul, emblemized already in an earlier chapter (Nine), bombinates in the damp dark at the bright window of my room, comfortably Krug returns unto the bosom of his maker.

September 9, 1963 —VLADIMIR NABOKOV
*Montreux*

# 1

AN OBLONG PUDDLE inset in the coarse asphalt; like a fancy footprint filled to the brim with quicksilver; like a spatulate hole through which you can see the nether sky. Surrounded. I note, by a diffuse tentacled black dampness where some dull dun dead leaves have stuck. Drowned, I should say, before the puddle had shrunk to its present size.

It lies in shadow but contains a sample of the brightness beyond, where there are trees and two houses. Look closer. Yes, it reflects a portion of pale blue sky—mild infantile shade of blue—taste of milk in my mouth because I had a mug of that colour thirty-five years ago. It also reflects a brief tangle of bare twigs and the brown sinus of a stouter limb cut off by its rim and a transverse bright cream-coloured band. You have dropped something, this is yours, creamy house in the sunshine beyond.

When the November wind has its recurrent icy spasm, a rudimentary vortex of ripples creases the brightness of the puddle.

Two leaves, two triskelions, like two shuddering three-legged bathers coming at a run for a swim, are borne by their impetus right into the middle where with a sudden slowdown they float quite flat. Twenty minutes past four. View from a hospital window.

November trees, poplars, I imagine, two of them growing straight out of the asphalt: all of them in the cold bright sun, bright richly furrowed bark and an intricate sweep of numberless burnished bare twigs, old gold—because getting more of the falsely mellow sun in the higher air. Their immobility is in contrast with the spasmodic ruffling of the inset reflection—for the visible emotion of a tree is the mass of its leaves, and there remain hardly more than thirty-seven or so here and there on one side of the tree. They just flicker a little, of a neutral tint, but burnished by the sun to the same ikontinct as the intricate trillions of twigs. Swooning blue of the sky crossed by pale motionless superimposed cloud wisps.

The operation has not been successful and my wife will die.

Beyond a low fence, in the sun, in the bright starkness, a slaty house front has for frame two cream-coloured lateral pilasters and a broad blank unthinking cornice: the frosting of a shopworn cake. Windows look black by day. Thirteen of them; white lattice, green shutters. All very clear, but the day will not last. Something has moved in the blackness of one window: an ageless housewife—ope as my dentist in my milktooth days used to say, a Dr. Wollison—opens the window, shakes out something and you may now close.

The other house (to the right, beyond a jutting garage) is quite golden now. The many-limbed poplars cast their alembic ascending shadow bands upon it, in between their own burnished black-shaded spreading and curving limbs. But it all fades, it fades, she used to sit in a field, painting a sunset that would never stay, and a peasant child, very small and quiet and bashful in spite of its mousy persistence would stand at her elbow, and look at the easel, at the paints, at her wet aquarelle brush poised like the tongue of a snake—but the sunset had gone, leaving only a clutter of the purplish remnants of the day, piled up anyhow—ruins, junk.

The dappled surface of that other house is crossed by an outer stairway, and the dormer window to which this leads is now as bright as the puddle was—for the latter has now changed to a dull liquid white traversed by dead black, so that it looks like an achromatic copy of the painting previously seen.

I shall probably never forget the dull green of the narrow lawn in front of the first house (to which the dappled one stands sideways). A lawn both dishevelled and baldish, with a middle parting of asphalt, and all studded with pale dun leaves. The colours go. There is a last glow in the window to which the stairs of the day still lead. But it is all up, and if the lights were turned on inside they would kill what remains of the outside day. The cloud wisps are flushed with flesh pink, and the trillions of twigs are becoming extremely distinct: and now there is no more colour below: the houses, the lawn, the fence, the vistas in between, everything has been toned down to a kind of auburn grey. Oh, the glass of the puddle is bright mauve.

They have turned on the lights in the house I am in, and the view in the window has died. It is all inky black with a pale blue inky sky—'runs blue, writes black' as that ink bottle said, but it did not, nor does the sky, but the trees do with their trillions of twigs.

# 2

KRUG HALTED in the doorway and looked down at her upturned face. The movement (pulsation, radiation) of its features (crumpled ripples) was due to her speaking, and he realized that this movement had been going on for some time. Possibly all the way down the hospital stairs. With her faded blue eyes and long wrinkled upper lip she resembled someone he had known for years but could not recall—funny. A side line of indifferent cognition led him to place her as the head nurse. The continuation of her voice came into being as if a needle had found its groove. Its groove in the disc of his mind. Of his mind that had started to revolve as he halted in the doorway and looked down at her upturned face. The movement of its features was now audible.

She pronounced the word that meant "fighting" with a north-western accent: "*fakhtung*" instead of "*fahtung*." The person (male?) whom she resembled peered out of the mist and was gone before he could identify her—or him.

"They are still fighting," she said. "... dark and dangerous. The town is dark, the streets are dangerous. Really, you had better spend the night here.... In a hospital bed" (*gospitalisha kruvka*—again that marshland accent and he felt like a heavy crow—*kruv*—flapping against the sunset). "Please! Or you could wait at least for Dr. Krug who has a car."

"No relative of mine," he said. "Pure coincidence."

"I know," she said, "but still you ought not to not to not to not to"—(the world went on revolving although it had expended its sense).

"I have," he said, "a pass." And, opening his wallet, he went so far as to unfold the paper in question with trembling fingers. He had thick (let me see) clumsy (there) fingers which always trembled slightly. The inside of his cheeks was methodically sucked in and smacked ever so slightly when he was in the act of unfolding something. Krug—for it was he—showed her the blurred paper. He was a huge tired man with a stoop.

"But it might not help," she whined, "a stray bullet might hit you."

(You see the good woman thought that bullets were still *flukhtung* about in the night, meteoric remnants of the firing that had long ceased.)

"I am not interested in politics," he said. "And I have only the river to cross. A friend of mine will come to fix things tomorrow morning."

He patted her on the elbow and went on his way.

He yielded, with what pleasure there was in the act, to the soft warm pressure of tears. The sense of relief did not last, for as soon as he let them flow they became atrociously hot and abundant so as to interfere with his eyesight and respiration. He walked through a spasmodic fog down the cobbled Omigod Lane towards the embankment. Tried clearing his throat but it merely led to another gasping sob. He was sorry now he had yielded to that temptation for he could not stop yielding and the throbbing man in him was soaked. As usual he discriminated between the throbbing one and the one that looked on: looked on with concern, with sympathy, with a sigh, or with bland surprise. This was the last stronghold of the dualism he abhorred. The square root of I is I. Footnotes, forget-me-nots. The stranger quietly watching the torrents of local grief from an abstract bank. A familiar figure, albeit anonymous and aloof. He saw me crying when I was ten and led me to a looking glass in an unused room (with an empty parrot cage in the corner) so that I might study my dissolving face. He has listened to me with raised eyebrows when I said things which I had no business to say. In every mask I tried on, there were slits for his eyes. Even at the very moment when I was rocked by the convulsion men value most. My saviour. My witness. And now Krug reached for his handkerchief which was a dim white blob somewhere in the depths of his private night. Having at last crept out of a labyrinth of pockets, he mopped and wiped the dark sky and amorphous houses; then he saw he was nearing the bridge.

On other nights it used to be a line of lights with a certain lilt, a metrical incandescence with every foot rescanned and prolonged by reflections in the black snaky water. This night there was only a diffused glow where a Neptune of granite loomed upon his square rock which rock continued as a parapet which parapet was lost in the mist. As Krug, trudging steadily, approached, two Ekwilist soldiers barred his way. More were lurking around, and when a lantern moved, knight-wise, to check him, he noticed a little man dressed as a *meshchaniner* [petty bourgeois] standing with folded arms and smiling a sickly smile. The two soldiers (both, oddly enough, had pockmarked faces) were asking, Krug understood, for his

(Krug's) papers. While he was fumbling for the pass they bade him hurry and mentioned a brief love affair they had had, or would have, or invited him to have with his mother.

"I doubt," said Krug as he went through his pockets, "whether these fancies which have bred maggot-like from ancient taboos could be really transformed into acts—and this for various reasons. Here it is" (it almost wandered away while I was talking to the orphan—I mean, the nurse).

They grabbed it as if it had been a hundred krun note. While they were subjecting the pass to an intense examination, he blew his nose and slowly put back his handkerchief into the left-hand pocket of his overcoat; but on second thought transferred it to his right-hand trouser pocket.

"What's this?" asked the fatter of the two, marking a word with the nail of the thumb he was pressing against the paper. Krug, holding his reading spectacles to his eyes, peered over the man's hand. "University," he said. "Place where things are taught—nothing very important."

"No, this," said the soldier.

"Oh, 'philosophy.' *You* know. When you try to imagine a *mirok* [small pink potato] without the least reference to any you have eaten or will eat." He gestured vaguely with his glasses and then slipped them into their lecture-hall nook (vest pocket).

"What is your business? Why are you loafing near the bridge?" asked the fat soldier while his companion tried to decipher the permit in his turn.

"Everything can be explained," said Krug. "For the last ten days or so I have been going to the Prinzin Hospital every morning. A private matter. Yesterday my friends got me this document because they foresaw that the bridge would be guarded after dark. My home is on the south side. I am returning much later than usual."

"Patient or doctor?" asked the thinner soldier.

"Let me read you what this little paper is meant to convey," said Krug, stretching out a helpful hand.

"Read on while I hold it," said the thin one, holding it upside down.

"Inversion," said Krug, "does not trouble me, but I need my glasses." He went through the familiar nightmare of overcoat—coat—trouser pockets, and found an empty spectacle case. He was about to resume his search.

"Hands up," said the fatter soldier with hysterical suddenness.

Krug obeyed, holding the case heavenward.

The left part of the moon was so strongly shaded as to be almost invisible in the pool of clear but dark ether across which it seemed to be swiftly floating, an illusion due to the moonward movement of some small chinchilla clouds; its right part, however, a somewhat porous but thoroughly talcpowdered edge or cheek, was vividly illumined by the artificial-looking blaze of an invisible sun. The whole effect was remarkable.

The soldiers searched him. They found an empty flask which quite recently had contained a pint of brandy. Although a burly man, Krug was ticklish and he uttered little grunts and squirmed slightly as they rudely investigated his ribs. Something jumped and dropped with a grasshopper's click. They had located the glasses.

"All right," said the fat soldier. "Pick them up, you old fool."

Krug stooped, groped, side-stepped—and there was a horrible scrunch under the toe of his heavy shoe.

"Dear, dear, this is a singular position," he said. "For now there is not much to choose between my physical illiteracy and your mental one."

"We are going to arrest you," said the fat soldier. "It will put an end to your clowning, you old drunkard. And when we get fed up with guarding you, we'll chuck you into the water and shoot at you while you drown."

Another soldier came up idly juggling with a flashlight and again Krug had a glimpse of a pale-faced little man standing apart and smiling.

"I want some fun too," the third soldier said.

"Well, well," said Krug. "Fancy seeing you here. How is your cousin, the gardener?"

The newcomer, an ugly, ruddy-cheeked country lad, looked at Krug blankly and then pointed to the fat soldier.

"It is his cousin, not mine."

"Yes, of course," said Krug quickly. "Exactly what I meant. How is he, that gentle gardener? Has he recovered the use of his left leg?"

"We have not seen each other for some time," answered the fat soldier moodily. "He lives in Bervok."

"A fine fellow," said Krug. "We were all so sorry when he fell into that gravel pit. Tell him, since he exists, that Professor Krug often recalls the talks we had over a jug of cider. Anyone can create the future but only a wise man can create the past. Grand apples in Bervok."

"This is his permit," said the fat moody one to the rustic ruddy one, who took the paper gingerly and at once handed it back.

"You had better call that *ved' min syn* [son of a witch] there," he said.

It was then that the little man was brought forward. He seemed to labour under the impression that Krug was some sort of superior in relation to the soldiers for he started to complain in a thin almost feminine voice, saying that he and his brother owned a grocery store on the other side and that both had venerated the Ruler since the blessed seventeenth of that month. The rebels were crushed, thank God, and he wished to join his brother so that a Victorious People might obtain the delicate foods he and his deaf brother sold.

"Cut it out," said the fat soldier, "and read this."

The pale grocer complied. Professor Krug had been given full liberty by the Committee of Public Welfare to circulate after dusk. To cross from the south town to the north one. And back. The reader desired to know why ne could not accompany the professor across the bridge. He was briskly kicked back into the darkness. Krug proceeded to cross the black river.

This interlude had turned the torrent away: it was now running unseen behind a wall of darkness. He remembered other imbeciles he and she had studied, a study conducted with a kind of gloating enthusiastic disgust. Men who got drunk on beer in sloppy bars, the process of thought satisfactorily replaced by swine-toned radio music. Murderers. The respect a business magnate evokes in his home town. Literary critics praising the books of their friends or partisans. Flaubertian *farceurs*. Fraternities, mystic orders. People who are amused by trained animals. The members of reading clubs. All those who *are* because they do *not* think, thus refuting Cartesianism. The thrifty peasant. The booming politician. Her relatives—her dreadful humourless family. Suddenly, with the vividness of a praedormital image or of a bright-robed lady on stained glass, she drifted across his retina, in profile, carrying something—a book, a baby, or just letting the cherry paint on her fingernails dry—and the wall dissolved, the torrent was loosed again.

Krug stopped, trying to control himself, with the palm of his ungloved hand resting on the parapet as in former days frock-coated men of parts used to be photographed in imitation of portraits by old masters—hand on book, on chair back, on globe—but as soon as the camera had clicked everything started to move, to gush, and he walked on—jerkily, because of the sobs shaking his ungloved soul. The lights of the thither side were nearing in a shudder of concentric prickly iridescent circles, dwindling again to a blurred glow when you blinked, and extravagantly expanding immediately afterwards. He was a big heavy man. He felt an intimate connection with the black lacquered water lapping and heaving under the stone arches of the bridge.

Presently he stopped again. Let us touch this and look at this. In the faint light (of the moon? of his tears? of the few lamps the dying fathers of the city had lit from a mechanical sense of duty?) his hand found a certain pattern of roughness: a furrow in the stone of the parapet and a knob and a hole with some moisture inside—all of it highly magnified as the 30,000 pits in the crust of the plastic moon are on the large glossy print which the proud selenographer shows his young wife. On this particular night, just after they had tried to turn over to me her purse, her comb, her cigarette holder, I found and touched this—a selected combination, details of the bas-relief. I had never touched this particular knob before and shall never find it again. This moment of conscious contact holds a drop of solace. The emergency brake of time. Whatever the present moment is, I have stopped it. Too late. In the course of our, let me see, twelve, twelve and three months, years of life together, I ought to have immobilized by this simple method millions of moments;

paying perhaps terrific fines, but stopping the train. Say, why did you do it? the popeyed conductor might ask. Because I liked the view. Because I wanted to stop those speeding trees and the path twisting between them. By stepping on its receding tail. What happened to her would perhaps not have happened, had I been in the habit of stopping this or that bit of our common life, prophylactically, prophetically, letting this or that moment rest and breathe in peace. Taming time. Giving her pulse respite. Pampering life, life—our patient.

Krug—for it was still he—walked on, with the impression of the rough pattern still tingling and clinging to the ball of his thumb. This end of the bridge was brighter. The soldiers who bade him halt looked livelier, better shaven, wore neater uniforms. There was also more of them, and more nocturnal travellers had been held up: two old men with their bicycles and what might be termed a gentleman (velvet collar of overcoat set up, hands thrust into pockets) and his girl, a bedraggled bird of paradise.

Pietro—or at least the soldier resembled Pietro, the head waiter at the University Club—Pietro the soldier examined Krug's pass and said in cultured accents:

"I fail to understand, Professor, what enabled you to effect the crossing of the bridge. You had no right whatever to do so since this pass has not been signed by my colleagues of the north side guard. I am afraid you must go back and have it done by them according to emergency regulations. Otherwise I cannot let you enter the south side of the city. *Je regrette* but a law is a law."

"Quite true," said Krug. "Unfortunately they are unable to read, let alone write."

"This does not concern us," said bland grave handsome Pietro—and his companions nodded in grave judicious assent. "No, I cannot let you pass, unless, I repeat, your identity and innocence are guaranteed by the signature of the opposite sentry."

"But cannot we turn the bridge the other way round, so to speak?" said Krug patiently. "I mean—give it a full turn. You sign the permits of those who cross over from the south side to the north one, don't you? Well, let us reverse the process. Sign this valuable paper and suffer me to go to my bed in Peregolm Lane."

Pietro shook his head: "I do not follow you, Professor. We have exterminated the enemy—aye, we have crushed him under our heels. But one or two hydra heads are still alive, and we cannot take any chances. In a week or so, Professor, I can assure you the city will go back to normal conditions. Isn't that a promise, lads?" Pietro added, turning to the other soldiers who assented eagerly, their honest intelligent faces lit up by that civic ardour which transfigures even the plainest man.

"I appeal to your imagination," said Krug. "Imagine I was going the other way. In fact, I *was* going the other way this morning, when the bridge was not guarded. To place sentries only at nightfall is a very conventional notion—but let it pass. Let me pass too."

"Not unless this paper is signed," said Pietro and turned away.

"Aren't you lowering to a considerable extent the standards by which the function, if any, of the human brain is judged?" rumbled Krug.

"Hush, hush," said another soldier, putting his finger to his cleaved lip and then quickly pointing at Pietro's broad back. "Hush. Pietro is perfectly right. Go."

"Yes, go," said Pietro *who had overheard the last words.* "And when you come again with your pass signed and everything in order—think of the inner satisfaction you will feel when we countersign it. And for us, too, it will be a pleasure. The night is still young, and anyway, we should not shirk a certain amount of physical exertion if we want to be worthy of our Ruler. Go, Professor."

Pietro looked at the two bearded old men patiently gripping their bicycle handles, their knuckles white in the lamplight, their lost dog eyes watching him intently. "You may go, too," said the generous fellow.

With an alacrity that was in odd contrast with their advanced age and spindle legs, the bearded ones jumped upon their mounts and pedalled off, wobbling in their eagerness to get away and exchanging rapid guttural remarks. What were they discussing? The pedigree of their bicycles? The price of some special make? The condition of the race track? Were their cries exclamations of encouragement? Friendly taunts? Did they banter the ball of a joke seen years before in the *Simplizissimus* or the *Strekoza?* One always desires to find out what people who ride by are saying to each other.

Krug walked as fast as he could. Clouds had masked our siliceous satellite. Somewhere near the middle of the bridge he overtook the grizzled cyclists. Both were inspecting the anal ruby of one of the bicycles. The other lay on its side like a stricken horse with half-raised sad head. He walked fast and held his pass in his fist. What would happen if I threw it into the Kur? Doomed to walk back and forth on a bridge which has ceased to be one since neither bank is really attainable. Not a bridge but an hourglass which somebody keeps reversing, with me, the fluent fine sand, inside. Or the grass stalk you pick with an ant running up it, and you turn the stalk upside down the moment he gets to the tip, which becomes the pit, and the poor little fool repeats his performance. The old men overtook him in their turn, clattering lickety-split through the mist, gallantly galloping, goading their old black horses with blood-red spurs.

" 'Tis I again," said Krug as his slovenly friends clustered around him. "You forgot to sign my pass. Here it is. Let us get it over with promptly. Scrawl a cross, or a telephone booth curlicue, or a gammadion, or something. I dare not hope that you have one of those stamping affairs at hand."

While still speaking, he realized that they did not recognize him at all. They looked at his pass. They shrugged their shoulders as if ridding themselves of the burden of knowledge. They even scratched their heads, a quaint method used in that country because supposed to prompt a richer flow of blood to the cells of thought.

"Do you live on the bridge?" asked the fat soldier.

"No," said Krug. "Do try to understand. *C'est simple comme bonjour*, as Pietro would say. They sent me back because they had no evidence that you let me pass. From a formal point of view I am not on the bridge at all."

"He may have climbed up from a barge," said a dubious voice.

"No, no," said Krug. "I not bargee-bargee. You still do not understand. I am going to put it as simply as possible. They of the solar side saw heliocentrically what you tellurians saw geocentrically, and unless these two aspects are somehow combined, I, the visualized object, must keep shuttling in the universal night."

"It is the man who knows Gurk's cousin," cried one of the soldiers in a burst of recognition.

"Ah, excellent," said Krug much relieved. "I was forgetting the gentle gardener. So one point is settled. Now, come on, do something."

The pale grocer stepped forward and said:

"I have a suggestion to make. I sign his, he signs mine, and we both cross."

Somebody was about to cuff him, but the fat soldier, *who seemed to be the leader of the group*, intervened and remarked that it was a sensible idea.

"Lend me your back," said the grocer to Krug; and hastily unscrewing his fountain pen, he proceeded to press the paper against Krug's left shoulder blade. "What name shall I put, brothers?" he asked of the soldiers.

They shuffled and nudged each other, none of them willing to disclose a cherished incognito.

"Put Gurk," said the bravest at last, pointing to the fat soldier.

"Shall I?" asked the grocer, turning nimbly to Gurk.

They got his consent after a little coaxing. Having dealt with Krug's pass, the grocer in his turn stood before Krug. Leapfrog, or the admiral in his cocked hat resting the telescope on the young sailor's shoulder (the grey horizon going seesaw, a white gull veering, but no land in sight).

"I hope," said Krug, "that I will be able to do it as nicely as I would if I had my glasses."

On the dotted line it will not be. Your pen is hard. Your back is soft. Cucumber. Blot it with a branding iron.

Both papers were passed around and bashfully approved of.

Krug and the grocer started walking across the bridge; at least Krug walked: his little companion expressed his delirious joy by running in circles around Krug, he ran in widening circles and imitated a railway engine: chug-chug, his elbows pressed to his ribs, his feet moving almost together, taking small firm staccato steps with knees slightly bent. Parody of a child—*my* child.

"*Stoy, chort* [stop, curse you]," cried Krug, for the first time that night using his real voice.

The grocer ended his gyrations by a spiral that brought him back into Krug's orbit whereupon he fell in with the latter's stride and walked beside him, chatting airily.

"I must apologize," he said, "for my demeanor. But I am sure you feel the same as I do. This has been quite an ordeal. I thought they would never let me go—and those allusions to strangling and drowning were a bit tactless. Nice boys, I admit, hearts of gold, but uncivilized—their only defect really. Otherwise, I agree with you, they are grand. While I was standing——"

This is the fourth lamp-post, and one tenth of the bridge. Few of them are alight.

". . . My brother who is practically stone deaf has a store on Theod—sorry, Emrald Avenue. In fact we are partners, but I have a little business of my own which keeps me away most of the time. In view of the present events he needs my help, as we all do. You might think——"

Lamp-post number ten.

". . . but I look at it this way. Of course our Ruler is a great man, a genius, a one-man-in-a-century-man. The kind of boss people like you and me have been always wanting. But he is bitter. He is bitter because for the last ten years our so-called liberal government has kept hounding him, torturing him, clapping him into jail for every word he said. I shall always remember—and shall pass it on to our grandsons—what he said that time they arrested him at the big meeting in the Godeon: "I," he said, "am born to lead as naturally as a bird flies." I think it is the greatest thought ever expressed in human language, and the most poetical one. Name me the writer who has said anything approaching it? I shall go even further and say——"

This is number fifteen. Or sixteen?

". . . if we look at it from another angle. We are quiet

people, we want a quiet life, we want our business to go on smoothly. We want the quiet pleasures of life. For instance, everybody knows that the best moment of the day is when one comes back from work, unbuttons one's vest, turns on some light music, and sits in one's favourite armchair, enjoying the jokes in the evening paper or discussing one's neighbours with the little woman. That is what we mean by true culture, true human civilization, the things for the sake of which so much blood and ink have been shed in ancient Rome or Egypt. But nowadays you continuously hear silly people say that for the likes of you and me that kind of life has gone. Do not believe them—it has not. And not only has it not gone——"

Are there more than forty? This must be at least half of the bridge.

"...shall I tell you what has really been going on all those years? Well, firstly, we were made to pay impossible taxes; secondly, all those Parliament members and Ministers of State whom we never saw or heard, kept drinking more and more champagne and sleeping with fatter and fatter whores. That is what they call liberty! And what happened in the meantime? Somewhere deep in the woods, in a log cabin, the Ruler was writing his manifestos, like a tracked beast. The things they did to his followers! Jesus! I have heard dreadful stories from my brother-in-law who has belonged to the party since his youth. He is certainly the brainiest man I have ever met. So you see——"

No, less than half.

"...you are a professor I understand. Well, Professor, from now on a great future lies before you. We must now educate the ignorant, the moody, the wicked—but educate them in a new way. Just think of all the trash we used to be taught.... Think of the millions of unnecessary books accumulating in libraries. The books they print! You know—you will never believe me—but I have been told by a reliable person that in one bookshop there actually is a book of at least a hundred pages which is wholly devoted to the anatomy of bedbugs. Or things in foreign languages which nobody can read. And all the money spent on nonsense. All those huge museums—just one long hoax. Makes you gape at a stone that somebody picked up in his backyard. Less books and more commonsense—that's my motto. People are made to live together, to do business with one another, to talk, to sing songs together, to meet in clubs and stores, and at street corners—and in churches and stadiums on Sundays—and not sit alone, thinking dangerous thoughts. My wife had a lodger——"

The man with the velvet collar and his girl passed by quickly with pit-a-pat of fugitive footfalls, not looking back.

". . . change it all. You will teach young people to count, to spell, to tie a parcel, to be tidy and polite, to take a bath every Saturday, to speak to prospective buyers—oh, thousands of necessary things, all the things that make sense to all people alike. I wish I was a teacher myself. Because I maintain that every man, no matter how humble, the last gaberloon, the last——"

If all were alight I should not have got so confused.

". . . for which I paid a ridiculous fine. And now? Now it is the State that will help me along with my business. It will be there to control my earnings—and what does that mean? It means that my brother-in-law who belongs to the party and now sits in a big office, if you please, at a big glass-topped writing desk will help me in every possible way to get my accounts straight: I shall make much more than I ever did because from now on we all belong to one happy community. It is all in the family now—

one huge family, all linked up, all snug and no questions asked. Because every man has some kind of relative in the party. My sister says how sorry she is that our old father is no more, he who was so afraid of bloodshed. Greatly exaggerated. What I say is the sooner we shoot the smart fellows who raise hell because a few dirty anti-Ekwilists at last got what was coming to them——"

This is the end of the bridge. And lo—there is no one to greet us.

Krug was perfectly right. The south side guards had deserted their post and only the shadow of Neptune's twin brother, a compact shadow that looked like a sentinel but was not one, remained as a reminder of those that had gone. True, some paces ahead, on the embankment, three or four, possibly uniformed, men, smoking two or three glowing cigarettes, relaxed on a bench while a seven-stringed amorandola was being discreetly, romantically thumbed in the dark, but they did not challenge Krug and his delightful companion, nor indeed pay any attention to them as the two passed.

# 3

HE ENTERED THE ELEVATOR which greeted him with the small sound he knew, half stamp, half shiver, and its features lit up. He pressed the third button. The brittle, thin-walled, old-fashioned little room blinked but did not move. He pressed again. Again the blink, the uneasy stillness, the inscrutable stare of a thing that does not work and knows it will not. He walked out. And at once, with an optical snap, the lift closed its bright brown eyes. He went up the neglected but dignified stairs.

Krug, a hunchback for the nonce, inserted his latchkey and slowly reverting to normal stature stepped into the hollow, humming, rumbling, rolling, roaring silence of his flat. Alone, a mezzotint of the Da Vinci miracle—thirteen persons at such a narrow table (crockery lent by the Dominican monks) stayed aloof. The lightning struck her stubby tortoiseshell-handled umbrella as it leant away from his own gamp, which was spared. He took off the one glove he had on, disposed of his overcoat and hung up his wide-brimmed black felt hat. His wide-brimmed black hat, no longer feeling at home, fell off the peg and was left lying there.

He walked down the long passage on the walls of which

black oil-paintings, the overflow from his study, showed nothing but cracks in the blindly reflected light. A rubber ball the size of a large orange was asleep on the floor.

He entered the dining-room. A plate of cold tongue garnished with cucumber slices and the painted cheek of a cheese were quietly expecting him.

The woman had a remarkable ear. She slipped out of her room next to the nursery and joined Krug. Her name was Claudina and for the last week or so she had been the sole servant in Krug's household: the male cook had left, disapproving of what he had neatly described as its "subversive atmosphere."

"Thank goodness," she said, "you have come safely home. Would you like some hot tea?"

He shook his head, turning his back to her, groping in the vicinity of the sideboard as if he were looking for something.

"How is madame tonight?" she asked.

Not answering, in the same slow blundering fashion, he made for the Turkish sitting-room which nobody used and, traversing it, reached another bend of the passage. There he opened a closet, lifted the lid of an empty trunk, looked inside and then came back.

Claudina was standing quite still in the middle of the dining-room where he had left her. She had been in the family for several years and, as conventionally happens in such cases, was pleasantly plump, middle-aged, and sensitive. There she stood staring at him with dark liquid eyes, her mouth slightly opened showing a gold spotted tooth, her coral earrings staring too and one hand pressed to her formless grey-worsted bosom.

"I want you to do something for me," said Krug. "Tomorrow I am taking the child to the country for a few days and while I am away will you please collect all her dresses and put them into the empty black trunk. Also her personal affairs, the umbrella and such things. Put it all, please, into the closet and lock it up. Anything you find. The trunk may be too small——"

He wandered out of the room without looking at her, was about to inspect another closet but thought better of it, turned on his heel and then automatically switched into tiptoe gear as he approached the nursery. There at the white door he stopped and the thumping of his heart was suddenly interrupted by his little son's special bedroom voice, detached and courteous, employed by David with graceful precision to notify his parents (when they returned, say, from a dinner in town) that he was still awake and ready to receive anybody who would like to wish him a second goodnight.

This was bound to happen. Only a quarter past ten. I thought the night was almost over. Krug closed his eyes for a moment, then went in.

He distinguished a rapid dim tumbling movement of bedclothes; the switch of a bed lamp clicked and the boy sat up, shielding his eyes. At that age (eight) children cannot be said to smile in any settled way. The smile is not localized; it is diffused throughout the whole frame—if the child is happy of course. This child was still a happy child. Krug said the conventional thing about time and sleep. No sooner had he said it than a fierce rush of rough tears started from the bottom of his chest, made for his throat, was stopped by inferior forces, remained in wait, manoeuvering in black depths, getting ready for another leap. *Pourvu qu'il ne pose pas la question atroce.* I pray thee, local deity.

"Have they been shooting at you?" David asked.

"What nonsense," he said. "Nobody shoots at night."

"But they have. I heard the pops. Look, here's a new way of wearing pyjamas."

He stood up nimbly, spreading his arms, balancing on small powdery-white, blue-veined feet that seemed to cling monkey-wise to the disarranged linen on the dimpled creaking mattress. Blue pants, pale-green vest (the woman must be colour-blind).

"I dropped the right ones into my bath," he explained cheerfully.

Possibilities of buoyancy exerted a sudden attraction, and with the collaboration of popping sounds he jumped, once, twice, three times, higher, higher—then from a dizzy suspension fell down on his knees, rolled over, stood up again on the tossed bed, tottering, swaying.

"Lie down, lie down," said Krug, "it is getting very late. I must go now. Come, lie down. Quick."

(He may not ask.)

He fell this time on his bottom and, fumbling with incurved toes, got them under the blanket, between blanket and sheet, laughed, got them right this time, and Krug rapidly tucked him in.

"There has been no story tonight," said David, lying quite flat, his own long upper lashes sweeping up, his elbows thrown back and resting like wings on both sides of his head on the pillow.

"I shall tell you a double one tomorrow."

As he bent over the child, Krug was held at arm's length for a moment, both looking into each other's faces: the child hurriedly trying hard to think up something to ask in order to gain time, the father frantically praying that one particular question would not be asked. How tender the skin looked in its bedtime glory, with a touch of the palest violet above the eyes and with the golden bloom on the forehead, below the thick ruffled fringe of golden brown hair. The perfection of nonhuman creatures—birds, young dogs, moths asleep, colts—and these little mammals. A combination of three tiny brown spots, birthmarks on the faintly flushed cheek near the nose recalled some combination he had seen, touched, taken in recently—what was it? The parapet.

He quickly kissed them, turned off the light and went out. Thank God, it has not been asked—he thought as he closed the door. But, as he gently released the handle, there it came, high-pitched, brightly remembered.

"Soon," he replied. "As soon as the doctor tells her she can. Sleep. I beg you."

At least a merciful door was between him and me.

In the dining-room, on a chair near the sideboard, Claudina sat crying lustily into a paper napkin. Krug settled down to his meal, dispatched it in haste, briskly handling the unnecessary pepper and salt, clearing his throat, moving plates, dropping a fork and catching it on his instep, while she sobbed intermittently.

"Please, go to your room," he said at last. "The child is not asleep. Call me at seven tomorrow. Mr. Ember will probably attend to the arrangements tomorrow. I shall leave with the child as early as possible."

"But it's so sudden," she moaned. "You said yesterday ——Oh, it ought not to have happened like this!"

"And I shall wring your neck," added Krug, "if you breathe one blessed word to the child."

He pushed away his plate, went to his study, locked the door.

Ember might be out. The telephone might not work. But from the feel of the receiver as he took it up he knew the faithful instrument was alive. I could never remember Ember's number. Here is the back of the telephone book on which we used to jot down names and figures, our hands mixed, slanting and curving in opposite directions. Her concavity fitting my convexity exactly. Extraordinary—I am able to make out the shadow of eyelashes on the child's cheek but fail to decipher my own handwriting. He found his spare glasses and then the familiar number with the six in the middle resembling Ember's Persian nose, and Ember put down his pen, removed the long amber cigarette-holder from his thickly pursed lips and listened.

"I was in the middle of this letter when Krug rang up and told me a terrible thing. Poor Olga is no more. She died today following an operation of the kidney. I had gone to see her at the hospital last Tuesday and she was as sweet as ever and admired so much the really lovely orchids I had brought her; there was no real danger in sight—or if there was, the doctors did not tell him. I have registered the shock but cannot analyse yet the impact of the news. I shall probably not be able to sleep for several nights. My own tribulations, all those petty theatrical intrigues I have just described, will, I am afraid, seem as trivial to you as they now seem to me.

"At first I was struck by the unpardonable thought that he was delivering himself of a monstrous joke like the time he read backwards from end to beginning that lecture on space to find out whether his students would react in any manner. They did not, nor do I for the moment. You will see him probably before you receive this muddled epistle; he is going tomorrow to the Lakes with his poor little boy. It is a wise decision. The future is not too clear but I suppose the University will resume its functions before long, though of course nobody knows what sudden changes may occur. Of late there have been some appalling rumours; the only newspaper I read has not come for at least a fortnight. He asked me to take care of the cremation tomorrow, and I wonder what people will think when he does not turn up; but of course his attitude towards death prevents his going to the ceremony though it will be as brief and formal as I can possibly make it—if only Olga's family does not intrude. Poor dear fellow—she was a brilliant helper to him in his brilliant career. In normal times, I suppose, I would be supplying her picture to American newspapermen."

Ember put down his pen again and sat lost in thought. He too had participated in that brilliant career. An obscure scholar, a translator of Shakespeare in whose green, damp country he had spent his studious youth—he innocently shambled into the limelight when a publisher asked him to apply the reverse process to the *Komparatiwn Stuhdar en Sophistat tuen Pekrekh* or, as the title of the American edition had it, a little more snappily, *The Philosophy of Sin* (banned in four states and a best seller in the rest). What a strange trick of chance—this masterpiece of esoteric thought endearing itself at once to the middleclass reader and competing for first honours during one season with that robust satire *Straight Flush*, and then, next year, with Elisabeth Ducharme's romance of Dixieland, *When the Train Passes*, and for twenty-nine days (leap year) with the book club selection *Through Towns and Villages*, and for two consecutive years with that remarkable cross between a certain kind of wafer and a lollipop, Louis Sontag's *Annunciata*, which started so well in the Caves of St. Barthelemy and ended in the funnies.

In the beginning, Krug, although professing to be amused, was greatly annoyed by the whole business, while Ember felt abashed and apologetic and covertly wondered whether perhaps his particular brand of rich synthetic English had contained some outlandish ingredient, some dreadful additional spice that might account for the unexpected excitement; but with a greater perspicacity than the two puzzled scholars showed, Olga prepared herself to enjoy thoroughly, for years to come, the success of a work whose very special points she knew better than its ephemeral reviewers could know. She it was who made the horrified Ember persuade Krug to go on that American lecture tour, as if she foresaw that its plangent reverberations would win him at home the esteem which his work in its native garb had neither wrung from academic stolidity nor induced in the comatose mass of amorphous readerdom. Not that the trip itself had been displeasing. Far from it. Although Krug, being as usual chary of squandering in idle conversation such experiences as might undergo unpredictable metamorphoses later on (if left to pupate quietly in the alluvium of the mind), had spoken little of his tour, Olga had managed to recompose it in full and to relay it gleefully to Ember who had vaguely expected a flow of sarcastic disgust. "Disgust?" cried Olga. "Why, he has known enough of that here. Disgust, indeed! Elation, delight, a quickening of the imagination, a disinfection of the mind, *togliwn ochnat divodiv* [the daily surprise of awakening]!"

"Landscapes as yet unpolluted with conventional poetry, and life, that self-conscious stranger, being slapped on the back and told to relax." He had written this upon his return, and Olga, with devilish relish, had pasted into a shagreen album indigenous allusions to the most original thinker of our times. Ember evoked her ample being, her thirty-seven resplendent years, the bright hair, the full lips, the heavy chin which went so well with the cooing undertones of her voice—something ventriloquial about her, a continuous soliloquy following in willowed shade the meanderings of her actual speech. He saw Krug, the ponderous dandruffed maestro, sitting there with a satisfied and sly smile on his big swarthy face (recalling that of Beethoven in the general correlation of its rugged features) —yes, lolling in that old rose armchair while Olga buoyantly took charge of the conversation—and how vividly one remembered the way she had of letting a sentence bounce and ripple over the three quick bites she took at the raisin cake she held, and the brisk triple splash of her plump hand over the sudden stretch of her lap as she brushed the crumbs away and went on with her story. Almost extravagantly healthy, a regular *radabarbára* [full-blown handsome woman]: those wide radiant eyes, that flaming cheek to which she would press the cool back of her hand, that shining white forehead with a whiter scar—the consequence of an automobile accident in the gloomy Lagodan mountains of legendary fame. Ember could not see how one might dispose of the recollection of such a life, the insurrection of such a widowhood. With her small feet and large hips, with her girlish speech and her matronly bosom, with her bright wits and the torrents of tears she shed that night, while dripping with blood herself, over the crippled crying doe that had rushed into the blinding lights of the car, with all this and with many other things that Ember knew he could not know, she would lie now, a pinch of blue dust in her cold columbarium.

He had liked her enormously, and he loved Krug with the same passion that a big sleek long-flewed hound feels for the high-booted hunter who reeks of the marsh as he leans towards the red fire. Krug could take aim at a flock of the most popular and sublime human thoughts and bring down a wild goose any time. But he could not kill death.

Ember hesitated, then dialled fluently. The line was engaged. That sequence of small bar-shaped hoots was like the long vertical row of superimposed I's in an index by first lines to a verse anthology. I am a lake. I am a tongue. I am a spirit. I am fevered. I am not covetous. I am the Dark Cavalier. I am the torch. I arise. I ask. I blow. I bring. I cannot change. I cannot look. I climb the hill. I come. I dream. I envy. I found. I heard. I intended an Ode. I know. I love. I must not grieve, my love. I never. I pant. I remember. I saw thee once. I travelled. I wandered. I will. I will. I will. I will.

He thought of going out to mail his letter as bachelors are wont to do around eleven o'clock at night. He hoped a timely aspirin tablet had nipped his cold in the bud. The unfinished translation of his favourite lines in Shakespeare's greatest play—

*follow the perttaunt jauncing 'neath the rack*
*with her pale skeins-mate.*

crept up tentatively but it would not scan because in his native tongue 'rack' was anapaestic. Like pulling a grand piano through a door. Take it to pieces. Or turn the corner into the next line. But the berth there was taken, the table was reserved, the line was engaged.

It was not now.

"I thought perhaps you might like me to come. We might play chess or something. I mean, tell me frankly——"

"I would," said Krug. "But I have had an unexpected call from—well, an unexpected call. They want me to come immediately. They call it an emergency session—I don't know—important, they say. All rubbish, of course, but as I can neither work nor sleep, I thought I might go."

"Had you any trouble in getting home tonight?"

"I am afraid I was drunk. I broke my glasses. They are sending——"

"Is it what you alluded to the other day?"

"No. Yes. No—I do not remember. *Ce sont mes collègues et le vieux et tout le trimbala.* They are sending a car for me in a few minutes."

"I see. Do you think——"

"You will be at the hospital as early as possible, won't you?—At nine, at eight, even earlier. . . ."

"Yes, of course."

"I told the maid—and perhaps you will look into the matter too when I am gone—I told her——"

Krug heaved horribly, could not finish—crushed down the receiver. His study was unusually cold. All of them so blind and sooty, and hung up so high above the bookshelves, that he could hardly make out the cracked complexion of an upturned face under a rudimentary halo or the jigsaw indentures of a martyr's parchmentlike robe dissolving into grimy blackness. A deal table in one corner supported loads of unbound volumes of the *Revue de Psychologie* bought secondhand, crabbed 1879 turning into plump 1880, their dead-leaf covers frayed or crumpled at the edges and almost cut through by the crisscross string eating its way into their dusty bulk. Results of the pact never to dust, never to unmake the room. A comfortable hideous bronze stand lamp with a thick glass shade of lumpy garnet and amethyst portions set in asymmetrical interspaces between bronze veins had grown to a great height, like some enormous weed, from the old blue carpet beside the striped sofa where Krug will lie tonight. The spontaneous generation of unanswered letters, reprints, university bulletins, disembowelled envelopes, paper clips, pencils in various stages of development littered the desk. Gregoire, a huge stag beetle wrought of pig iron which had been used by his grandfather to pull off by the heel (hungrily gripped by these burnished mandibles) first one riding boot, then the other, peered, unloved, from under the leathern fringe of a leathern armchair. The only pure thing in the room was a copy of Chardin's "House of Cards," which she had once placed over the mantelpiece (to ozonize your dreadful lair, she had said)—the conspicuous cards, the flushed faces, the lovely brown background.

He walked down the passage again, listened to the rhythmic silence in the nursery—and Claudina again slipped out of the adjacent room. He told her he was going out and asked her to make his bed on the divan in the study. Then he picked up his hat from the floor and went downstairs to wait for the car.

It was cold outside and he regretted not having refilled his flask with that brandy which had helped him to live through the day. It was also very quiet—quieter than usual. The oldfashioned genteel house fronts across the cobbled lane had extinguished most of their lights. A man he knew, a former Member of Parliament, a mild bore who used to take out his two polite paletoted dachshunds at nightfall, had been removed a couple of days before from number fifty in a motor truck already crammed with other prisoners. Obviously the Toad had decided to make his revolution as conventional as possible. The car was late.

He had been told by University President Azureus that a Dr. Alexander, Assistant Lecturer in Biodynamics, whom Krug had never met, would come to fetch him. The man Alexander had been collecting people all evening and the President had been trying to get in touch with Krug since the early afternoon. A peppy, dynamic, efficient gentleman, Dr. Alexander—one of those people who in times of disaster emerge from dull obscurity to blossom forth suddenly with permits, passes, coupons, cars, connections, lists of addresses. The University bigwigs had crumpled up helplessly, and of course no such gathering would have been possible had not a perfect organizer been evolved from the periphery of their species by a happy mutation which almost suggested the discreet intermediation of a transcendental force. One could distinguish in the dubious light the emblem (bearing a remarkable resemblance to a crushed dislocated but still writhing spider) of the new government upon a red flaglet affixed to the bonnet, when the officially sanctioned car obtained by the magician in our midst drew up at the curb which it grazed with a purposeful tyre.

Krug seated himself beside the driver, who was none other than Dr. Alexander himself, a pink-faced, very blond, very well-groomed man in his thirties, with a pheasant's feather in his nice green hat and a heavy opal ring on his fourth finger. His hands were very white and soft, and lay lightly on the steering wheel. Of the two (?) persons in the back Krug recognized Edmond Beuret, the Professor of French literature.

"*Bonsoir, cher collègue,*" said Beuret. "*On m'ai tiré du lit au grand désepoir de ma femme. Comment va la vôtre?*"

"A few days ago," said Krug, "I had the pleasure of reading your article on—" (he could not recall the name of that French general, an honest if somewhat limited historical figure who had been driven to suicide by slanderous politicians).

"Yes," said Beuret, "it did me good to write it. '*Les morts, les pauvres morts ont de grandes douleurs. Et quand Octobre souffle*'——"

Dr. Alexander turned the wheel very gently and spoke without looking at Krug, then giving him a rapid glance, then looking again straight ahead:

"I understand, Professor, that you are going to be our saviour tonight. The fate of our Alma Mater lies in good hands."

Krug grunted noncommittally. He had not the vaguest —or was it a veiled allusion to the fact that the Ruler, colloquially known as the Toad, had been a schoolmate of his—but that would have been too silly.

The car was stopped in the middle of Skotoma (ex Liberty, ex Imperial) Place by three soldiers, two policemen, and the raised hand of poor Theodor the Third who permanently wanted a lift or to go to a smaller place, teacher; but they were motioned by Dr. Alexander to look at the little red and black flag—whereupon they saluted and retired into the darkness.

The streets were deserted as usually happens in the gaps of history, in the *terrains vagues* of time. Taken all in all the only live creature encountered was a young man going home from an ill-timed and apparently badly truncated fancy ball: he was dressed up as a Russian mujik—embroidered shirt spreading freely from under a tasselled sash, *culotte bouffante*, soft crimson boots, and wrist watch.

"*On va lui torcher le derrière, à ce gaillard-là,*" remarked Professor Beuret grimly. The other—anonymous—person in the back seat, muttered something inaudible and replied to himself in an affirmative but likewise inarticulate way.

"I cannot drive much faster," said Dr. Alexander steadily looking ahead, "because the wrestle-cap of the lower slammer is what they call muckling. If you will put your hand into my right-hand pocket, Professor, you will find some cigarettes."

"I am a non-smoker," said Krug. "And anyway I do not believe there are any there."

They drove on for some time in silence.

"Why?" asked Dr. Alexander, gently treading, gently releasing.

"A passing thought," said Krug.

Discreetly the gentle driver allowed one hand to leave

the wheel and grope, then the other. Then, after a moment, the right one again.

"I must have mislaid them," he said after another minute of silence. "And you, Professor, are not only a non-smoker —and not only a man of genius, everybody knows that, but also (quick glance) an exceedingly lucky gambler."

"Eez eet zee verity," said Beuret, suddenly shifting to English, which he knew Krug understood, and speaking it like a Frenchman in an English book, "eez eet zee verity zat, as I have been informed by zee reliably sources, zee disposed *chef* of the state has been captured together with a couple of other blokes (when the author gets bored by the process—or forgets) somewhere in the hills—and shot? But no, I ziss cannot credit—eet eez too orrible" (when the author remembers again).

"Probably a slight exaggeration," observed Dr. Alexander in the vernacular. "Various kinds of ugly rumours are apt to spread nowadays, and although of course *domusta barbarn kapusta* [the ugliest wives are the truest], still I do not think that in this particular case," he trailed off with a pleasant laugh and there was another silence.

O my strange native town! Your narrow lanes where the Roman once passed dream in the night of other things than do the evanescent creatures that tread your stones. O you strange town! Your every stone holds as many old memories as there are motes of dust. Every one of your grey quiet stones has seen a witch's long hair catch fire, a pale astronomer mobbed, a beggar kicked in the groin by another beggar—and the King's horses struck sparks from you, and the dandies in brown and the poets in black repaired to the coffee houses while you dripped with slops to the merry echoes of gardyloo. Town of dreams, a changing dream, O you, stone changeling. The little shops all shuttered in the clean night, the gaunt walls, the niche shared by the homeless pigeon with a sculptured churchman, the rose window, the exuded gargoyle, the jester who slapped Christ—lifeless carvings and dim life mingling their feathers.... Not for the wheels of oil-maddened engines were your narrow and rough streets designed—and as the car stopped at last and bulky Beuret crawled out in the wake of his beard, the anonymous muser who had been sitting beside him was observed to split into two, producing by sudden gemination Gleeman, the frail Professor of Medieval Poetry, and the equally diminutive Yanovsky, who taught Slavic scansion—two newborn homunculi now drying on the paleolithic pavement.

"I shall lock the car and follow you presently," said Dr. Alexander with a little cough.

An Italianate mendicant in picturesque rags who had overdone it by having an especially dramatic hole in the one place which normally would never have had any—the bottom of his expectant hat—stood, shaking diligently with the ague in the lamplight at the front door. Three consecutive coppers fell—and are still falling. Four silent professors flocked up the rococo stairs.

But they did not have to ring or knock or anything for the door on the topmost landing was flung open to greet them by the prodigious Dr. Alexander who was there already, having zoomed perhaps, up some special backstairs, or by means of those nonstop things as when I used to rise from the twinned night of the Keeweenawatin and the horrors of the Laurentian Revolution, through the ghoul-haunted Province of Perm, through Early Recent, Slightly Recent, Not So Recent, Quite Recent, Most Recent—warm, warm!—up to *my* room number on *my* hotel floor in a remote country, up, up, in one of those express elevators manned by the delicate hands—my own in a negative picture—of dark-skinned men with sinking stomachs and rising hearts, never attaining Paradise, which is not a roof garden; and from the depths of the stag-headed hall old President Azureus came at a quick pace, his arms open, his faded blue eyes beaming in advance, his long wrinkled upper lip quivering——

"Yes, of course—how stupid of me," thought Krug, the circle in Krug, one Krug in another one.

# 4

OLD AZUREUS'S MANNER of welcoming people was a silent rhapsody. Ecstatically beaming, slowly, tenderly, he would take your hand between his soft palms, hold it thus as if it were a long sought treasure or a sparrow all fluff and heart, in moist silence, peering at you the while with his beaming wrinkles rather than with his eyes, and then, very slowly, the silvery smile would start to dissolve, the tender old hands would gradually release their hold, a blank expression replace the fervent light of his pale fragile face, and he would leave you as if he had made a mistake, as if after all you were not the loved one—the loved one whom, the next moment, he would espy in another corner, and again the smile would dawn, again the hands would enfold the sparrow, again it would all dissolve.

A score of prominent representatives of the University, some of them Dr. Alexander's recent passengers, were standing or sitting in the spacious, more or less glittering drawing-room (not all the lamps were lit under the green cumuli and cherubs of its ceiling) and perhaps half a dozen more co-existed in the adjacent *mussikisha* [music room], for the old gentleman was a mediocre harpist *à ses heures* and liked to fix up trios, with himself as the hypotenuse, or have some very great musician do things to the piano, after which the very small and not overabundant sandwiches and some triangled *bouchées,* which he fondly believed, had a special charm of their own due to their shape, were passed around by two maids and his unmarried daughter, who smelt vaguely of eau de Cologne and distinctly of sweat. Tonight, in lieu of these dainties, there were tea and hard biscuits; and a tortoiseshell cat (stroked alternately by the Professor of Chemistry, and Hedron, the Mathematician) lay on the dark-shining Bechstein. At the dry-leaf touch of Gleeman's electric hand, the cat rose like boiling milk and proceeded to purr intensely; but the little medievalist was absent-minded and wandered away. Economics, Divinity, and Modern History stood talking near one of the heavily draped windows. A thin but virulent draught was perceptible in spite of the drapery. Dr. Alexander had sat down at a small table, had carefully removed to its north-western corner the articles upon it (a glass ashtray, a porcelain donkey with paniers for matches, a box made to mimic a book) and was going through a list of names, crossing out some of them by means of an incredibly sharp pencil. The President hovered over him in a mixed state of curiosity and concern. Now and then Dr. Alexander would stop to ponder, his unoccupied hand cautiously stroking the sleek fair hair at the back of his head.

"What about Rufel?" (Political Science) asked the President. "Could you not get him?"

"Not available," replied Dr. Alexander. "Apparently arrested. For his own safety, I am told."

"Let us hope so," said old Azureus thoughtfully. "Well, no matter. I suppose we may start."

Edmond Beuret, rolling his big brown eyes, was telling

a phlegmatic fat person (Drama) of the bizarre sight he had witnessed.

"Oh, yes," said Drama. "Art students. I know all about it."

"*Ils ont du toupet pourtant*," said Beuret.

"Or merely obstinacy. When young people cling to tradition they do so with as much passion as the riper man shows when demolishing it. They broke into the *Klumba* [Pigeon Hole—a well-known theatre] since all the dancing halls proved closed. Perseverance."

"I hear that the *Parlamint* and the *Zud* [Court of Justice] are still burning," said another Professor.

"You hear wrongly," said Drama, "because we are not talking of that, but of the sad case of history encroaching upon an annual ball. They found a provision of candles and danced on the stage," he went on, turning again to Beuret, who stood with his stomach protruding and both hands thrust deep into his trouser pockets. "Before an empty house. A picture which has a few nice shadows."

"I think we may start," said the President, coming up to them and then passing through Beuret like a moonbeam, to notify another group.

"Then it is admirable," said Beuret, as he suddenly saw the thing in a different light. "I do hope the *pauvres gosses* had some fun."

"The police," said Drama, "dispersed them about an hour ago. But I presume it was exciting while it lasted."

"I think we may start in a moment," said the President confidently, as he drifted past them again. His smile gone long ago, his shoes faintly creaking, he slipped in between Yanovksy and the Latinist and nodded yes to his daughter, who was showing him surreptitiously a bowl of apples through the door.

"I have heard from two sources (one was Beuret, the

other Beuret's presumable informer)," said Yanovsky—and sank his voice so low that the Latinist had to bring down and lend him a white-fluffed ear.

"I have heard another version," the Latinist said, slowly unbending. "They were caught while attempting to cross the frontier. One of the Cabinet Ministers whose identity is not certain was executed on the spot, but (he subdued his voice as he named the former President of the State) . . . was brought back and imprisoned."

"No, no," said Yanovsky, "not Me Nisters. He all alone. Like King Lear."

"Yes, this will do nicely," said Dr. Azureus with sincere satisfaction to Dr. Alexander who had shifted some of the chairs and had brought in a few more, so that by magic the room had assumed the necessary poise.

The cat slid down from the piano and slowly walked out, on the way brushing for one mad instant against the pencil-striped trouser leg of Gleeman who was busy peeling a dark-red Bervok apple.

Orlik, the Zoologist, stood with his back to the company as he intently examined at various levels and from various angles the spines of books on the shelves beyond the piano, now and then pulling out one which showed no title—and hurriedly putting it back: they were all zwiebacks, all in German—German poetry. He was bored and had a huge noisy family at home.

"I disagree with you there—with both of you," the Professor of Modern History was saying. "My client never repeats herself. At least not when people are all agog to see the repetition coming. In fact, it is only unconsciously that Clio can repeat herself. Because her memory is too short. As with so many phenomena of time, recurrent combinations are perceptible as such only when they cannot affect us any more—when they are imprisoned so to speak in the past, which *is* the past just because it is disinfected. To try to map our tomorrows with the help of data supplied by our yesterdays means ignoring the basic element of the future which is its complete non-existence. The giddy rush of the present into this vacuum is mistaken by us for a rational movement.

"Pure Krugism," murmured the Professor of Economics.

"To take an example"—continued the Historian without noticing the remark: "no doubt we can single out occasions in the past that parallel our own period, when the snowball of an idea had been rolled and rolled by the red hands of schoolboys and got bigger and bigger until it became a snowman in a crumpled top hat set askew and with a broom perfunctorily affixed to his armpit—and then suddenly the bogey eyes blinked, the snow turned to flesh, the broom became a weapon and a full-fledged tyrant beheaded the boys. Oh, yes, a parliament or a senate has been upset before, and it is not the first time that an obscure and unlovable but marvellously obstinate man has gnawed his way into the bowels of a country. But to those who watch these events and would like to ward them, the past offers no clues, no *modus vivendi*—for the simple reason that it had none itself when toppling over the brink of the present into the vacuum it eventually filled."

"If this be so," said the Professor of Divinity, "then we go back to the fatalism of inferior nations and disown the thousands of past occasions when the capacity to reason, and act accordingly, proved more beneficial than scepticism and submission would have been. Your academic distaste for applied history rather suggests its vulgar utility, my friend."

"Oh, I was not talking of submission or anything in that line. That is an ethical question for one's own conscience to solve. I was merely refuting your contention that history could predict what Paduk would say or do tomorrow. There can be no submission—because the very fact of our discussing these matters implies curiosity, and curiosity in its turn is insubordination in its purest form. Speaking of curiosity, can you explain the strange infatuation of our President for that pink-faced gentleman yonder—the kind gentleman who brought us here? What is his name, who is he?"

"One of Maler's assistants, I think; a laboratory worker or something like that," said Economics.

"And last term," said the Historian, "we saw a stuttering imbecile being mysteriously steered into the Chair of Paedology because he happened to play the indispensable contrabass. Anyhow the man must be a very Satan of persuasiveness considering that he has managed to get Krug to come here."

"Did he not use," asked the Professor of Divinity with a mild suggestion of slyness, "did he not use somewhere that simile of the snowball and the snowman's broom?"

"Who?" asked the Historian. "Who used it? That man?"

"No," said the Professor of Divinity. "The other. The one whom it was so hard to get. It is curious the way ideas he expressed ten years ago——"

They were interrupted by the President who stood in the middle of the room asking for attention and lightly clapping his hands.

The person whose name had just been mentioned, Professor Adam Krug, the philosopher, was seated somewhat apart from the rest, deep in a cretonned armchair, with his hairy hands on its arms. He was a big heavy man in his early forties, with untidy, dusty, or faintly grizzled locks and a roughly hewn face suggestive of the uncouth chess master or of the morose composer, but more intelligent.

The strong compact dusky forehead had that peculiar hermetic aspect (a bank safe? a prison wall?) which the brows of thinkers possess. The brain consisted of water, various chemical compounds and a group of highly specialized fats. The pale steely eyes were half closed in their squarish orbits under the shaggy eyebrows which had protected them once from the poisonous droppings of extinct birds—Schneider's hypothesis. The ears were of goodly size with hair inside. Two deep folds of flesh diverged from the nose along the large cheeks. The morning had been shaveless. He wore a badly creased dark suit and a bow tie, always the same, hyssop violet with (pure white in the type, here Isabella) interneural macules and a crippled left hindwing. The not so recent collar was of the low open variety, i.e., with a comfortable triangular space for his namesake's apple. Thick-soled shoes and old-fashioned black spats were the distinctive characters of his feet. What else? Oh, yes—the absent-minded beat of his forefinger against the arm of his chair.

Under this visible surface, a silk shirt enveloped his robust torso and tired hips. It was tucked deep into his long underpants which in their turn were tucked into his socks: it was rumoured, he knew, that he wore none (hence the spats) but that was not true; they were in fact nice expensive lavender silk socks.

Under this was the warm white skin. Out of the dark an ant trail, a narrow capillary caravan, went up the middle of his abdomen to end at the brink of his navel; and a blacker and denser growth was spread-eagled upon his chest.

Under this was a dead wife and a sleeping child.

The President bent his head over a rosewood bureau which had been drawn by his assistant into a conspicuous position. He put on his spectacles using one hand, shaking his silvery head to get their bows into place, and proceeded to collect, equate, tap, tap, the papers he had been counting. Dr. Alexander tiptoed into a far corner where he sat down on an introduced chair. The President put down his thick even batch of typewritten sheets, removed his spectacles and, holding them away from his right ear, began his preliminary speech. Soon Krug became aware that he was a kind of focal centre in respect to the Argus-eyed room. He knew that except for two people in the assembly, Hedron and, perhaps, Orlik, nobody really liked him. To each, or about each, of his colleagues he had said at one time or other, something ... something impossible to recall in this or that case and difficult to define in general terms—some careless bright and harsh trifle that had grazed a stretch of raw flesh. Unchallenged and unsought, a plump pale pimply adolescent entered a dim classroom and looked at Adam who looked away.

"I have called you together, gentlemen, to inform you of certain very grave circumstances, circumstances which it would be foolish to ignore. As you know, our University has been virtually closed since the end of last month. I have now been given to understand that unless our intentions, our programme and conduct are made clear to the Ruler, this organism, this old and beloved organism, will cease to function altogether, and some other institution with some other staff be established in its stead. In other words, the glorious edifice which those bricklayers, Science and Administration, have built stone by stone during centuries, will fall.... It will fall because of our lack of initiative and tact. At the eleventh hour a line of conduct has been planned which, I hope, may prevent the disaster. Tomorrow it might have been too late.

"You all know how distasteful the spirit of compromise is to me. But I do not think the gallant effort in which we shall all join can be branded by that obnoxious term. Gentlemen! When a man has lost a beloved wife, when an animal has lost his feet in the aging ocean; when a great executive sees the work of his life shattered to bits—he regrets. He regrets too late. So let us not by our own fault place ourselves in the position of the bereaved lover, of the admiral whose fleet is lost in the raging waves, of the bankrupt administrator—let us take our fate like a flaming torch into both hands.

"First of all, I shall read you a short memorandum—a kind of manifesto if you wish—which is to be submitted to the Government and duly published . . . and here comes the second point I wish to raise—a point which some of you have already guessed. In our midst we have a man . . . a great man let me add, who by a singular coincidence happened in bygone days to be the schoolmate of another great man, the man who leads our State. Whatever political opinions we hold—and during my long life I have shared most of them—it cannot be denied that a government is a government and as such cannot be expected to suffer a tactless demonstration of unprovoked dissension or indifference. What seemed to us a mere trifle, the mere snowball of a transient political creed gathering no moss, has assumed enormous proportions, has become a flaming banner while we were blissfully slumbering in the security of our vast libraries and expensive laboratories. Now we are awake. The awakening is rough, I admit, but perhaps this is not solely the fault of the bugler. I trust that the delicate task of wording this . . . this that has been prepared . . . this historical paper which we all will promptly sign, has been accomplished with a deep sense of the enormous importance this task presents. I trust too that Adam Krug will recall his happy schooldays and carry this document in person to the Ruler, who, I know, will appreciate greatly the visit of a beloved and world-famous former playmate, and thus will lend a kinder ear to our sorry plight and good resolutions than he would if this miraculous coincidence had not been granted us. Adam Krug, will you save us?"

Tears stood in the old man's eyes and his voice had trembled while uttering this dramatic appeal. A page of foolscap skimmed off the table and gently settled on the green roses of the carpet. Dr. Alexander noiselessly walked over to it and restored it to the desk. Orlik, the old zoologist, opened a little book lying next to him and discovered that it was an empty box with a lone pink peppermint on the bottom.

"You are the victim of a sentimental delusion, my dear Azureus," said Krug. "What I and the Toad hoard *en fait de souvenirs d'enfance* is the habit I had of sitting upon his face."

There was a sudden crash of wood against wood. The zoologist had looked up and at the same time put down *Buxum biblioformis* with too much force. A hush followed. Dr. Azureus slowly sat down and said in a changed voice:

"I do not quite follow you, Professor. I do not know who the... whom the word or name you used refers to and—what you mean by recalling that singular game—probably some childish tussle... lawn tennis or something like that."

"Toad was his nickname," said Krug. "And it is doubtful whether you would call it lawn tennis—or even leapfrog for that matter. *He* did not. I was something of a bully, I am afraid, and I used to trip him up and sit upon his face—a kind of rest cure."

"Please, my dear Krug, please," said the President, wincing. "This is in questionable taste. You were boys at school, and boys will be boys, and I am sure you have many enjoyable memories in common—discussing lessons or talking of your grand plans for the future as boys will do———"

"I sat upon his face," said Krug stolidly, "every blessed day for about five school years—which makes, I suppose, about a thousand sittings."

Some looked at their feet, others at their hands, others again got busy with cigarettes. The zoologist, after showing a momentary interest in the proceedings, turned to a newfound bookcase. Dr. Alexander negligently avoided the shifting eye of old Azureus, who apparently was seeking help in that unexpected quarter.

"The details of the ritual," continued Krug—but was interrupted by the ching-ching of a little cowbell, a Swiss trinket that the old man's desperate hand had found on the bureau.

"All this is quite irrelevant," cried the President. "I really must call you to order, my dear colleague. We have wandered away from the main———"

"But look here," said Krug. "Really, I have not said anything dreadful, have I? I do not suggest for instance that the present face of the Toad retains after twenty-five years the immortal imprint of my weight. In those days, although thinner than I am now———"

The President had slipped out of his chair and fairly ran towards Krug.

"I have remembered," he said with a catch in his voice, "something I wanted to tell you—most important—*sub rosa*—will you please come with me into the next room for a minute?"

"All right," said Krug, heaving out of his armchair.

The next room was the President's study. Its tall clock had stopped at a quarter past six. Krug calculated rapidly, and the blackness inside him sucked at his heart. Why am I here? Shall I go home? Shall I stay?

"... My dear friend, you know well my esteem for you. But you are a dreamer, a thinker. You do not realize the circumstances. You say impossible, unmentionable things. Whatever we think of—of that person, we must keep it to ourselves. We are in deathly danger. You are jeopardizing the—everything...."

Dr. Alexander, whose courtesy, assistance and *savoir vivre* were really supreme, slipped in with an ash tray which he placed at Krug's elbow.

"In that case," said Krug, ignoring the redundant article, "I have to note with regret that the tact you mentioned was but its helpless shadow—namely an afterthought. You ought to have warned me, you know, that for reasons I still cannot fathom you intended to ask me to visit the———"

"Yes, to visit the Ruler," interpolated Azureus hurriedly. "I am sure that when you take cognizance of the manifesto, the reading of which has been so unexpectedly postponed———"

The clock began striking. For Dr. Alexander, who was an expert in such matters and a methodical man, had not been able to curb the tinkerer's instinct and was now standing on a chair and pawing the danglers and the naked face. His ear and dynamic profile were reflected in pink pastel by the opened glass door of the clock.

"I think I prefer going home," said Krug.

"Stay, I implore you. We shall now quickly read and sign that really historical document. And you must agree, you must be the messenger, you must be the dove———"

"Confound that clock," said Krug. "Can't you stop its striking, man? You seem to confuse the olive branch with the fig leaf," he went on, turning again to the President. "But this is neither here nor there, since for the life of me———"

"I only beg you to think it over, to avoid any rash decision. Those school recollections are delightful *per se*—little quarrels—a harmless nickname—but we must be serious now. Come, let us go back to our colleagues and do our duty."

Dr. Azureus, whose oratorical zest seemed to have waned, briefly informed his audience that the declaration which all had to read and sign, had been typed in the same number of copies as there would be signatures. He had been given to understand, he said, that this would lend a dash of individuality to every copy. What was the real object of this arrangement he did not explain, and, let us hope, did not know, but Krug thought he recognized in the apparent imbecility of the procedure the eerie ways of the Toad. The good doctors, Azureus and Alexander, distributed the sheets with the celerity that a conjuror and his assistant display when passing around for inspection articles which should not be examined too closely.

"You take one, too," said the older doctor to the younger one.

"No, really," exclaimed Dr. Alexander, and everybody could see his handsome face express a rosy confusion. "Indeed, no. I would not dare. My humble signature must not hobnob with those of this august assembly. I am nothing."

"Here—this is yours," said Dr. Azureus with an odd burst of impatience.

The zoologist did not bother to read his, signed it with a borrowed pen, returned the pen over his shoulder and became engrossed again in the only inspectable stuff he had found so far—an old Baedeker with views of Egypt and ships of the desert in silhouette. Poor collecting ground on the whole—except perhaps for the orthopterist.

Dr. Alexander sat down at the rosewood desk, unbuttoned his jacket, shot out his cuffs, tuned the chair proximally, checked its position as a pianist does; then produced from his vest pocket a beautiful glittering instrument made of crystal and gold; looked at its nib; tested it on a bit of paper; and, holding his breath, slowly unfolded the convolutions of his name. Having completed the ornamentation of its complex tail, he raised his pen and surveyed the glamour he had wrought. Unfortunately at this precise moment, his golden wand (perhaps resentful of the concussions that its master's various exertions had been transmitting to it throughout the evening) shed a big black tear on the valuable typescript.

Really flushing this time, the V vein swelling on his forehead, Dr. Alexander applied the leech. When the corner of the blotting paper had drunk its fill without touching the bottom, the unfortunate doctor gingerly dabbed the remains. Adam Krug from a vantage point near by saw these pale blue remains: a fancy footprint or the spatulate outline of a puddle.

Gleeman re-read the document twice, frowned twice, remembered the grant and the stained-glass window frontispiece and the special type he had chosen, and the footnote on page 306 that would explode a rival theory concerning the exact age of a ruined wall, and affixed his dainty but strangely illegible signature.

Beuret who had been brusquely roused from a pleasant nap in a screened armchair, read, blew his nose, cursed the day he had changed his citizenship—then told himself that after all it was not his business to combat exotic politics, folded his handkerchief and seeing that others signed, signed.

Economics and History held a brief consultation during which a sceptic but slightly strained smile appeared on the latter's face. They appended their signatures in unison and then noticed with dismay that while comparing notes they had somehow swapped copies, for each copy had the name and address of the potential undersigner typed out in the left-hand corner.

The rest sighed and signed, or did not sigh and signed, or signed—and sighed afterwards, or did neither the one nor the other, but then thought better of it and signed. Adam Krug too, he too, he too, unclipped his rusty wobbly fountain pen. The telephone rang in the adjacent study.

Dr. Azureus had personally handed the document to him and had hung around while Krug had leisurely put on his spectacles and had started to read, throwing his head back so as to rest it on the antimacassar and holding the sheets rather high in his slightly trembling thick fingers. They trembled more than usually because it was after midnight and he was unspeakably tired. Dr. Azureus stopped hovering and felt his old heart stumble as it went upstairs (metaphorically) with its guttering candle when Krug nearing the end of the manifesto (three pages and a half, sewn) pulled at the pen in his breast pocket. A sweet aura of intense relief made the candle rear its flame as old Azureus saw Krug spread the last page on the flat wooden arm of his cretonned armchair and unscrew the muzzle part of his pen, turning it into a cap.

With a quick flip-like delicately precise stroke quite out of keeping with his burly constitution, Krug inserted a comma in the fourth line. Then (*chmok*) he remuzzled, reclipped his pen (*chmok*) and handed the document to the distracted President.

"Sign it," said the President in a funny automatic voice.

"Legal documents excepted," answered Krug, "and not all of them at that, I never have signed, nor ever shall sign, anything not written by myself."

Old Azureus glanced around, his arms slowly rising. Somehow nobody was looking his way save Hedron, the mathematician, a gaunt man with a so-called "British" moustache and a pipe in his hand. Dr. Alexander was in the next room attending to the telephone. The cat was asleep in the stuffy room of the President's daughter who was dreaming of not being able to find a certain pot of apple jelly which she knew was a ship she had once seen in Bervok and a sailor was leaning and spitting overboard, watching his spit fall, fall, fall into the apple jelly of the heart-rending sea for her dream was shot with golden-yellow, as she had not put out the lamp, wishing to keep awake until her old father's guests had gone.

"Moreover," said Krug, "the metaphors are all mongrels whereas the sentence about being ready to add to the curriculum such matters as would prove necessary to promote political understanding and to do our utmost is miserable grammar which even my comma cannot save. I want to go home now."

"*Prakhtata meta!*" poor Dr. Azureus cried to the very quiet assembly. "*Prakhta tuen vadust, mohen kern! Profsar Krug malarma ne donje . . . Prakhtata!*"

Dr. Alexander, faintly resembling the fading sailor, reappeared and signalled, then called the President, who, still clutching the unsigned paper, sped wailing towards his faithful assistant.

"Come on, old boy, don't be a fool. Sign that darned

thing," said Hedron, leaning over Krug and resting the fist with the pipe on Krug's shoulder. "What on earth does it matter? Affix your commercially valuable scrawl. Come on! Nobody can touch our circles—but we must have some place to draw them."

"Not in the mud, sir, not in the mud," said Krug, smiling his first smile of the evening.

"Oh, don't be a pompous pedant," said Hedron. "Why do you want to make me feel so uncomfortable? I signed it—and my gods did not stir."

Without looking, Krug put up his hand to touch lightly Hedron's tweed sleeve.

"It's all right," he said. "I don't care a damn for your morals so long as you draw your circles and show conjuring tricks to my boy."

For one dangerous moment he felt again the hot black surge of grief and the room was almost melted . . . but Dr. Azureus was speeding back.

"My poor friend," said the President with great gusto. "You are a hero to have come. Why did not you tell me? I understand everything now! Of course, you could not have given the necessary attention—your decision and signature may be postponed—and I am sure we all are heartily ashamed of ourselves for having bothered you at such a moment."

"Go on speaking," said Krug. "Go on. Your words are conundrums to me but don't let that stop you."

With an awful feeling that a piece of utter misinformation had bedeviled him, Azureus stared, then stammered:

"I hope, I am not . . . I mean, I hope I am . . . I mean, haven't you . . . isn't there sorrow in your family?"

"If there is, it is no concern of yours," said Krug. "I want to go home," he added, blasting out suddenly in the terrible voice that would come like a thunderclap when he arrived at the climax of a lecture. "Will that man—what's his name—drive me back?"

From afar Dr. Alexander nodded to Dr. Azureus.

The mendicant had been relieved. Two soldiers sat huddled on the treadboard of the car, presumably guarding it. Krug, being eager to avoid a chat with Dr. Alexander, promptly got into the back. To his great annoyance, however, Dr. Alexander, instead of taking the wheel, joined him there. With one of the soldiers driving while the other protruded a comfortable elbow, the car screeched, cleared its throat and hummed through the dark streets.

"Perhaps you would like———" said Dr. Alexander, and, groping on the floor, attempted to draw up a rug so as to unite under it his and his bedfellow's legs. Krug grunted and kicked the thing off. Dr. Alexander tugged, fidgeted, tucked himself in all alone, and then relaxed, one hand languidly resting in the strap on his side of the car. An incidental street lamp found and mislaid his opal.

"I must confess I admired you, Professor. Of course you were the only real man among those poor dear fossils. I understand, you do not see much of your colleagues, do you? Oh, you must have felt rather out of place———"

"Wrong again," said Krug, breaking his vow to keep silent. "I esteem my colleagues as I do my own self, I esteem them for two things: because they are able to find perfect felicity in specialized knowledge and because they are not apt to commit physical murder."

Dr. Alexander mistook this for one of the obscure quips which, he had been told, Adam Krug liked to indulge in and laughed cautiously.

Krug glanced at him through the running darkness and turned away for good.

"And you know," continued the young biodynamicist,

"I have a curious feeling, Professor, that somehow or other the numerous sheep are prized less than the one lone wolf. I wonder what is going to happen next. I wonder, for instance, what would be your attitude if our whimsical government with apparent inconsistency ignored the sheep but offered the wolf the most munificent position imaginable. It is a passing thought of course and you may laugh at the paradox (the speaker briefly demonstrated the way it might be done) but this and other possibilities, perhaps of a quite opposite nature, somehow or other come to the mind. You know, when I was a student and lived in a garret, my landlady, the wife of the grocer below, used to insist that I should end by setting the house on fire, so many candles did I burn every night while poring over the pages of your admirable in every respect——"

"Shut up, will you?" said Krug, all of a sudden revealing a queer streak of vulgarity and even cruelty, for nothing in the innocent and well-meaning, if not very intelligent prattle of the young scientist (who quite obviously had been turned into a chatterbox by the shyness characteristic of overstrung and perhaps undernourished young folks, victims of capitalism, communism and masturbation, when they find themselves in the company of really big men, such as for instance someone whom they know to be a personal friend of the boss, or the head of the firm himself, or even the head's brother-in-law Gogolevitch, and so on) warranted the rudeness of the interjection; which interjection however had the effect of ensuring complete silence for the rest of the trip.

Only when the somewhat roughly driven car swerved into Peregolm Lane, did the unrestful young man, who realized no doubt the bewildered state of mind of the widower, open his mouth again.

"Here we are," he said genially, "I hope you have your *sesamka* [latchkey]. We must be dashing back, I'm afraid. Good night! Happy dreams! *Proshchevantze!*" [jocose "adieu"].

The car vanished while the square echo of its slammed door was still suspended in mid-air like an empty picture frame of ebony. But Krug was not alone: a thing that resembled a helmet had rolled down the steps of the porch and lay at his feet.

Close up, close up! In the farewell shadows of the porch, his moon-white monstrously padded shoulder in pathetic disharmony with his slender neck, a youth, dressed up as an American Football Player, stood in one last deadlock with a sketchy little Carmen—and even the sum of their years was at least ten less than the spectator's age. Her short black skirt with its suggestion of jet and petal half veiled the quaint garb of her lover's limbs. A spangled wrap drooped from her left hand and the inner side of her limp arm shone through black gauze. Her other arm circled up and around the boy's neck and the tense fingers were thrust from behind into his dark hair; yes, one distinguished everything—even the short clumsily lacquered fingernails, the rough schoolgirl knuckles. He, the tackler, held Laocoön, and a brittle shoulder-blade, and a small rhythmical hip, in his throbbing coils through which glowing globules were travelling in secret, and her eyes were closed.

"I am really sorry," said Krug, "but I have to pass. *Donje te zankoriv* [do please excuse me]."

They separated and he caught a glimpse of her pale, dark-eyed, not very pretty face with its glistening lips as she slipped under his door-holding arm and after one backward glance from the first landing ran upstairs trailing her wrap with all its constellation—Cepheus and Cassiopeia in their eternal bliss, and the dazzling tear of Capella, and Polaris the snowflake on the grizzly fur of the Cub, and the swooning galaxies—those mirrors of infinite space *qui m'effrayent, Blaise*, as they did you, and where Olga is not, but where mythology stretches strong circus nets, lest thought, in its ill-fitting tights, should break its old neck instead of rebouncing with a hep and a hop—hopping down again into this urine-soaked dust to take that short run with the half pirouette in the middle and display the extreme simplicity of heaven in the acrobat's amphiphorical gesture, the candidly open hands that start a brief shower of applause while he walks backwards and then, reverting to virile manners, catches the little blue handkerchief, which his muscular flying mate, after her own exertions, takes from her heaving hot bosom—heaving more than her smile suggests—and tosses to him, so that he may wipe the palms of his aching weakening hands.

# 5

It bristled with farcical anachronisms; it was suffused with a sense of gross maturity (as in Hamlet the churchyard scene); its somewhat meager setting was patched up with odds and ends from other (later) plays; but still the recurrent dream we all know (finding ourselves in the old classroom, with our homework not done because of our having unwittingly missed ten thousand days of school) was in Krug's case a fair rendering of the atmosphere of the original version. Naturally, the script of daytime memory is far more subtle in regard to factual details, since a good deal of cutting and trimming and conventional recombination has to be done by the dream producers (of whom there are usually several, mostly illiterate and middle-class and pressed by time); but a show is always a show, and the embarrassing return to one's former existence (with the off-stage passing of years translated in terms of forgetfulness, truancy, inefficiency) is somehow better enacted by a popular dream than by the scholarly precision of memory.

But is it really as crude as all that? Who is behind the timid producers? No doubt, this desk at which Krug finds himself sitting has been hastily borrowed from a different set and is more like the general equipment of the university auditorium than like the individual affair of Krug's boyhood, with its smelly (prunes, rust) inkhole and the penknife scars on its lid (which could bang) and that special inkstain in the shape of Lake Malheur. No doubt, too, there is something wrong about the position of the door, and some of Krug's students, vague supes (Danes today, Romans tomorrow), have been hurriedly rounded up to fill gaps left by those of his schoolmates who proved less mnemogenic than others. But among the producers or stagehands responsible for the setting there has been one . . . it is hard to express it . . . a nameless, mysterious genius who took advantage of the dream to convey his own peculiar code message which has nothing to do with school days or indeed with any aspect of Krug's physical existence, but which links him up somehow with an unfathomable mode of being, perhaps terrible, perhaps blissful, perhaps neither, a kind of transcendental madness which lurks behind the corner of consciousness and which cannot be defined more accurately than this, no matter how Krug strains his brain. O yes—the lighting is poor and one's field of vision is oddly narrowed as if the memory of closed eyelids persisted intrinsically within the sepia shading of the dream, and the orchestra of the senses is limited to a few native instruments, and Krug reasons in his dream worse than a drunken fool; but a closer inspection (made when the dream-self is dead for the ten thousandth time and the day-self inherits for the ten thousandth time those dusty trifles, those debts, those bundles of illegible letters) reveals the presence of someone in the know. Some intruder has been there, has tiptoed upstairs, has opened closets and very slightly disarranged the order of things. Then the shrunken, chalk-dusty, incredibly light and dry sponge imbibes water until it is as plump as a fruit; it makes glossy black arches all over the livid blackboard as it sweeps away the dead white symbols; and we start afresh now combining dim dreams with the scholarly precision of memory.

You entered a tunnel of sorts; it ran through the body of an irrelevant house and brought you into an inner court coated with old grey sand which turned to mud at the first spatter of rain. Here soccer was played in the windy pale interval between two series of lessons. The yawn of the tunnel and the door of the school, at the opposite ends of the yard, became football goals much in the same fashion as the commonplace organ of one species of animal is dramatically modified by a new function in another.

At times, a regular association football with its red liver tightly tucked in under its leather corset and the name of an English maker running across the almost palatable sections of its hard ringing rotundity, would be surreptitiously brought and cautiously dribbled about in a corner, but this was a forbidden object in the yard, bounded as it was by brittle windows.

Here is the ball, the ball, the smooth indiarubber ball, approved by the authorities, suddenly disclosed in a glass case like some museum exhibit: three balls, in fact, in three cases, for we are shown all its instars: first the new one, so clean as to be almost white—the white of a shark's belly; then the dirty grey adult with grains of gravel adhering to its weather-beaten cheek; then a flabby and formless corpse. A bell tinkles. The museum gets dark and empty again.

Pass the ball, Adamka! A shot wide of the mark or a deliberate punt seldom resulted in a crash of broken glass; but, conversely, a puncture would usually follow the collision with a certain vicious projection formed by an angle of the roofed porch. The stricken ball's collapse would not be noticeable at once. Then, at the next hard kick, its life-air would start to ooze, and presently it would be flopping about like an old galosh, before coming to rest, a miserable jellyfish of soiled indiarubber, on the muddy ground where fiendishly disappointed boots would at last kick it to pieces. The end of the *ballona* [festive gathering with dances]. She doffs her diamond tiara before her mirror.

Krug played football [*vooter*], Paduk did not [*nekht*]. Krug, a burly, fat-faced, curly-headed boy, sporting tweed knickerbockers with buttons below the knee (soccer shorts were taboo), pounded through the mud with more zest than skill. Now he found himself running (by night, ugly? Yah, by night, folks) down something that looked like a railway track through a long damp tunnel (the dream stage management having used the first set available for rendering "tunnel," without bothering to remove either the rails or the ruby lamps that glowed at intervals along the rocky black sweating walls). There was a heavy ball at his toes; he kept treading upon it whenever he tried to kick it; finally it got stuck somehow or other on a ledge of the rock wall, which, here and there, had small inset show windows, neatly illumined and enlivened by a quaint aquarian touch (corals, sea urchins, champagne bubbles). Within one of them she sat, taking off her dew-bright rings and unclasping the diamond *collier de chien* that encircled her full white throat; yes, divesting herself of all earthly jewels. He groped for the ball on the ledge and fished out a slipper, a little red pail with the picture of a sailing boat upon it and an eraser, all of which somehow summed up to the ball. It was difficult to go on dribbling through the tangle of rickety scaffolding where he felt he was getting in the way of the workmen who were fixing wires or something, and when he reached the diner the ball had rolled under one of the tables, and there, half hidden by a fallen napkin, was the threshold of the goal, because the goal was a door.

If you opened that door you found a few [*zaftpupen*] "softies" mooning on the broad window seats behind the clothes racks, and Paduk would be there, too, eating something sweet and sticky given him by the janitor, a bemedaled veteran with a venerable beard and lewd eyes. When the bell rang, Paduk would wait for the bustle of flushed begrimed classbound boys to subside, whereupon he would quietly make his way up the stairs, his agglutinate palm caressing the banisters. Krug, whom the putting away of the ball had detained (there was a big box for playthings and fake jewellery under the stairs), overtook him and pinched his plump buttocks in passing.

Krug's father was a biologist of considerable repute. Paduk's father was a minor inventor, a vegetarian, a theosophist, a great expert in cheap Hindu lore; at one time he seems to have been in the printing business—printing mainly the works of cranks and frustrated politicians. Paduk's mother, a flaccid lymphatic woman from the Marshland, had died in childbirth, and soon after this the widower had married a young cripple for whom he had been devising a new type of braces (she survived him, braces and all, and is still limping about somewhere). The boy Paduk had a pasty face and a grey-blue cranium with bumps: his father shaved his head for him personally once a week—some kind of mystic ritual, no doubt.

It is not known how the nickname "toad" originated, for there was nothing in his face suggestive of that animal. It was an odd face with all its features in their proper position but somehow diffuse and abnormal as if the little fellow had undergone one of those facial operations when the skin is borrowed from some other part of the body. The impression was due perhaps to the motionless cast of his features: he never laughed and when he happened to sneeze he had a way of doing it with a minimum of contraction and no sound at all. His small dead-white nose and neat blue galatea made him resemble *en laid* the wax schoolboys in the shop windows of tailors, but his hips were much plumper than those of mannikins, and he walked with a slight waddle and wore sandals which used to provoke a good deal of caustic comment. Once, when he was being badly mauled it was discovered that he had right against the skin a green undershirt, green as a billiard cloth and apparently made of the same texture. His hands were permanently clammy. He spoke in a curiously smooth nasal voice with a strong north-western accent and had an irritating trick of calling his classmates by anagrams of their names—Adam Krug for instance was Gumakrad or Dramaguk; this he did not from any sense of humour, which he totally lacked, but because, as he carefully explained to new boys, one should constantly bear in mind that all men consist of the same twenty-five letters variously mixed.

Such traits would have been readily excused had he been a likable fellow, a good pal, a co-operative vulgarian or a pleasantly queer boy with most matter-of-fact muscles (Krug's case). Paduk, in spite of his oddities, was dull, commonplace and insufferably mean. Thinking of it later, one comes to the unexpected conclusion that he was a veritable hero in the domain of meanness, since every time he indulged in it he must have known that he was heading again towards that hell of physical pain which his revengeful classmates put him through every time. Curiously enough, we cannot recall any single definite example of his meanness, albeit vividly remembering what Paduk had to suffer in retaliation of his recondite crimes. There was for instance the case of the padograph.

He must have been fourteen or fifteen when his father invented this only contraption of his which was destined to have some commercial success. It was a portable affair looking like a typewriter made to reproduce with repellent perfection the hand of its owner. You supplied the inventor with numerous specimens of your penmanship, he would study the strokes and the linkage, and then turn out your individual padograph. The resulting script copied exactly the average "tone" of your handwriting while the minor variations of each character were taken care of by the several keys serving each letter. Punctuation marks were carefully diversified within the limits of this or that individual manner, and such details as spacing and what experts call "clines" were so rendered as to mask mechanical regularity. Although, of course, a close examination of the script never failed to reveal the presence of a mechanical medium, a good deal of more or less foolish deceit could be practised. You could, for instance, have your padograph based on the handwriting of a correspondent and then play all kinds of pranks on him and his friends. Despite this inane undertow of clumsy forgery, the thing caught the fancy of the honest consumer: devices which in some curious new way imitate nature are attractive to simple minds. A really good padograph, reproducing a multitude of shades, was a very expensive article. Orders, however, poured in, and one purchaser after another enjoyed the luxury of seeing the essence of his incomplex personality distilled by the magic of an elaborate instrument. In the course of a year, three thousand padographs were sold, and of this number, more than one tenth were optimistically used for fraudulent purposes (both cheaters and cheated displaying remarkable stupidity in the process). Paduk senior had been just about to build a special factory for production on a grand scale when a Parliamentary decree put a ban on the manufacture and sale of padographs throughout the country. Philosophically speaking, the padograph subsisted as an Ekwilist symbol, as a proof of the fact that a mechanical device can reproduce personality, and that Quality is merely the distribution aspect of Quantity.

One of the first samples issued by the inventor was a birthday present for his son. Young Paduk applied it to the needs of homework. His handwriting was a thin arachnoid scrawl of the reverse type with strongly barred *t*'s standing out conspicuously among the other limp letters, and all this was perfectly mimicked. He had never got rid of infantile inkstains, so his father had thrown in additional keys for an hourglass-shaped blot and two round ones. These adornments, however, Paduk ignored, and quite rightly. His teachers only noticed that his work had become somewhat tidier and that such question marks as he happened to use were in darker and purpler ink than the rest of the characters: by one of those mishaps which are typical of a certain kind of inventor, his father had forgotten that sign.

Soon, however, the pleasures of secrecy waned and one morning Paduk brought his machine to school. The teacher of mathematics, a tall, blue-eyed Jew with a tawny beard, had to attend a funeral, and the resulting free hour was devoted to a demonstration of the padograph. It was a beautiful object and a shaft of spring sunlight promptly located it; snow was melting and dripping outside, jewels glittered in the mud, iridescent pigeons cooed on the wet window ledge, the roofs of the houses beyond the yard shone with a diamond shimmer; and Paduk's stumpy fingers (the edible part of each fingernail gone except for a dark linear limit embedded in a roll of yellowish flesh) drummed upon the bright keys. One must admit that the whole procedure showed considerable pluck on his part: he was surrounded by rough boys who disliked him intensely and there was nothing to prevent their pulling his magic instrument to pieces. But there he sat coolly transcribing some text and explaining in his high-pitched drawl the niceties of the demonstration. Schimpffer, a red-haired boy of Alsatian descent, with extremely efficient fingers, said: "Now let me try!" and Paduk made room for him and directed his—at first somewhat suspensive—taps. Krug tried next, and Paduk helped him, too, until he realized that his mechanized double under Krug's strong thumb was submissively setting down: I am an imbecile imbecile am I and I promise to pay ten fifteen twenty-five kruns—"Please, oh, please," said Paduk quickly, "somebody is coming, let us put it away." He clapped it into his desk, pocketed the key and hurried to the lavatory, as he always did when he got excited.

Krug conferred with Schimpffer and a simple plan of action was devised. After lessons they coaxed Paduk into giving them another look at the instrument. As soon as its case was unlocked, Krug removed Paduk and sat upon him, while Schimpffer laboriously typed out a short letter. This he slipped into the mailbox and Paduk was released.

On the following day the young wife of the rheumy and dithering teacher of history received a note (on lined paper with two holes punched out in the margin) pleading for a rendezvous. Instead of complaining to her husband, as was expected, this amiable woman, wearing a heavy blue veil, waylaid Paduk, told him he was a big naughty boy and with an eager jiggle of her rump (which in those days of tight waists looked like an inverted heart) suggested taking a *kuppe* [closed carriage] and driving to a certain unoccupied flat, where she might scold him in peace. Although since the preceding day Paduk had been on the lookout for something nasty to happen, he was not prepared for anything of this particular sort and actually followed her into the dowdy cab before recovering his wits. A few minutes later, in the traffic jam of Parliament Square, he slithered out and ignominiously fled. How all these *trivesta* [details of amorous doings] reached his comrades, is difficult to conjecture; anyway, the incident became a school legend. For a few days Paduk kept away; nor did Schimpffer appear for some time: by an amusing coincidence the latter's mother had been badly burned by a mysterious explosive that some practical joker had put into her bag while she was out shopping. When Paduk turned up again, he was his usual quiet self but he did not refer to his padograph or bring it to school any more.

That same year, or perhaps the next, a new headmaster with ideas resolved to develop what he termed "the politico-social consciousness" of the older boys. He had quite a programme—meetings, discussions, the formation of party groups—oh, lots of things. The healthier boys avoided these gatherings for the simple reason that, being held after class or during recess, they encroached upon one's freedom. Krug made violent fun of the fools or trucklers who fell for this civic nonsense. The headmaster, while stressing the purely voluntary nature of attendance, warned Krug (who was at the top of his class) that his individualistic behavior constituted a dreadful example. There was an etching representing the Sand Bread Riot, 1849, above the headmaster's horsehair couch. Krug did not dream of yielding and stoically ignored the mediocre marks which from that moment fell to his lot despite his work's remaining on the same level. Again the headmaster spoke to him. There was also a coloured print depicting a lady in cherry red, sitting before her mirror. The position was interesting: here was this headmaster, a liberal with robust leanings towards the left, an eloquent advocate of Uprightness and Impartiality, ingeniously blackmailing the brightest boy in this school and acting thus not because he wished him to join a certain definite group (say a Leftist one), but because the boy would not join any group whatsoever. For it should be remarked in all fairness to the headmaster that, far from enforcing his own political predilections, he allowed his pupils to adhere to any party they chose, even if this proved to be a new combination unrelated to any of the factions represented in the then flourishing Parliament. Indeed, so broadminded was he that he positively *wanted* the richer boys to form strongly capitalistic clusters, or the sons of reactionary nobles to keep in tune with their caste and unite in "*Rutterheds.*" All he asked for was that they follow their social and economic instincts, while the only thing he condemned was the complete absence of such instincts in an individual. He saw the world as a lurid interplay of class passions amid a landscape of conventional gauntness, with Wealth and Work emitting Wagnerian thunder in their predetermined parts; a refusal to act in the show appeared to him as a vicious insult to his dynamic myth as well as to the Trade Union to which the actors belonged. Under these circumstances he felt justified in pointing out to the teachers that if Adam Krug passed the final examinations with honours, his success would be dialectically unfair in regard to those of Krug's schoolmates who had less brains but were better citizens. The teachers entered so heartily into the spirit of the thing that it is a wonder how our young friend managed to pass at all.

That last term was also marked by the sudden rise of Paduk. Although he had seemed to be disliked by all, a kind of small court and bodyguard was there to greet him when he gently rose to the surface and gently founded the party of the Average Man. Every one of his followers had some little defect or "background of insecurity" as an educationist after a fruit cocktail might put it: one boy suffered from permanent boils, another was morbidly shy, a third had by accident beheaded his baby sister, a fourth stuttered so badly that you could go out and buy yourself a chocolate bar while he was wrestling with an initial *p* or *b:* he would never try to by-pass the obstacle by switching to a synonym, and when finally the explosion did occur, it convulsed his whole frame and sprayed his interlocutor with triumphant saliva. A fifth disciple was a more sophisticated stutterer, since the flaw in his speech took the form of an additional syllable coming *after* the critical word like a kind of halfhearted echo. Protection was provided by a truculent simian youth who at seventeen could not memorize the multiplication tables but was able to hold up a chair majestically occupied by yet another disciple, the fattest boy in the school. Nobody had noticed how this rather incongruous, little crowd had gathered around Paduk and nobody could understand what exactly had given Paduk the leadership.

A couple of years before these events his father had become acquainted with Fradrik Skotoma of pathetic fame. The old iconoclast as he liked to be called, was at the time steadily slipping into misty senility. With his moist bright red mouth and fluffy white whiskers he had begun to look, if not respectable, at least harmless, and his shrunken body assumed such a gossamery aspect that the matrons of his dingy neighbourhood, as they watched him shuffle along in the fluorescent halo of his dotage, felt almost like crooning over him and would buy him cherries and hot raisin cakes and the loud socks he affected. People who had been stirred in their youth by his writings had long forgotten that passionate flow of insidious pamphlets and mistook the shortness of their own memory for the curtailment of his objective existence, so that they would frown a quick frown of incredulity if told that Skotoma, the *enfant terrible* of the sixties, was still alive. Skotoma himself, at eighty-five, was inclined to consider his tumultuous past as a preliminary stage far inferior to his present philosophical period, for, not unnaturally, he saw his decline as a ripening and an apotheosis, and was quite sure that the rambling treatise he had Paduk senior print would be recognized as an immortal achievement.

He expressed his new-found conception of mankind with the solemnity befitting a tremendous discovery. At every given level of world-time there was, he said, a certain computable amount of human consciousness distributed throughout the population of the world. This distribution was uneven and herein lay the root of all our woes. Human beings, he said, were so many vessels containing unequal portions of this essentially uniform consciousness. It was, however, quite possible, he maintained, to regulate the capacity of the human vessels. If, for instance, a given amount of water were contained in a given number of heterogeneous bottles—wine bottles, flagons and vials of varying shape and size, and all the crystal and gold scent bottles that were reflected in her mirror, the distribution of the liquid would be uneven and unjust, but could be made even and just either by grading the contents or by eliminating the fancy vessels and adopting a standard size. He introduced the idea of balance as a basis for universal bliss and called his theory "Ekwilism." This he claimed was quite new. True, socialism had advocated uniformity on an economic plane, and religion had grimly promised the same in spiritual terms as an inevitable status beyond the grave. But the economist had not seen that no levelling of wealth could be successfully accomplished, nor indeed was of any real moment, so long as there existed some individuals with more brains or guts than others; and similarly the priest had failed to perceive the futility of his metaphysical promise in relation to those favoured ones (men of bizarre genius, big game hunters, chess players, prodigiously robust and versatile lovers, the radiant woman taking her necklace off after the ball) for whom this world was a paradise in itself and who would be always one point up no matter what happened to everyone in the melting pot of eternity. And even, said Skotoma, if the last became the first and vice versa, imagine the patronizing smile of the *ci-devant* William Shakespeare on seeing a former scribbler of hopelessly bad plays blossom anew as the Poet Laureate of heaven.

It is important to note that while suggesting a remoulding of human individuals in conformity with a well-balanced pattern, the author prudently omitted to define both the practical method to be pursued and the kind of person or persons responsible for planning and directing the process. He contented himself with repeating throughout his book that the difference between the proudest intellect and the humblest stupidity depended entirely upon the degree of "world consciousness" condensed in this or that individual. He seemed to think that its redistribution and regulation would automatically follow as soon as his readers perceived the truth of his main assertion. It is also to be observed that the good Utopian had the whole misty blue world in view, not only his own morbidly self-conscious country. He died soon after his treatise appeared and so was spared the discomfort of seeing his vague and benevolent Ekwilism transformed (while retaining its name) into a violent and virulent political doctrine, a doctrine that proposed to enforce spiritual uniformity upon his native land through the medium of the most standardized section of the inhabitants, namely the Army, under the supervision of a bloated and dangerously divine State.

When young Paduk instituted the Party of the Average

Man as based on Skotoma's book, the metamorphosis of Ekwilism had only just started and the frustrated boys who conducted those dismal meetings in a malodorous classroom were still groping for the means to make the contents of the human vessel conform to an average scale. That year a corrupt politician had been assassinated by a college student called Emrald (not Amrald, as his name is usually misspelled abroad), who at the trial came out quite irrelevantly with a poem of his own composition, a piece of jagged neurotic rhetorism extolling Skotoma because he

> *. . . taught us to worship the Common Man,*
> *and showed us that no tree*
> *can exist without a forest,*
> *no musician without an orchestra,*
> *no wave without an ocean,*
> *and no life without death.*

Poor Skotoma, of course, had done nothing of the kind, but this poem was now sung to the tune of "*Ustra mara, donjet domra*" (a popular ditty lauding the intoxicating properties of gooseberry wine) by Paduk and his friends and later became an Ekwilist classic. In those days a blatantly bourgeois paper happened to be publishing a cartoon sequence depicting the home life of Mr. and Mrs. Etermon (Everyman). With conventional humour and sympathy bordering upon the obscene, Mr. Etermon and the little woman were followed from parlour to kitchen and from garden to garret through all the mentionable stages of their daily existence, which, despite the presence of cosy armchairs and all sorts of electric thingumbobs and one thing-in-itself (a car), did not differ essentially from the life of a Neanderthal couple. Mr. Etermon taking a z-nap on the divan or stealing into the kitchen to sniff with erotic avidity the sizzling stew, represented quite unconsciously a living refutation of individual immortality, since his whole habitus was a dead-end with nothing in it capable or worthy of transcending the mortal condition. Neither, however, could one imagine Etermon actually dying, not only because the rules of gentle humour forbade his being shown on his deathbed, but also because not a single detail of the setting (not even his playing poker with life-insurance salesmen) suggested the fact of absolutely inevitable death; so that in one sense Etermon, while personifying a refutation of immortality, was immortal himself, and in another sense he could not hope to enjoy any kind of afterlife simply because he was denied the elementary comfort of a death chamber in his otherwise well planned home. Within the limits of this airtight existence, the young couple were as happy as any young couple ought to be: a visit to the movies, a raise in one's salary, a yum-yum something for dinner—life was positively crammed with these and similar delights, whereas the worst that might befall one was hitting a traditional thumb with a traditional hammer or mistaking the date of the boss's birthday. Poster pictures of Etermon showed him smoking the brand that millions smoke, and millions could not be wrong, and every Etermon was supposed to imagine every other Etermon, up to the President of the State, who had just replaced dull, stolid Theodore the Last, returning at the close of the office day to the (rich) culinary and (meagre) connubial felicities of the Etermon home. Skotoma, quite apart from the senile divagations of his "Ekwilism" (and even they implied some kind of drastic change, some kind of dissatisfaction with given conditions), had viewed what he called "the petty bourgeois" with the wrath of orthodox anarchism and would have been appalled, just as Emrald the terrorist would have been, to know that a group of youths was worshiping

Ekwilism in the guise of a cartoon-engendered Mr. Etermon. Skotoma, however, had been the victim of a common delusion: his "petty bourgeois" existed only as a printed label on an empty filing box (the iconoclast, like most of his kind, relied entirely upon generalizations and was quite incapable of noting, say, the wallpaper in a chance room or talking intelligently to a child). Actually, with a little perspicacity, one might learn many curious things about Etermons, things that made them so different from one another that Etermon, except as a cartoonist's transient character, could not be said to exist. All of a sudden transfigured, his eyes narrowly glowing, Mr. Etermon (whom we have just seen mildly pottering about the house) locks himself up in the bathroom with his prize—a prize we prefer not to name; another Etermon, straight from his shabby office, slips into the silence of a great library to gloat over certain old maps of which he will not speak at home; a third Etermon with a fourth Etermon's wife anxiously discusses the future of a child she has managed to bear him in secret during the time her husband (now back in his armchair at home) was fighting in a remote jungle land where, in his turn, he has seen moths the size of a spread fan, and trees at night pulsating rhythmically with countless fireflies. No, the average vessels are not as simple as they appear: it is a conjuror's set and nobody, not even the enchanter himself, really knows what and how much they hold.

Skotoma had dwelt in his day upon the economic aspect of Etermon; Paduk deliberately copied the Etermon cartoon in its sartorial sense. He wore the tall collar of celluloid, the famous shirt-sleeve bands and the expensive footgear—for the only brilliance Mr. Etermon permitted himself was related to parts as far as possible removed from the anatomic centre of his being: glossy shoes, glossy hair.

With his father's reluctant consent, the top of Paduk's pale-blue cranium was allowed to grow just enough hair to resemble Etermon's beautifully groomed pate and Etermon's washable cuffs with starlike links were affixed to Paduk's weak wrists. Although in later years this mimetic adaptation was no longer consciously pursued (while on the other hand the Etermon strip was eventually discontinued, and afterwards seemed quite atypical when looked up at a different period of fashion) Paduk never got over this stiff superficial neatness; he was known to endorse the views of a doctor, belonging to the Ekwilist party, who affirmed that if a man kept his clothes scrupulously clean, he might, and should, limit his weekday ablutions to washing nothing but his face, ears, and hands. Throughout all his later adventures, in all places, under all circumstances, in the blurry back rooms of suburban cafés, in the miserable offices where this or that obstinate newspaper of his was concocted, in barracks, in public halls, in the forests and hills where he hid with a bunch of barefooted red-eyed soldiers, and in the palace where, through an incredible whim of local history, he found himself vested with more power than any national ruler had ever enjoyed, Paduk still retained something of the late Mr. Etermon, a sort of cartoon angularity, a cracked and soiled cellophane wrapper effect, through which, nevertheless, one could discern a brand-new thumbscrew, a bit of rope, a rusty knife and a specimen of the most sensitive of human organs wrenched out together with its blood-clotted roots.

In the classroom where the final examination was being held, young Paduk, his sleek hair resembling a wig too small for his shaven head, sat between Brun the Ape and a lacquered dummy representing an absentee. Adam Krug, wearing a brown dressing gown, sat directly behind. Somebody on his left asked him to pass a book to the family of his right-hand neighbour, and this he did. The book, he noticed, was in reality a rosewood box shaped and painted to look like a volume of verse and Krug understood that it contained some secret commentaries that would assist an unprepared student's panic-stricken mind. Krug regretted that he had not opened the box or book while it passed through his hands. The theme to be tackled was an afternoon with Mallarmé, an uncle of his mother, but the only part he could remember seemed to be "*le sanglot dont j'étais encore ivre.*"

Everybody around was scribbling with zest and a very black fly which Schimpffer had especially prepared for the occasion by dipping it into India ink was walking on the shaven part of Paduk's studiously bent head. It left a blot near his pink ear and a black colon on his shiny white collar. A couple of teachers—her brother-in-law and the teacher of mathematics—were busily arranging a curtained something which would be a demonstration of the next theme to be discussed. They reminded one of stagehands or morticians but Krug could not see well because of the Toad's head. Paduk and all the rest wrote on steadily, but Krug's failure was complete, a baffling and hideous disaster, for he had been busy becoming an elderly man instead of learning the simple but now unobtainable passages which they, mere boys, had memorized. Smugly, noiselessly, Paduk left his seat to take his paper to the examiner, tripped over the foot that Schimpffer shot out and through the gap which he left Krug clearly perceived the outlines of the next theme. It was now quite ready for demonstration but the curtains were still drawn. Krug found a scrap of clean paper and got ready to write his impressions. The two teachers pulled the curtains apart. Olga was revealed sitting before her mirror and taking off her jewels after the ball. Still clad in cherry-red velvet, her strong gleaming elbows thrown back and lifted like wings, she had begun to unclasp at the back of her neck her dazzling dog collar. He knew it would come off together with her vertebrae—that in fact it was the crystal of her vertebrae —and he experienced an agonizing sense of impropriety at the thought that everybody in the room would observe and take down in writing her inevitable, pitiful, innocent disintegration. There was a flash, a click: with both hands she removed her beautiful head and, not looking at it, carefully, carefully, dear, smiling a dim smile of amused recollection (who could have guessed at the dance that the real jewels were pawned?), she placed the beautiful imitation upon the marble ledge of toilet table. Then he knew that all the rest would come off too, the rings together with the fingers, the bronze slippers with the toes, the breasts with the lace that cupped them . . . his pity and shame reached their climax, and at the ultimate gesture of the tall cold stripteaser, prowling pumalike up and down the stage, with a horrible qualm Krug awoke.

# 6

"We met yesterday," said the room. "I am the spare bedroom in the Maximovs' *dacha* [country house, cottage]. These are windmills on the wallpaper." "That's right," replied Krug. Somewhere in the thin-walled, pine-fragrant house a stove was comfortably crackling and David was speaking in his tinkling voice—probably answering Anna Petrovna, probably having breakfast with her in the next room.

Theoretically there is no absolute proof that one's awakening in the morning (the finding oneself again in the saddle of one's personality) is not really a quite unprecedented event, a perfectly original birth. One day Ember and he had happened to discuss the possibility of their having invented *in toto* the works of William Shakespeare, spending millions and millions on the hoax, smothering with hush money countless publishers, librarians, the Stratford-on-Avon people, since in order to be responsible for all references to the poet during three centuries of civilization, these references had to be assumed to be spurious interpolations injected by the inventors into actual works which they had re-edited; there still was a snag here, a bothersome flaw, but perhaps it might be eliminated, too, just as a cooked chess problem can be cured by the addition of a passive pawn.

The same might be true of one's personal existence as perceived in retrospect upon waking up: the retrospective effect itself is a fairly simple illusion, not unlike the pictorial values of depth and remoteness produced by a paintbrush on a flat surface; but it takes something better than a paintbrush to create the sense of compact reality backed by a plausible past, of logical continuity, of picking up the thread of life at the exact point where it was dropped. The subtlety of the trick is nothing short of marvellous, considering the immense number of details to be taken into account, arranged in such a way as to suggest the action of memory. Krug at once knew that his wife had died; that he had beaten a hasty retreat to the country with his little son, and that the view framed in the casement (wet leafless trees, brown earth, white sky, a hill with a farmhouse in the distance) was not only a sample picture of that particular region but was also there to tell him that David had pulled the shade up and had left the room without awakening him; whereupon, with almost obsequious apropos, a couch at the other end of the room displayed by means of mute gestures—see this and this—all that was necessary to convince one that a child had slept there.

On the morning after her death her relatives had arrived. The night before Ember had informed them of her death. Note how smoothly the retrospective machinery works: everything fits into everything else. They (to switch into a lower past-gear) arrived, they invaded Krug's flat. David was finishing his velvetina. They came in full force: her sister Viola, Viola's revolting husband, a half brother of sorts and his wife, two remote female cousins scarcely visible in the mist and a vague old man whom Krug had never met before. Augment the vanity of the illusive depth. Viola had always disliked her sister; they had seldom seen each other during the last twelve years. She wore a heavily blotched little veil: it came down to the bridge of her freckled nose, no further than that, and behind its black violets one could distinguish a brightness which was both voluptuous and hard. Her blond-bearded husband gently supported her, although actually the solicitude with which the pompous rogue surrounded her sharp elbow only hampered her swift masterful movements. She soon shook him away. When last seen, he was staring in dignified silence through the window at two black limousines waiting at the kerb. A gentleman in black with powdered blue jowls, the representative of the incinerating firm, came to say that it was high time to start. Meanwhile Krug had escaped with David by the back door.

Carrying a suitcase, still wet from Claudina's tears, he led the child to the nearest trolley stop, and, in company with a band of sleepy soldiers who were going on to their barracks, arrived at the railway station. Before he was allowed to board the train for the Lakes, governmental agents examined his papers and the balls of David's eyes. The Lakes hotel turned out to be closed, and after they had wandered around for a while, a jovial postman in his yellow automobile took them (and Ember's letter) to the Maximovs. This completes the reconstruction.

The common bathroom in a friendly house is its only inhospitable section, especially when the water runs at first tepid, then stone cold. A long silvery hair was imbedded in a cake of cheap almond soap. Toilet paper had been difficult to get lately and was replaced by bits of newspaper impaled on a hook. At the bottom of the bowl a safety razor blade envelope with Dr. S. Freud's face and signature floated. If I stay for a week, he thought, this alien wood will be gradually tamed and purified by repeated contacts with my wary flesh. He rinsed the bath gingerly. The rubber tube of the spraying affair came off the tap with a plop. Two clean towels hung on a rope together with some black stockings that had been, or would be, washed. A bottle of mineral oil, half full, and a grey cardboard cylinder which had been the kernel of a toilet paper roll, stood side by side on a shelf. The shelf also held two popular novels (*Flung Roses* and *All Quiet on the Don*). David's toothbrush gave him a smile of recognition. He dropped his shaving soap on the floor and there was silvery hair sticking to it when he picked it up.

In the dining room Maximov was alone. The portly old gentleman slipped a marker into his book, stood up with a genial jerk and vigorously shook hands with Krug, as if a night's sleep had been a long and hazardous journey. "How did you rest [*Kak pochivali*]?" he asked, and then, with a worried frown, tested the temperature of the coffee pot under its coxcomb cozy. His shiny pink face was clean-shaven like that of an actor (old-fashioned simile); a tasselled skullcap protected his perfectly bald head; he wore a warm jacket with toggles. "I recommend this," he said, pointing with his fifth finger. "I find it is the only cheese of its kind that does not clog the bowels."

He was one of those persons whom one loves not because of some lustrous streak of talent (this retired businessman possessed none), but because every moment spent with them fits exactly the gauge of one's life. There are friendships like circuses, waterfalls, libraries; there are others comparable to old dressing gowns. You found nothing especially attractive about Maximov's mind if you took it apart: his ideas were conservative, his tastes undistinguished: but somehow or other these dull components formed a wonderfully comfortable and harmonious whole.

No subtlety of thought tainted his honesty, he was as reliable as iron and oak, and when Krug mentioned once that the word "loyalty" phonetically and visually reminded him of a golden fork lying in the sun on a smooth spread of pale yellow silk, Maximov replied somewhat stiffly that to *him* loyalty was limited to its dictionary denotation. Common sense with him was saved from smug vulgarity by a delicate emotional undercurrent, and the somewhat bare and birdless symmetry of his branching principles was ever so slightly disturbed by a moist wind blowing from regions which he naïvely thought did not exist. The misfortunes of others worried him more than did his own troubles, and had he been an old sea captain, he would have dutifully gone down with his ship rather than plump apologetically into the last lifeboat. At the present moment he was bracing himself to give a piece of his mind to Krug, and was playing for time by talking politics.

"The milkman," he said, "told me this morning that posters have been put up all over the village inviting the population to celebrate spontaneously the restoration of complete order. A plan of conduct is suggested. We are supposed to collect in our usual holiday haunts, in cafés, in clubs and in the halls of our corporations and sing communal songs in praise of the Government. Directors of civic *ballonas* have been elected for every district. One wonders of course what people who cannot sing and who do not belong to any corporation are expected to do."

"I dreamed of him," said Krug. "Apparently this is the only way that my old schoolmate can hope to associate with me nowadays."

"I understand you were not particularly fond of each other at school?"

"Well, that needs analysing. I certainly loathed him, but the question is—was it mutual? I remember one queer incident. The lights went out suddenly—short circuit or something."

"Does happen sometimes. Try that jam. Your son thought highly of it."

"I was in the classroom reading," continued Krug. "Goodness knows why it was in the evening. The Toad had slipped in and was fumbling in his desk—he kept candy there. It was then that the lights went out. I leaned back, waiting in perfect darkness. Suddenly I felt something wet and soft on the back of my hand. The Kiss of the Toad. He managed to bolt before I could catch him."

"Pretty sentimental, I should say," remarked Maximov.

"And loathsome," added Krug.

He buttered a bun and proceeded to recount the details of the meeting at the President's house. Maximov sat down too, pondered for a moment, then pounced across the table at a basket with *knakerbrod*, bumped it down near Krug's plate and said:

"I want to tell you something. When you hear it, you may be cross and call me a meddler, but I shall risk incurring your displeasure because the matter is really much too serious and I do not mind whether you growl or not. *Ia, sobstvenno, uzhe vchera khotel* [I should have broached the subject yesterday] but Anna thought you were too tired. It would be rash to postpone this talk any longer."

"Go ahead," said Krug, taking a bite and bending forward as the jam was about to drip.

"I perfectly understand your refusal to deal with those people. I should have acted likewise, I guess. They will make another attempt at getting you to sign things and you will refuse again. This point is settled."

"Most definitely," said Krug.

"Good. Now, since this point is settled, it follows that something else is settled too. Namely, your position under the new regime. It takes on a peculiar aspect, and what I wish to point out is that you do not seem to realize the danger of this aspect. In other words, as soon as the Ekwilists lose hope of obtaining your co-operation they will arrest you."

"Nonsense," said Krug.

"Precisely. Let us call this hypothetical occurrence an utterly nonsensical thing. But the utterly nonsensical is a natural and logical part of Paduk's rule. You have to take this into consideration, my friend, you have to prepare some kind of defence, no matter how unlikely the danger may seem."

"*Yer un dah* [stuff and nonsense]," said Krug. "He will go on licking my hand in the dark. I am invulnerable. Invulnerable—the rumbling sea wave [*volna*] rolling the rabble of pebbles as it recedes. Nothing can happen to Krug the Rock. The two or three fat nations (the one that is blue on the map and the one that is fallow) from which my Toad craves recognition, loans, and whatever else a bullet-riddled country may want to obtain from a sleek neighbour—these nations will simply ignore him and his government, if he . . . molests me. Is that the right kind of growl?"

"It is not. Your conception of practical politics is romantic and childish, and altogether false. We can imagine him forgiving you the ideas you expressed in your former works. We can also imagine him suffering an outstanding mind to exist in the midst of a nation which by his own law must be as plain as its plainest citizen. But in order to imagine these things we are forced to postulate an attempt on his part to put you to some special use. If nothing comes of it—then he will not bother about public opinion abroad, and on the other hand no state will bother about you if it finds some profit in dealing with this country."

"Foreign academies will protest. They will offer fabulous sums, my weight in *Ra*, to buy my liberty."

"You may jest as much as you please, but still I want to know—look here, Adam, what do you expect to do? I mean, you surely cannot believe you will be permitted to lecture or publish your works, or keep in touch with foreign scholars and publishers, or do you?"

"I do not. *Je resterai coi.*"

"My French is limited," said Maximov dryly.

"I shall," said Krug (beginning to feel very bored), "lie *doggo.* In due time what intelligence I have left will be dovetailed into some leisurely book. Frankly I do not give a damn for this or any other university. Is David out of doors?"

"But, my dear fellow, they will not let you sit still! This is the crux of the matter. I or any other plain citizen can and must sit still, but you cannot. You are one of the very few celebrities our country has produced in modern times, and——"

"Who are the other stars of this mysterious constellation?" queried Krug, crossing his legs and inserting a comfortable hand between thigh and knee.

"All right: the only one. And for this reason they will want you to be as active as possible. They will do all they can to make you boost their way of thinking. The style, the *begonia* [brilliancy], will be yours, of course. Paduk will be satisfied with merely arranging the programme."

"And I shall remain deaf and dumb. Really, my dear fellow, this is all journalism on your part. I want to be left alone."

"Alone is the wrong word!" cried Maximov, flushing. "You are not alone! You have a child."

"Come, come," said Krug, "let us please——"

"We shall not. I warned you that I would ignore your irritation."

"Well, what do you want me to do?" asked Krug with a sigh and helped himself to another cup of lukewarm coffee.

"Leave the country at once."

The stove crackled gently, and a square clock with two cornflowers painted on its white wooden face and no glass rapped out the seconds in pica type. The window attempted a smile. A faint infusion of sunshine spread over the distant hill and brought out with a kind of pointless distinction the little farm and its three pine trees on the opposite slope which seemed to move forward and then to retreat again as the wan sun swooned.

"I do not see the necessity of leaving right now," said Krug. "If they pester me too persistently I probably shall —but for the present the only move I care to make is to rook my king the long side."

Maximov got up and then sat down in another chair.

"I see it is going to be quite difficult to make you realize your position. Please, Adam, use your wits: neither today, nor tomorrow, nor at any time will Paduk allow you to go abroad. But today you can escape, as Berenz and Marbel and others have escaped; tomorrow it will be impossible, the frontiers are being stitched up more and more closely, there will not be a single interstice left by the time you make up your mind."

"Well, why then don't you escape yourself?" grunted Krug.

"My position is somewhat different," answered Maximov quietly. "And what is more, you know it. Anna and I are too old—and besides I am the perfect type of the average man and present no danger whatever to the Government. You are as healthy as a bull, and everything about you is criminal."

"Even if I thought it wise to leave the country I should not have the faintest idea how to manage the business."

"Go to Turok—he knows, he will put you in touch with the necessary people. It will cost you a good deal of money but you can afford it. I too do not know how it is done, but I know it can and has been done. Think of the peace in a civilized country, of the possibilities to work, of the schooling available for your child. Under your present circumstances——"

He checked himself. After an exceedingly awkward supper the night before he had told himself he would not refer again to the subject which this strange widower seemed so stoically to avoid.

"No," said Krug. "No. I am not up to it [*ne do tovo*] for the moment. It is kind of you to worry about me [*obo mne*] the way you do, but really [*pravo*] you exaggerate the danger. I shall keep your suggestion in mind, of course [*koneshno*]. Let us not talk of it any more [*bol'she*]. What is David doing?"

"Well, you know what I think at least [*po kraïneï mere*]," said Maximov, picking up the historical novel he had been reading when Krug came in. "But we are not through with you yet. I shall have Anna talk to you, too, whether you like it or not. She may fare better. I believe David is with her in the kitchen garden. We lunch at one."

The night had been stormy, heaving and gasping with brutal torrents of rain; and in the starkness of the cold quiet morning the sodden brown asters were in disorder and drops of quicksilver blotched the pungent-smelling purple cabbage leaves, between the coarse veins of which grubs had made ugly holes. David was dreamily sitting in a wheelbarrow and the little old lady was trying to push it along on the muddy clay of the path. "*Ne mogoo!* [I cannot]," she exclaimed with a laugh and brushed a strand of thin silvery hair away from her temple. David tumbled out of the wheelbarrow. Krug, not looking at her, said he wondered whether it was not too chilly for the boy to go about without his coat, and Anna Petrovna replied that the white sweater he had on was sufficiently thick and comfy. Olga somehow had never much liked Anna Petrovna and her sweet saintliness.

"I want to take him for a good long walk," said Krug. "You must have had quite enough of him. Lunch at one, is that right?"

What he said, what words he used, did not matter; he kept avoiding her brave kind eyes to which he felt he could not live up, and listened to his own voice stringing trivial sounds in the silence of a shrivelled world.

She stood watching them as father and son went hand in hand towards the road. Very still, fumbling keys and a thimble in the strained pockets of her black jumper.

Broken clusters of mountain ash corals lay here and there on the chocolate-brown road. The berries were puckered and soiled, but even if they had been juicy and clean you certainly could not eat them. Jam is a different matter. No, I said: No. To *taste* is the same as to eat. Some of the maples in the silent damp wood through which the road wandered retained their painted leaves but the birches were quite naked. David slipped and with great presence of mind prolonged the slide so as to have the pleasure of sitting down on the sticky earth. Get up, get up. But he kept sitting there for another moment looking up with sham stupefaction and laughing eyes. His hair was moist and hot. Get up. Surely, this is a dream, thought Krug, this silence, the deep ridicule of late autumn, miles away from home. Why are we here of all places? A sickly sun again attempted to enliven the white sky: for a second or two a couple of wavering shadows, K ghost and D ghost, marching on shadowy stilts, copied the human gait and then faded out. An empty bottle. If you like, he said, you can pick up that Skotomic bottle and throw it hard at the trunk of a tree. It will explode with a beautiful bang. But it fell intact into the rusty waves of the bracken, and he had to wade in after it himself, because the place was much too damp for the wrong pair of shoes David was wearing. Try again. It refused to break. All right, I shall do it myself. There was a post with a sign: Hunting Prohibited. Against this he hurled the green vodka bottle violently. He was a big heavy man. David backed. The bottle burst like a star.

Presently they emerged into open country. Who was that idly sitting on a fence? He wore long boots and a peaked cap but did not look like a peasant. He smiled and said: "Good morning, Professor." "Good morning to you," answered Krug without stopping. Possibly one of the people who supplied the Maximovs with game and berries.

The *dachas* on the right-hand side of the road were mostly deserted. Here and there, however, some remnants of vacational life still persisted. In front of one of the porches a black trunk with brass knobs, a couple of bundles, and a helpless looking bicycle with swathed pedals stood, sat, and lay, awaiting some means of transportation, and a child in town clothes was rocking for the last time in a doleful swing between the boles of two pine trees that had seen better days. A little further, two elderly women with tear-stained faces were engaged in burying a mercifully killed dog together with the old croquet ball that bore the signs of its gay young teeth. In yet another garden a white-bearded waltwhitmanesque man wearing a jaeger suit was seated before an easel, and although the time was a quarter to eleven of a nondescript morning, a cindery red-barred sunset sprawled on his canvas, and he was painting in the trees and various other details which, on the day before, advancing dusk had prevented him from completing. On a bench in a pine grove on the left a straight-backed girl was rapidly speaking (retaliation ... bombs ... cowards ... oh, Phokus, if I were a man ...) with nervous gestures of perplexity and dismay to a blue-capped student who sat with bent head and poked at scraps of paper, bus tickets, pine needles, the eye of a doll or a fish, the soft soil, with the point of the slim, tightly buttoned umbrella belonging to his pale companion. But otherwise the once cheerful resort was forlorn, the shutters were closed, a battered perambulator lay upside down in a ditch and the telegraph poles, those armless laggards, hummed in mournful unison with the blood that throbbed in one's head.

The road dipped slightly and then the village appeared, with a misty wilderness on one side and Lake Malheur on the other. The posters the milkman had mentioned gave a delightful touch of civilization and civic maturity to the humble hamlet squatting under its low mossy roofs. Several scrawny peasant women and their drum-bellied children had collected in front of the village hall, which was being prettily decorated for the coming festivities; and from the windows of the post office on the left and from the windows of the police station on the right uniformed clerks followed the progress of the good work with eager intelligent eyes full of pleasant anticipation. All of a sudden, with a sound akin to the cry of a newborn infant, a radio loud-speaker which had just been installed burst into life, then abruptly collapsed.

"There are some toys there," remarked David, pointing across the road towards a small but eclectic store which carried everything from groceries to Russian felt boots.

"All right," said Krug; "let us see what there is."

But as the impatient child started to cross alone, a big black automobile emerged at full speed from the direction of the district highway, and Krug, plunging forward, jerked David back as the car thundered by, leaving the mangled body of a hen in its tingling wake.

"You hurt me," said David.

Krug felt weak in the knees and bade David make haste so that he would not notice the dead bird.

"How many times——" said Krug.

A small replica of the murderous vehicle (the vibration of which still haunted Krug's solar plexus, although by that time it had probably reached or even passed the spot where the neighbourly loafer had been perched on his fence) was immediately detected by David among the cheap dolls and the tins of preserves. Though somewhat dusty and scratched, it had the kind of detachable tyres he approved of and was especially acceptable because it had been found in an out-of-the-way place. Krug asked the red-cheeked young grocer for a pocket flask of brandy (the Maximovs were teetotallers). As he was paying for it and for the little car which David was delicately rolling backwards and forwards upon the counter, the Toad's nasal tones, prodigiously magnified, burst forth from outside. The grocer stood to attention, fixing in civic fervour the flags decorating the village hall, which, together with a strip of white sky, could be seen through the doorway.

". . . and to those who trust me as they trust themselves," roared the loud-speaker, as it ended a sentence.

The clatter of applause that followed was presumably interrupted by the gesture of the orator's hand.

"From now on," continued the tremendously swollen Tyrannosaurus, "the way to total joy lies open. You will attain it, brothers, by dint of ardent intercourse with one another, by being like happy boys in a whispering dormitory, by adjusting ideas and emotions to those of a harmonious majority; you will attain it, citizens, by weeding out all such arrogant notions as the community does not and should not share; you will attain it, adolescents, by letting your person dissolve in the virile oneness of the State; then, and only then, will the goal be reached. Your groping individualities will become interchangeable and, instead of crouching in the prison cell of an illegal ego, the naked soul will be in contact with that of every other man in this land; nay, more: each of you will be able to make his abode in the elastic inner self of any other citizen, and to flutter from one to another, until you know not whether you are Peter or John, so closely locked will you be in the embrace of the State, so gladly will you be krum karum——"

The speech disintegrated in a succession of cackles. There was a kind of stunned silence: evidently the village radio was not yet in perfect working order.

"One could almost butter one's bread with the modulations of that admirable voice," remarked Krug.

What followed was most unexpected: the grocer gave him a wink.

"Good gracious," said Krug, "a gleam in the gloom!"

But the wink contained a specific injunction. Krug turned. An Ekwilist soldier was standing right behind him.

All he wanted however was a pound of sunflower seeds. Krug and David inspected a cardboard house which stood on the floor in a corner. David sank down on his little haunches to peep inside through the windows. But these were simply painted upon the wall. He slowly drew himself up, still looking at the house and automatically slipping his hand into Krug's.

They left the shop, and in order to overcome the monotony of the return journey, decided to skirt the lake and then to follow a path that meandered through meadows and would bring them back to the Maximovs' cottage after going round the wood.

Was the fool trying to save me? From what? From whom? Excuse me, I am invulnerable. Not much more foolish in fact than suggesting I grow a beard and cross the frontier.

There were a number of things to be settled before giving thought to political matters—if indeed that drivel could be called a political matter. If, moreover, in a fortnight or so some impatient admirer did not murder Paduk. Misunderstanding, so to speak, the drift of the spiritual cannibalism advocated by the poor fellow. One wondered also (at least somebody might wonder—the question was of little interest) what the peasants made of that eloquence. Maybe it vaguely reminded them of church. First of all I shall have to get him a good nurse—a picture-book nurse, kind and wise and scrupulously clean. Then I must do something about you, my love. We have imagined that a white hospital train with a white Diesel engine has taken you through many a tunnel to a mountainous country by the sea. You are getting well there. But you cannot write because your fingers are so very weak. Moonbeams cannot hold even a white pencil. The picture is pretty, but how long can it stay on the screen? We expect the next slide, but the magic-lantern man has none left. Shall we let the theme of a long separation expand till it breaks into tears?

Shall we say (daintily handling the disinfected white symbols) that the train is Death and the nursing home Paradise? Or shall we leave the picture to fade by itself, to mingle with other fading impressions? But we want to write letters to you even if you cannot answer. Shall we suffer the slow wobbly scrawl (we can manage our name and two or three words of greeting) to work its conscientious and unnecessary way across a post card which will never be mailed? Are not these problems so hard to solve because my own mind is not made up yet in regard to your death? My intelligence does not accept the transformation of physical discontinuity into the permanent continuity of a nonphysical element escaping the obvious law, nor can it accept the inanity of accumulating incalculable treasures of thought and sensation, and thought-behind-thought and sensation-behind-sensation, to lose them all at once and forever in a fit of black nausea followed by infinite nothingness. Unquote.

"See if you can climb on top of that stone. I don't think you can."

David trotted across a dead meadow towards a boulder shaped like a sheep (left behind by some careless glacier). The brandy was bad but would serve. He suddenly recalled a summer day when he had walked through these very fields in the company of a tall black-haired girl with thick lips and downy arms whom he had courted just before he met Olga.

"Yes, I *am* looking. Splendid. Now try to get down."

But David could not. Krug walked up to the boulder and tenderly removed him. This little body. They sat for a while on a lamb-boulder near by and contemplated an endless freight train puffing beyond the fields towards the station near the lake. A crow ponderously flapped by, the slow swish-swish of its wings making the rotting grassland and the colourless sky seem even sadder than they actually were.

"You will lose it that way. Better let me put it into my pocket."

Presently they started moving again, and David was curious to know how far they had to walk yet. Only a little way. They followed the edge of the forest and then turned into a very muddy road which led them to what was for the moment home.

A cart was standing in front of the cottage. The old white horse looked at them across its shoulder. On the threshold of the porch two people were sitting side by side: the farmer who lived on the hill and his wife who did the housework for the Maximovs.

"They are gone," said the farmer.

"I hope they did not go out to meet us on the road because we came by another way. Go in, David, and wash your hands."

"No," said the farmer. "They are quite gone. They have been taken away in a police car."

At this point his wife became very voluble. She had just come down from the hill when she saw the soldiers leading the aged couple away. She had been afraid to come near. Her wages had not been paid since October. She would take, she said, all the jars of jam in the house.

Krug went in. The table was laid for four. David wanted to have his toy which, he hoped, his father had not lost. A piece of raw meat was lying on the kitchen table.

Krug sat down. The farmer had also come in and was stroking his grizzled chin.

"Could you drive us to the station?" asked Krug after a while.

"I might get into trouble," said the farmer.

"Oh, come, I offer you more than the police will ever pay you for whatever you do for them."

"You are not the police and so cannot bribe me," replied the honest and meticulous old farmer.

"You mean you refuse?"

The farmer was silent.

"Well," said Krug, getting to his feet, "I am afraid I shall have to insist. The child is tired, I do not intend to carry him and the bag."

"How much was it again?" asked the farmer.

Krug put on his glasses and opened his wallet.

"You will stop at the police station on the way," he added.

The toothbrushes and the pyjamas were quickly packed. David accepted the sudden departure with perfect equanimity but suggested eating something first. The kind woman got him some biscuits and an apple. A fine rain had set in. David's hat could not be found and Krug gave him his own broad-brimmed black one, but David kept taking it off because it covered his ears and he wanted to hear the sloshing hoofs, the creaking wheels.

As they were passing the spot where two hours before a man with a heavy moustache and twinkling eyes had been sitting on a rustic fence, Krug noticed that now, instead of the man, there were but a couple of *rudobrustki* or *ruddocks* [a small bird allied to the robin] and that a square of cardboard had been nailed to the fence. It bore a rough inscription in ink (already somewhat affected by the drizzle):

*Bon Voyage!*

To this Krug drew the attention of the driver; who, without turning his head, remarked that there were many inexplicable things happening *nowadays* (a euphemism for "new regime") and that it was better not to study current phenomena too closely. David tugged at his father's sleeve and wanted to know what it was all about. Krug explained that they were discussing the strange ways of people who arranged picnics in dreary November.

"I had better drive you straight on, folks, or you might miss the one-forty," said the farmer tentatively, but Krug made him pull up at the brick house where the local police had their headquarters. Krug got out and entered an office room where a bewhiskered old man, his uniform unbuttoned at the neck, was sipping tea from a blue saucer and blowing upon it between sips. He said he knew nothing about the business. It was, he said, the City Guard, and not his department, which had made the arrest. He could only presume that they had been taken to some prison in town as political offenders. He suggested that Krug stop playing the busybody and thank his stars for not having been in the house when the arrest took place. Krug said that, on the contrary, he intended doing everything in his power to find out why two aged and respectable persons who had lived quietly in the country for a number of years and had no connection whatever with——The police officer, interrupting him, said that the best a professor could do (if Krug *was* a professor) would be to keep his mouth shut and leave the village. Again the saucer was lifted to the bearded lips. Two young members of the force hovered around and stared at Krug.

He stood there for a moment looking at the wall, at a poster calling attention to the plight of aged policemen, at a calendar (monstrously *in copula* with a barometer); pondered a bribe: decided that they really knew nothing here; and with a shrug of his heavy shoulders walked out.

David was not in the cart.

The farmer turned his head, looked at the empty seat and said the child had probably followed Krug into the police station. Krug went back. The chief eyed him with irritation and suspicion and said that he had seen the cart from the window and that there had been no child in it from the very start. Krug tried to open another door in the corridor but it was locked. "Stop that," growled the man, losing his temper, "or else we'll arrest you for making a nuisance of yourself."

"I want my little boy," said Krug (another Krug, horribly handicapped by a spasm in the throat and a pounding heart).

"Hold your horses," said one of the younger policemen. "This is not a kindergarten, there are no children here."

Krug (now a man in black with an ivory face) pushed him aside and went out again. He cleared his throat and bellowed for David. Two villagers in medieval *kappen* who stood near the cart gazed at him and then at each other, and then one of them turned and glanced in a given direction. "Have you——?" asked Krug. But they did not reply and looked once more at each other.

I must not lose my head, thought Adam the Ninth—for by now there were quite a number of these serial Krugs: turning this way and that like the baffled buffeted seeker in a game of blindman's buff: battering with imaginary fists a cardboard police station to pulp; running through nightmare tunnels; half-hiding together with Olga behind a tree to watch David warily tiptoe around another, his whole body ready for a little shiver of glee; searching an intricate dungeon where, somewhere, a shrieking child was being tortured by experienced hands; hugging the boots of a uniformed brute; strangling the brute amid a chaos of overturned furniture; finding a small skeleton in a dark cellar.

At this point it may be mentioned that David wore on the fourth finger of his left hand a child's enamelled ring.

He was about to attack the police once more, but then noticed that a narrow lane fringed with shrivelled nettles ran along the side of the brick police house (the two peasants had been glancing in that direction for quite a while) and turned into it, stumbling painfully over a log as he did so.

"Take care, don't break your pins, you'll need 'em," said the farmer with an amiable laugh.

In the lane, a barefooted scrofulous boy in a pink red-patched shirt was whipping a top and David stood looking on with his hands behind his back.

"This is intolerable," cried Krug. "You ought never, never to wander away like that. Shut up! Yes. I *will* hold you. Get in. Get in."

One of the peasants tapped his temple slightly with a judicious air, and his crony nodded. In an open window a young policeman aimed a half-eaten apple at Krug's back but was restrained by a staider comrade.

The cart moved on. Krug groped for his handkerchief, did not find it, wiped his face with the palm of his still shaking hand.

The well-named lake was a featureless expanse of grey water, and as the cart turned on to the highway that ran along the shore to the station, a cold breeze lifted with invisible finger and thumb the thin silvery mane of the old mare.

"Will my mummy be back when we come?" asked David.

# 7

A FLUTED GLASS with a blue-veined violet and a jug of hot punch stand on Ember's bedtable. The buff wall directly above his bed (he has a bad cold) bears a sequence of three engravings.

Number one represents a sixteenth-century gentleman in the act of handing a book to a humble fellow who holds a spear and a bay-crowned hat in his left hand. Note the sinistral detail (Why? Ah, "that is the question," as Monsieur Homais once remarked, quoting *le journal d'hier;* a question which is answered in a wooden voice by the Portrait on the title page of the First Folio). Note also the legend: "Ink, a Drug." Somebody's idle pencil (Ember highly treasures this scholium) has numbered the letters so as to spell *Grudinka* which means "bacon" in several Slavic languages.

Number two shows the rustic (now clad in the clothes of the gentleman) removing from the head of the gentleman (now writing at a desk) a kind of shapska. Scribbled underneath in the same hand: "*Ham-let,* or *Homelette au Lard.*"

Finally, number three has a road, a traveller on foot (wearing the stolen shapska) and a road sign "To High Wycombe."

His name is protean. He begets doubles at every corner. His penmanship is unconsciously faked by lawyers who happen to write a similar hand. On the wet morning of November 27, 1582, he is Shaxpere and she is a Wately of Temple Grafton. A couple of days later he is Shagspere and she is a Hathway of Stratford-on-Avon. Who is he? William X, cunningly composed of two left arms and a mask. Who else? The person who said (not for the first time) that the glory of God is to hide a thing, and the glory of man is to find it. However, the fact that the Warwickshire fellow wrote the plays is most satisfactorily proved on the strength of an applejohn and a pale primrose.

There are two themes here: the Shakespearian one rendered in the present tense, with Ember presiding in his ruelle; and another theme altogether, a complex mixture of past, present, and future, with Olga's monstrous absence causing dreadful embarrassment. This was, this is, their first meeting since she died. Krug will not speak of her, will not even inquire about her ashes; and Ember, who feels the shame of death too, does not know what to say. Had he been able to move about freely, he might have embraced his fat friend in silence (a miserable defeat in the case of philosophers and poets accustomed to believe that words are superior to deeds), but this is not feasible when one of the two lies in bed. Krug, semi-intentionally, keeps out of reach. He is a difficult person. Describe the bedroom. Allude to Ember's bright brown eyes. Hot punch and a touch of fever. His strong shining blue-veined nose and the bracelet on his hairy wrist. Say something. Ask about David. Relate the horror of those rehearsals.

"David is also laid up with a cold [*ist auk beterkeltet*] but that is not why we had to come back [*zueruk*]. What [*shto bish*] were you saying about those rehearsals [*repetitia*]?"

Ember gratefully adopts the subject selected. He might

have asked: "why then?" He will learn the reason a little later. Vaguely he perceives emotional dangers in that dim region. So he prefers to talk shop. Last chance of describing the bedroom.

Too late. Ember gushes. He exaggerates his own gushing manner. In a dehydrated and condensed form Ember's new impressions as Literary Adviser to the State Theatre may be rendered thus:

"The two best Hamlets we had, indeed the only respectable ones, have both left the country in disguise and are now said to be fiercely intriguing in Paris after having almost murdered each other en route. None of the youngsters we have interviewed are any good, though one or two have at least the full habit of body required for the part. For reasons I shall presently make clear Osric and Fortinbras have acquired a tremendous ascendancy over the rest of the cast. The Queen is with child. Laertes is constitutionally unable to learn the elements of fencing. I have lost all interest in the staging of the thing as I am helpless to change the grotesque course it has taken. My sole poor object now is to have the players adopt my own translation instead of the abominable one to which they are used. On the other hand this work of love commenced long ago is not yet quite finished and the fact of having to speed it up for what is a rather incidental purpose (to say the least) causes me intense irritation, which, however, is nothing to the horror of hearing the actors lapse with a kind of atavistic relief into the gibberish of the traditional version (Kronberg's) whenever Wern, who is weak and prefers ideas to words, allows them to behind my back."

Ember goes on to explain why the new Government found it worth while to suffer the production of a muddled Elizabethan play. He explains the idea on which the production is based. Wern, who humbly submitted the project, took his conception of the play from the late Professor Hamm's extraordinary work "The Real Plot of *Hamlet*."

" 'Iron and ice' (wrote the Professor) '—this is the physical amalgamation suggested by the personality of the strangely rigid and ponderous Ghost. Of this union Fortinbras (Ironside) will be presently born. According to the immemorial rules of the stage what is boded must be embodied: the eruption must come at all cost. In *Hamlet* the exposition grimly promises the audience a play founded upon young Fortinbras' attempt to recover the lands lost by his father to King Hamlet. This is the conflict, this is the plot. To surreptitiously shift the stress from this healthy, vigorous and clearcut Nordic theme to the chameleonic moods of an impotent Dane would be, on the modern stage, an insult to determinism and common sense.

" 'Whatever Shakespeare's or Kyd's intentions were, there can be no doubt that the keynote, the impelling power of the action, is the corruption of civil and military life in Denmark. Imagine the morale of an army where a soldier, who must fear neither thunder nor silence, says that he is sick at heart! Consciously or unconsciously, the author of *Hamlet* has created the tragedy of the masses and thus has founded the sovereignty of society over the individual. This, however, does not mean that there is no tangible hero in the play. But he is not Hamlet. The real hero is of course Fortinbras, a blooming young knight, beautiful and sound to the core. With God's sanction, this fine Nordic youth assumes the control of miserable Denmark which had been so criminally misruled by degenerate King Hamlet and Judeo-Latin Claudius.

" 'As with all decadent democracies, everybody in the Denmark of the play suffers from a plethora of words. If the state is to be saved, if the nation desires to be worthy of a new robust government, then everything must be changed; popular commonsense must spit out the caviar of moonshine and poetry, and the simple words, *verbum sine ornatu*, intelligible to man and beast alike, and accompanied by fit action, must be restored to power. Young Fortinbras possesses an ancient claim and hereditary rights to the throne of Denmark. Some dark deed of violence or injustice, some base trick on the part of degenerate feudalism, some masonic manoeuvre engendered by the Shylocks of high finance, has dispossessed his family of their just claims, and the shadow of this crime keeps hanging in the dark background until, with the closing scene, the idea of mass justice impresses upon the whole play its seal of historical significance.

" 'Three thousand crowns and a week or so of available time would not have been sufficient to conquer Poland (at least in those days); but they proved amply sufficient for another purpose. Wine-besotted Claudius is completely deceived by young Fortinbras' suggestion, that he, Fortinbras, pass through the dominion of Claudius on his (singularly roundabout) way to Poland with an army levied for quite a different purpose. No, the bestial Polacks need not tremble: *that* conquest will not take place; it is not *their* bogs and forests that our hero covets. Instead of proceeding to the port, Fortinbras, that soldier of genius, will be lying in waiting and the "go softly on" (which he whispers to his troops after sending a captain to greet Claudius) can only mean one thing: go softly into hiding while the enemy (the Danish King) thinks you have embarked for Poland.

" 'The real plot of the play will be readily grasped if the following is realized: the Ghost on the battlements of Elsinore is not the ghost of King Hamlet. It is that of Fortinbras the Elder whom King Hamlet has slain. The ghost of the victim posing as the ghost of the murderer—what a wonderful bit of farseeing strategy, how deeply it excites our intense admiration! The glib and probably quite untrue account of old Hamlet's death which this admirable imposter gives is intended solely to create *innerliche Unruhe* in the state and to soften the morale of the Danes. The poison poured into the sleeper's ear is a symbol of the subtle injection of lethal rumours, a symbol which the groundlings of Shakespeare's day could hardly have missed. Thus, old Fortinbras, disguised as his enemy's ghost, prepares the peril of his enemy's son and the triumph of his own offspring. No, the "judgments" were not so accidental, the "slaughters" not so casual as they seemed to Horatio the Recorder, and there is a note of deep satisfaction (which the audience cannot help sharing) in the young hero's guttural exclamation—Ha-ha, this quarry cries on havoc (meaning: the foxes have devoured one another)—as he surveys the rich heap of dead bodies, all that is left of the rotten state of Denmark. We can easily imagine him adding in an outburst of rough filial gratitude: Yah, the old mole has done a good job!

" 'But to return to Osric. Garrulous Hamlet has just been speaking to the skull of a jester; now it is the skull of jesting death that speaks to Hamlet. Note the remarkable juxtaposition: the skull—the shell; "Runs away with a shell on his head." Osric and Yorick almost rhyme, except that the yolk of one has become the bone (os) of the other. Mixing as he does the language of the shop and the ship, this middleman, wearing the garb of a fantastic courtier, is in the act of selling death, the very death that Hamlet has just escaped at sea. The winged doublet and the aureate innuendoes mask a deep purpose, a bold and cunning mind. Who is this master of ceremonies? He is young Fortinbras' most brilliant spy.' Well, this gives you a fair sample of what I have to endure."

Krug cannot help smiling at little Ember's complaints.

He remarks that somehow or other the whole business reminds him of Paduk's mannerisms. I mean these intricate convolutions of sheer stupidity. To stress the artist's detachment from life, Ember says he does not know and does not care to know (a telltale dismissal) who this Paduk or Padock—*bref, la personne en question*—is. By way of explanation Krug tells Ember about his visit to the Lakes and how it all ended. Naturally Ember is aghast. He vividly visualizes Krug and the child wandering through the rooms of the deserted cottage whose two clocks (one in the dining-room, the other in the kitchen) are probably still going, alone, intact, pathetically sticking to man's notion of time after man has gone. He wonders whether Maximov had time to receive the well-written letter he sent him about Olga's death and Krug's helpless condition. What shall I say? The priest mistook a blear-eyed old man belonging to Viola's party for the widower and while making his oration, and while the beautiful big body was burning behind a thick wall, kept addressing himself to that person (who nodded back). Not even an uncle, not even her mother's lover.

Ember turns his face to the wall and bursts into tears. In order to bring things back to a less emotional level Krug tells him about a curious character with whom he once travelled in the States, a man who was fanatically eager to make a film out of *Hamlet.*

"We'd begin, he had said, with
Ghostly apes swathed in sheets
haunting the shuddering Roman streets.
And the mobled moon...

Then: the ramparts and towers of Elsinore, its dragons and florid ironwork, the moon making fish scales of its shingle tiles, the integument of a mermaid multiplied by the gable roof, which shimmers in an abstract sky, and the green star of a glowworm on the platform before the dark castle. Hamlet's first soliloquy is delivered in an unweeded garden that has gone to seed. Burdock and thistle are the main invaders. A toad breathes and blinks on the late king's favourite garden seat. Somewhere the cannon booms as the new king drinks. By dream law and screen law the cannon is gently transformed into the obliquity of a rotten tree trunk in the garden. The trunk points cannonwise at the sky where for one instant the deliberate loops of canescent smoke form the floating word "self-slaughter."

"Hamlet at Wittenberg, always late, missing G. Bruno's lectures, never using a watch, relying on Horatio's timepiece which is slow, saying he will be on the battlements between eleven and twelve and turning up after midnight.

"The moonlight following on tiptoe the Ghost in complete steel, a gleam now settling on a rounded pauldron, now stealing along the taces.

"We shall also see Hamlet dragging the dead Ratman from under the arras and along the floor and up the winding stairs, to stow him away in an obscure passage, with some weird light effects anon, when the torch-bearing Switzers are sent to find the body. Another thrill will be provided by Hamlet's sea-gowned figure, unhampered by the heavy seas, heedless of the spray, clambering over bales and barrels of Danish butter and creeping into the cabin where Rosenstern and Guildenkranz, those gentle interchangeable twins 'who came to heal and went away to die,' are snoring in their common bunk. As the sagebrush country and leopard-spotted hills sped past the window of the men's lounge, more and more pictorial possibilities were evolved. We might be shown, he said (he was a hawkfaced shabby man whose academic career had been suddenly brought to a close by an awkwardly timed love affair), R. following young L. through the Quartier Latin, Polonius in his youth acting Caesar at the University Playhouse, the skull in Hamlet's gloved hands developing the features of a live jester (with the censor's permission); perhaps even lusty old King Hamlet smiting with a poleaxe the Polacks skidding and sprawling on the ice. Then he produced a flask from his hip pocket and said: 'take a shot.' He added he had thought she was eighteen at least, judging by her bust, but, in fact, she was hardly fifteen, the little bitch. And then there was Ophelia's death. To the sounds of Liszt's *Les Funérailles* she would be shown wrestling—or, as another rivermaid's father would have said, 'wrustling' —with the willow. A lass, a salix. He recommended here a side shot of the glassy water. To feature a phloating leaph. Then back again to her little white hand, holding a wreath trying to reach, trying to wreathe a phallacious sliver. Now comes the difficulty of dealing in a dramatic way with what had been in prevocal days the *pièce de résistance* of comic shorts—the getting-unexpectedly-wet stunt. The hawk-man in the toilet lounge pointed out (between cigar and cuspidor) that the difficulty might be neatly countered by showing only her shadow, her falling shadow, falling and glancing across the edge of the turfy bank amid a shower of shadowy flowers. See? Then: a garland afloat. That puritanical leather (on which they sat) was the very last remnant of a phylogenetic link between the modern highly differentiated Pullman idea and a bench in the primitive stagecoach: from oats to oil. Then—and only then—we see her, he said, on her back in the brook (which table-forks further on to form eventually the Rhine, the Dnepr and the Cottonwood Canyon or Nova Avon) in a dim ectoplastic cloud of soaked, bulging bombast-quilted garments and dreamily droning hey non nonny nonny or any other old laud. This is transformed into a tinkling of bells, and now we are shown a liberal shepherd on marshy ground where *Orchis mascula* grows: period rags, sun-margined beard, five sheep and one cute lamb. An important point this lamb, despite the brevity—one heartthrob—of the bucolic theme. Song moves to Queen's shepherd, lamb moves to brook."

Krug's anecdote has the desired effect. Ember stops sniffling. He listens. Presently he smiles. Finally, he enters into the spirit of the game. Yes, she was found by a shepherd. In fact her name can be derived from that of an amorous shepherd in Arcadia. Or quite possibly it is an anagram of Alpheios, with the "S" lost in the damp grass—Alpheus the rivergod, who pursued a long-legged nymph until Artemis changed her into a stream, which of course suited his liquidity to a tee (*cp.* Winnipeg Lake, ripple 585, Vico Press edition). Or again we can base it on the Greek rendering of an old Danske serpent name. Lithe, lithping, thin-lipped Ophelia, Amleth's wet dream, a mermaid of Lethe, a rare water serpent, *Russalka letheana* of science (to match your long purples). While he was busy with German servant maids, she at home, in an embayed window, with the icy spring wind rattling the pane, innocently flirted with Osric. Her skin was so tender that if you merely looked at it a rosy spot would appear. The uncommon cold of a Botticellian angel tinged her nostrils with pink and suffused her upperlip—you know, when the rims of the lips merge with the skin. She proved to be a kitchen wench too—but in the kitchen of a vegetarian. Ophelia, serviceableness. Died in passive service. The fair Ophelia. A first Folio with some neat corrections and a few bad mistakes. "My dear fellow" (we might have Hamlet say to Horatio), "she was as hard as nails in spite of her physical softness. And slippery: a posy made of eels. She was one of those thin-blooded pale-eyed lovely slim slimy ophidian maidens that are both hotly hysterical and hopelessly frigid. Quietly, with a kind of devilish daintiness she minced her dangerous course the way her father's ambition pointed. Even mad, she went on teasing her secret with the dead man's finger. Which kept pointing at me. Oh, of course I loved her like forty thousand brothers, as thick as thieves (terracotta jars, a cypress, a fingernail moon) but we all were Lamord's pupils, if you know what I mean." He might add that he had caught a cold in the head during the dumb show. Undine's pink gill, iced watermelon, *l'aurore grelottant en robe rose et verte.* Her sleazy lap.

Speaking of the word-droppings on a German scholar's decrepit hat, Krug suggests tampering with Hamlet's name too. Take "Telemachos," he says, which means "fighting from afar"—which again was Hamlet's idea of warfare. Prune it, remove the unnecessary letters, all of them secondary additions, and you get the ancient "Telmah." Now read it backwards. Thus does a fanciful pen elope with a lewd idea and Hamlet in reverse gear becomes the son of Ulysses slaying his mother's lovers. *Worte, worte, worte.* Warts, warts, warts. My favourite commentator is Tschischwitz, a madhouse of consonants—or a *soupir de petit chien.*

Ember, however, has not quite finished with the girl. After hurriedly noting that Elsinore is an anagram of Roseline, which has possibilities, he returns to Ophelia. He likes her, he says. Quite apart from Hamlet's notions about her, the girl had charm, a kind of heartbreaking charm: those quick grey-blue eyes, the sudden laugh, the small even teeth, the pause to see whether you were not making fun of her. Her knees and calves, though quite shapely, were a little too sturdy in comparison with her thin arms and light bosom. The palms of her hands were like a damp Sunday and she wore a cross round her neck where a tiny raisin of flesh, a coagulated but still transparent bubble of dove's blood, seemed always in danger of being sliced off by that thin golden chain. Then too, there was her morning breath, it smelled of narcissi before breakfast and of curdled milk after. She had something the matter with her liver. The lobes of her ears were naked, though they had been minutely pierced for small corals—not pearls. The combination of these details, her sharp elbows, very fair hair, tight glossy cheekbones and the ghost of a blond fluff (most delicately bristly to the eye) at the corners of her mouth, remind him (says Ember remembering his childhood) of a certain anaemic Esthonian housemaid, whose pathetically parted poor little breasts palely dangled in her blouse when she went low, very low, to pull on for him his striped socks.

Here Ember suddenly raises his voice to a petulant scream of distress. He says that instead of this authentic Ophelia the impossible Gloria Bellhouse, hopelessly plump, with a mouth like the ace of hearts, has been selected for the part. He is especially incensed at the greenhouse carnations and lilies that the management gives her to play with in the "mad" scene. She and the producer, like Goethe, imagine Ophelia in the guise of a canned peach: "her whole being floats in sweet ripe passion," says Johann Wolfgang, Ger. poet, nov., dram. & phil. Oh, horrible.

"Or her father. . . . We all know him and love him, don't we? and it would be so simple to have him right: Polonius-Pantolonius, a pottering dotard in a padded robe, shuffling about in carpet slippers and following the sagging spectacles at the end of his nose, as he waddles from room to room, vaguely androgynous, combining the pa and the ma, a hermaphrodite with the comfortable pelvis of a eunuch—instead of which they have a stiff tall man who played Metternich in *The World Waltzes* and insists on remaining a wise and wily statesman for the rest of his days. Oh, most horrible."

But there is worse to come. Ember asks his friend to hand him a certain book—no, the red one. Sorry, the *other* red one.

"As you have noticed, perhaps, the Messenger mentions a certain Claudio as having given him letters which Claudio 'received . . . of him that brought them [from the ship]'; there is no reference to this person anywhere else in the play. Now let us open the great Hamm's second book. What does he do? Here we are. He takes this Claudio and—well, just listen.

"That he was the King's fool is evident from the fact that in the German original (*Bestrafter Brudermord*) it is the clown Phantasmo who brings the news. It is amazing that nobody as yet has troubled to follow up this prototypical clue. No less obvious is the fact that in his quibbling mood Hamlet would of course make a special point of having the sailors deliver his message to the *King's fool,* since he, Hamlet, has *fooled* the *King*. Finally, when we recall that in those days a court jester would often assume the name of his master, with only a slight change in the ending, the picture becomes complete. We have thus the interesting figure of this Italian or Italianate jester haunting the gloomy halls of a Northern castle, a man in his forties, but as alert as he was in his youth, twenty years ago, when he replaced Yorick. Whereas Polonius had been the 'father' of good news, Claudio is the 'uncle' of bad news. His character is more subtle than that of the wise and good old man. He is afraid to confront the King directly with a message with which his nimble fingers and prying eye have already acquainted themselves. He knows that he cannot very well come to the King and tell him 'your beer is sour' with a quibble on 'beer,' meaning 'your beard is soar'd' (to soar —to pull, to twitch off). So, with superb cunning he invents a stratagem which speaks more for his intelligence than for his moral courage. What is this stratagem? It is far deeper than anything 'poor Yorick' could ever have devised. While the sailors hurry away to such abodes of pleasure as a long-yearned-for port can provide, Claudio, the dark-eyed schemer, neatly refolds the dangerous letter and casually hands it to *another messenger*, the 'Messenger' of the play, who innocently takes it to the King."

But enough of this, let us hear Ember's rendering of some famous lines:

> *Ubit' il' ne ubit'? Vot est' oprosen.*
> *Vto bude edler: v rasume tzerpieren*
> *Ogneprashchi i strely zlovo roka——*

(or as a Frenchman might have it:)

> *L'égorgerai-je ou non? Voici le vrai problème.*
> *Est-il plus noble en soi de supporter quand même*
> *Et les dards et le feu d'un accablant destin——*

Yes, I am still jesting. We now come to the real thing.

> *Tam nad ruch'om rostiot naklonno iva,*
> *V vode iavliaia list'ev sedinu;*
> *Guirliandy fantasticheskie sviv*
> *Iz etikh list'ev—s primes'u romashek,*
> *Krapivy, lutikov——*
> (over yon brook there grows aslant a willow
> Showing in the water the hoariness of its leaves;
> Having tressed fantastic garlands
> of these leaves, with a sprinkling of daisies,
> Nettles, crowflowers——)

You see I have to choose my commentators.

Or this difficult passage:

*Ne dumaete-li vy, sudar', shto vot eto* (the song about the wounded deer), *da les per'ev na shliape, a dve kamchatye rozy na proreznykh bashmakakh, mogli by, kol' fortuna zadala by mne turku, zasluzhit' mne uchast'e v teatralnoí arteli; a, sudar'?*

Or the beginning of my favourite scene:

As he sits listening to Ember's translation, Krug cannot help marvelling at the strangeness of the day. He imagines himself at some point in the future recalling this particular moment. He, Krug, was sitting beside Ember's bed. Ember, with knees raised under the counterpane, was reading bits of blank verse from scraps of paper. Krug had recently lost his wife. A new political order had stunned the city. Two people he was fond of had been spirited away and perhaps executed. But the room was warm and quiet and Ember was deep in *Hamlet*. And Krug marvelled at the strangeness of the day. He listened to the rich-toned voice (Ember's father had been a Persian merchant) and tried to simplify the terms of his reaction. Nature had once produced an Englishman whose domed head had been a hive of words; a man who had only to breathe on any particle of his stupendous vocabulary to have that particle live and expand and throw out tremulous tentacles until it became a complex image with a pulsing brain and correlated limbs. Three centuries later, another man, in another country, was trying to render these rhythms and metaphors in a different tongue. This process entailed a prodigious amount of labour, for the necessity of which no real reason could be given. It was as if someone, having seen a certain oak tree (further called Individual T) growing in a certain land and casting its own unique shadow on the green and brown ground, had proceeded to erect in his garden a prodigiously intricate piece of machinery which in itself was as unlike that or any other tree as the translator's inspiration and language were unlike those of the original author, but which, by means of ingenious combinations of parts, light effects, breeze-engendering engines, would, when completed, cast a shadow exactly similar to that of Individual T—the same outline, changing in the same manner, with the same double and single spots of suns rippling in the same position, at the same hour of the day. From a practical point of view, such a waste of time and material (those headaches, those midnight triumphs that turn out to be disasters in the sober light of morning!) was almost criminally absurd, since the greatest masterpiece of imitation presupposed a voluntary limitation of thought, in submission to another man's genius. Could this suicidal limitation and submission be compensated by the miracle of adaptive tactics, by the thousand devices of shadography, by the keen pleasure that the weaver of words and their witness experienced at every wile in the warp, or was it, taken all in all, but an exaggerated and spiritualized replica of Paduk's writing machine?

"Do you like it, do you accept it?" asked Ember anxiously.

"I think it is wonderful," said Krug, frowning. He got up and paced the room. "Some lines need oiling," he continued, "and I do not like the colour of dawn's coat—I see 'russet' in a less leathery, less proletarian way, but you may be right. The whole thing is really quite wonderful."

He went to the window as he spoke, unconsciously peering into the yard, a deep well of light and shade (for, curiously enough, it was some time in the afternoon, and not in the middle of the night).

"I am so pleased," said Ember. "Of course, there are lots of little things to be changed. I think I shall stick to '*laderod kappe.*' "

"Some of his puns——" said Krug. "Hullo, that's queer."

He had become aware of the yard. Two organ-grinders were standing there, a few paces from each other, neither of them playing—in fact, both looked depressed and self-conscious. Several heavy-chinned urchins with zigzag profiles (one little chap holding a toy cart by a string) gaped at them quietly.

"Never in my life," said Krug, "have I seen *two* organ-grinders in the same back yard at the same time."

"Nor have I," admitted Ember. "I shall now proceed to show you——"

"I wonder what has happened?" said Krug. "They look most uncomfortable, and they do not, or cannot play."

"Perhaps one of them butted into the other's beat," suggested Ember, sorting out a fresh set of papers.

"Perhaps," said Krug.

"And perhaps each is afraid that the other will plunge into some competitive music as soon as one of them starts to play."

"Perhaps," said Krug. "All the same—it is a very singular picture. An organ-grinder is the very emblem of oneness. But here we have an absurd duality. They do not play but they do glance upwards."

"I shall now proceed," said Ember, "to read you——"

"I know of only one other profession," said Krug, "that has that upward movement of the eyeballs. And that is our clergy."

"Well, Adam, sit down and listen. Or am I boring you?"

"Oh nonsense," said Krug, going back to his chair. "I was only trying to think what exactly was wrong. The children seem also perplexed by their silence. There is something familiar about the whole thing, something I cannot quite disentangle—a certain line of thought. . . ."

"The chief difficulty that assails the translator of the following passage," said Ember, licking his fat lips after a draught of punch and readjusting his back to his large pillow, "the chief difficulty——"

The remote sound of the doorbell interrupted him.

"Are you expecting someone?" asked Krug.

"Nobody in particular. Maybe some of those actor fellows have come to see whether I am dead. They will be disappointed."

The footfalls of the valet passed down the corridor. Then returned.

"Gentleman and lady to see you, sir," he said.

"Curse them," said Ember. "Could you, Adam, . . . ?"

"Yes of course," said Krug. "Shall I tell them you are asleep?"

"And unshaven," said Ember. "And anxious to go on with my reading."

A handsome lady in a dove-grey tailor-made suit and a gentleman with a glossy red tulip in the buttonhole of his cutaway coat stood side by side in the hall.

"We——" began the gentleman, fumbling in his left trouser pocket and accompanying this gesture with a kind of wriggle as if he had a touch of cramp or were uncomfortably clothed.

"Mr. Ember is in bed with a cold," said Krug. "And he asked me——"

The gentleman bowed: "I understand perfectly, but this (his free hand proffered a card) will tell you my name and standing. I have my orders as you can see. Prompt submission to them tore me away from my very private duties as host. I too was giving a party. And no doubt Mr. Ember, if that is his name, will act as promptly as I did. This is my secretary—in fact, something more than a secretary."

"Oh, come, Hustav," said the lady, nudging him.

"Surely, Professor Krug is not interested in our relations."

"Our relations?" said Hustav, looking at her with an expression of fond facetiousness on his aristocratic face. "Say that again. It sounded lovely."

She lowered her thick eyelashes and pouted.

"I did not mean what you mean, you bad boy. The Professor will think *Gott weiss was.*"

"It sounded," pursued Hustav tenderly, "like the rhythmic springs of a certain blue couch in a certain guest room."

"All right. It is sure not to happen again if you go on being so nasty."

"Now she is cross with us," sighed Hustav, turning to Krug. "Beware of women, as Shakespeare says! Well, I have to perform my sad duty. Lead me to the patient, Professor."

"One moment," said Krug. "If you are not actors, if this is not some fatuous hoax——"

"Oh, I know what you are going to say"—purred Hustav; "this element of gracious living strikes you as queer, does it not? One is accustomed to consider such things in terms of sordid brutality and gloom, rifle butts, rough soldiers, muddy boots—*und so weiter*. But headquarters knew that Mr. Ember was an artist, a poet, a sensitive soul, and it was thought that something a little dainty and uncommon in the way of arrests, an atmosphere of high life, flowers, the perfume of feminine beauty, might sweeten the ordeal. Please, notice that I am wearing civilian clothes. Whimsical perhaps, I grant you, but then—imagine his feelings if my uncouth assistants (the thumb of his free hand pointed in the direction of the stairs) crashed in and started to rip up the furniture.

"Show the Professor that big ugly thing you carry about in your pocket, Hustav."

"Say that again?"

"I mean your pistol of course," said the lady stiffly.

"I see," said Hustav. "I misunderstood you. But we shall go into that later. You need not mind her, Professor, she is apt to exaggerate. There is really nothing special about this weapon. A humdrum official article, No. 184682, of which you can see dozens any time."

"I think I have had enough of this," said Krug. "I do not believe in pistols and—well, no matter. You can put it back. All I want to know is: do you intend to take him away right now?"

"Yep," said Hustav.

"I shall find some way to complain about these monstrous intrusions," rumbled Krug. "It cannot go on like this. They were a perfectly harmless old couple, both in rather indifferent health. You shall certainly regret it."

"It has just occurred to me," remarked Hustav to his fair companion, as they moved through the flat in Krug's wake, "that the Colonel had one schnapps too many when we left him, so that I doubt whether your little sister will be quite the same by the time we get back."

"I thought that story he told about the two sailors and the *barbok* [a kind of pie with a hole in the middle for melted butter] most entertaining," said the lady. "You must tell it to Mr. Ember; he is a writer and might put it into his next book."

"Well, for that matter, your own pretty mouth——" began Hustav—but they had reached the bedroom door and the lady modestly remained behind while Hustav, again thrusting a fumbling hand into his trouser pocket, jerkily went in after Krug.

The valet was in the act of removing a *mida* [small table with incrustations] from the bedside. Ember was inspecting his uvula in a hand mirror.

"This idiot here has come to arrest you," said Krug in English.

Hustav, who had been quietly beaming at Ember from the threshold, suddenly frowned and glanced at Krug suspiciously.

"But surely this is a mistake," said Ember. "Why should anyone want to arrest me?"

"*Heraus, Mensch, marsch,*" said Hustav to the valet and, when the latter had left the room:

"We are not in a classroom, Professor," he said, turning to Krug, "so please use language that everybody can understand. Some other time I may ask you to teach me Danish or Dutch; at this moment, however, I am engaged in the performance of duties which are perhaps as repellent to me and to Miss Bachofen as they are to you. Therefore I must call your attention to the fact that, although I am not averse to a little mild bantering——"

"Wait a minute, wait a minute," cried Ember. "I know what it is. It is because I did not open my windows when those very loud speakers were on yesterday. But I can explain.... My doctor will certify I was ill. Adam, it is all right, there is no need to worry."

The sound of an idle finger touching the keys of a cold piano came from the drawing room, as Ember's valet returned with some clothes over his arm. The man's face was the colour of veal and he avoided looking at Hustav. To his master's exclamation of surprise he replied that the lady in the drawing room had told him to get Ember dressed or be shot.

"But this is ridiculous!" cried Ember, "I cannot just jump into my clothes. I must have a bath first, I must shave."

"There is a barber at the nice quiet place you are going to," remarked the kindly Hustav. "Come, get up, you really must not be so disobedient."

(How if I answer "no"?)

"I refuse to dress while you are all staring at me," said Ember.

"We are not looking," said Hustav.

Krug left the room and walked past the piano towards the study. Miss Bachofen rose up from the piano stool and nimbly overtook him.

"*Ich will etwas sagen* [I want to say something]," she said, and dropped her light hand upon his sleeve. "Just now, when we were talking, I had the impression you thought Hustav and I were rather absurd young people. But that is only a way he has, you know, always making *witze* [jokes] and teasing me, and really I am not the sort of girl you may think I am."

"These odds and ends," said Krug, touching a shelf near which he was passing, "have no special value, but he treasures them, and if you have slipped a little porcelain owl—which I do not see—into your bag——"

"Professor, we are not thieves," she said very quietly, and he must have had a heart of stone who would not have felt ashamed of his evil thought as she stood there, a narrow-hipped blonde with a pair of symmetrical breasts moistly heaving among the frills of her white silk blouse.

He reached the telephone and dialled Hedron's number. Hedron was not at home. He talked to Hedron's sister. Then he discovered that he had been sitting on Hustav's hat. The girl came towards him again and opened her white bag to show him she had not purloined anything of real or sentimental value.

"And you may search me, too," she said defiantly, unbuttoning her jacket. "Provided you do not tickle me," added the doubly innocent, perspiring German girl.

He went back to the bedroom. Near the window Hustav was turning the pages of an encyclopaedia in search of exciting words beginning with M and V. Ember stood half-dressed, a yellow tie in his hand.

"*Et voilà . . . et me voici . . .*" he said with an infantile little whine in his voice. "*Un pauvre bonhomme qu'on traine en prison.* Oh, I don't want to go *at all!* Adam, isn't there anything that can be done? Think up something, please! *Je suis souffrant, je suis en détresse.* I shall confess I had been preparing a *coup d'état* if they start torturing me."

The valet whose name was or had been Ivan, his teeth chattering, his eyes half-closed, helped his poor master into his coat.

"May I come in now?" queried Miss Bachofen with a kind of musical coyness. And slowly she sauntered in, rolling her hips.

"Open your eyes wide, Mr. Ember," exclaimed Hustav. "I want you to admire the lady who has consented to grace your home."

"You are incorrigible," murmured Miss Bachofen with a slanting smile.

"Sit down, dear. On the bed. Sit down, Mr. Ember. Sit down, Professor. A moment of silence. Poetry and philosophy must brood, while beauty and strength—your apartment is nicely heated, Mr. Ember. Now, if I were *quite, quite* sure that you two would not try to get shot by the men outside, I might ask you to leave the room, while Miss Bachofen and I remain here for a brisk business conference. I need it badly."

"No, *Liebling*, no," said Miss Bachofen. "Let us get moving. I am sick of this place. We'll do it at home, honey."

"I think it is a beautiful place," muttered Hustav reproachfully.

"*Il est saoul,*" said Ember.

"In fact, these mirrors and rugs suggest certain tremendous Oriental sensations which I cannot resist."

"*Il est complètement saoul,*" said Ember and began to weep.

Pretty Miss Bachofen took her boy friend firmly by the arm and after some coaxing he was made to convey Ember to the black police car waiting for them. When they had gone, Ivan became hysterical, produced an old bicycle from the attic, carried it downstairs and rode away. Krug locked the apartment and slowly went home.

# 8

The town was curiously bright in the late sunlight: this was one of the Painted Days peculiar to the region. They came in a row after the first frost, and happy the foreign tourist who visited Padukgrad at such a time. The mud left by the recent rains made one's mouth water, so rich did it look. The house fronts on one side of the street were bathed in an amber light which brought out every, oh, every, detail; some displayed mosaic designs; the principal city bank, for instance, had seraphs amid a yuccalike flora. On the fresh blue paint of the boulevard benches children had made with their fingers the words: Glory to Paduk—a sure way of enjoying the properties of the sticky substance without getting one's ears twisted by the policeman, whose strained smile indicated the quandary in which he found himself. A ruby-red toy balloon hung in the cloudless sky. Grimy chimney sweeps and flour-powdered baker boys were fraternizing in open cafés, where they drowned their ancient feud in cider and grenadine. A man's rubber overshoe and a bloodstained cuff lay in the middle of the sidewalk and passers-by gave them a wide berth without, however, slowing down or looking at those two articles or indeed revealing their awareness of them in any way beyond stepping off the curb into the mud and then stepping back on to the sidewalk. The window of a cheap toyshop had been starred by a bullet, and, as Krug approached, a soldier came out carrying a clean paper bag into which he proceeded to cram the overshoe and the cuff. You remove the obstacle and the ants resume a straight course. Ember never wore detachable cuffs, nor would he have dared jump out of a moving vehicle and run, and gasp, and run and duck as that unfortunate person had done. This is becoming a nuisance. I must awake. The victims of my nightmares are increasing in numbers too fast, thought Krug as he walked, ponderous, black-overcoated, black-hatted, the overcoat flappily unbuttoned, the wide-brimmed felt hat in his hand.

Weakness of habit. A former official, a very *ancien régime* old party, had avoided arrest, or worse, by slipping out from his genteel plush-and-dust apartment, Peregolm Lane 4, and transferring his quarters to the dead elevator in the house where Krug dwelt. In spite of the "Not Working" sign on the door, that strange automaton Adam Krug would invariably try to get in and would be met by the frightened face and white goatee of the harassed refugee. Fright, however, would at once be replaced by a worldly display of hospitality. The old fellow had managed to transform his narrow abode into quite a comfortable little den. He was neatly dressed and carefully shaven and with pardonable pride would show you such fixtures as, for example, an alcohol lamp and a trousers press. He was a Baron.

Krug boorishly refused the cup of coffee he was offered and tramped up to his own flat. Hedron was waiting for him in David's room. He had been told of Krug's telephone call; had come over at once. David did not want them to leave the nursery and threatened to get out of bed if they did. Claudina brought the boy his supper but he refused to eat. From the study to which Krug and Hedron retired, they could indistinctly hear him arguing with the woman.

They discussed what could be done: planning a certain course of action; well knowing that neither this course nor any other would avail. Both wanted to know why people of no political importance had been seized: though, to be sure, they might have guessed the answer, the simple answer that was to be given them half an hour later.

"Incidentally, we are having another meeting on the twelfth," remarked Hedron. "I am afraid you are going to be the guest of honour again."

"Not I," said Krug. "I shall not be there."

Hedron carefully scooped out the black contents of his pipe into the bronze ash tray at his elbow.

"I must be getting back," he said with a sigh. "Those Chinese delegates are coming to dinner."

He was referring to a group of foreign physicists and mathematicians who had been invited to take part in a congress that had been called off at the last moment. Some of the least important members had not been notified of this cancellation and had come all the way for nothing.

At the door, just before leaving, he looked at the hat in his hand and said:

"I hope she did not suffer . . . I——"

Krug shook his head and hurriedly opened the door.

The staircase presented a remarkable spectacle. Hustav, now in full uniform, with a look of utter dejection on his swollen face, was sitting on the steps. Four soldiers in various postures formed a martial bas-relief along the wall. Hedron was immediately surrounded and shown the order for his arrest. One of the men pushed Krug out of the way. There was a vague sort of scuffle, in the course of which Hustav lost his footing and bumpily fell down the steps, dragging Hedron after him. Krug tried to follow the soldiers downstairs but was made to desist. The clatter subsided. One imagined the Baron cowering in the darkness of his unconventional hiding place and still not daring to believe that he remained uncaptured.

# 9

Holding your cupped hands together dear, and progressing with the cautious and tremulous steps of tremendous age (although hardly fifteen) you crossed the porch; stopped; gently worked open the glass door by means of your elbow; made your way past the caparisoned grand piano, traversed the sequence of cool carnation-scented rooms, found your aunt in the *chambre violette*——

I think I want to have the whole scene repeated. Yes, from the beginning. As you came up the stone steps of the porch, your eyes never left your cupped hands, the pink chink between the two thumbs. Oh, what were you carrying? Come on now. You wore a striped (dingy white and pale-blue) sleeveless jersey, a dark-blue girl-scout skirt, untidy orphan-black stockings and a pair of old chlorophyl-stained tennis shoes. Between the pillars of the porch geometrical sunlight touched your reddish brown bobbed hair, your plump neck and the vaccination mark on your sunburned arm. You moved slowly through a cool and sonorous drawing room, then entered a room where the carpet and armchairs and curtains were purple and blue. From various mirrors your cupped hands and lowered head came towards you and your movements were mimicked behind your back. Your aunt, a lay figure, was writing a letter.

"Look," you said.

Very slowly, rosewise, you opened your hands. There, clinging with all its six fluffy feet to the ball of your thumb, the tip of its mouse-grey body slightly excurved, its short, red, blue-ocellated inferior wings oddly protruding forward from beneath the sloping superior ones which were long and marbled and deeply notched——

I think I shall have you go through your act a third time, but in reverse—carrying that hawk moth back into the orchard where you found it.

As you went the way you had come (now with the palm of your hand open), the sun that had been lying in state on the parquetry of the drawing-room and on the flat tiger (spread-eagled and bright-eyed beside the piano), leaped at you, climbed the dingy soft rungs of your jersey and struck you right in the face so that all could see (crowding, tier upon tier, in the sky, jostling one another, pointing, feasting their eyes on the young *radabarbára*) its high colour and fiery freckles, and the hot cheeks as red as the hind wings basally, for the moth was still clinging to your hand and you were still looking at it as you progressed towards the garden, where you gently transferred it to the lush grass at the foot of an apple tree far from the beady eyes of your little sister.

Where was I at the time? An eighteen-year-old student sitting with a book (*Les Pensées*, I imagine) on a station bench miles away, not knowing you, not known to you. Presently I shut the book and took what was called an omnibus train to the country place where young Hedron was spending the summer. This was a cluster of rentable cottages on a hillside overlooking the river, the opposite bank of which revealed in terms of fir trees and alder bushes the heavily timbered acres of your aunt's estate.

We shall now have somebody else arrive from nowhere —*à pas de loup*, a tall boy with a little black moustache and other signs of hot uncomfortable puberty. Not I, not Hedron. That summer we did nothing but play chess. The boy was your cousin, and while my comrade and I, across the river, poured over Tarrash's collection of annotated games, he would drive you to tears during meals by some intricate and maddening piece of teasing and then, under the pretence of reconciliation, would steal after you into some attic where you were hiding your frantic sobbing, and there would kiss your wet eyes, and hot neck and tumbled hair and try to get at your armpits and garters for you were a remarkably big ripe girl for your age; but he, in spite of his fine looks and hungry hard limbs, died of consumption a year later.

And still later, when you were twenty and I twenty-three, we met at a Christmas party and discovered that we had been neighbours that summer, five years before—five years lost! And at the precise moment when in awed surprise (awed by the bungling of destiny) you put your hand to your mouth and looked at me with very round eyes and muttered: "But that's where *I* lived!"—I recalled in a flash a green lane near an orchard and a sturdy young girl carefully carrying a lost fluffy nestling, but whether it had been really you no amount of probing and poking could either confirm or disprove.

Fragment from a letter addressed to a dead woman in heaven by her husband in his cups.

# 10

He got rid of her furs, of all her photographs, of her huge English sponge and supply of lavender soap, of her umbrella, of her napkin ring, of the little porcelain owl she had bought for Ember and never given him—but she refused to be forgotten. When (some fifteen years before) both his parents had been killed in a railway accident, he had managed to alleviate the pain and the panic by writing Chapter III (Chapter IV in later editions) of his "*Mirokonzepsia*" wherein he looked straight into the eyesockets of death and called him a dog and an abomination. With one strong shrug of his burly shoulders he shook off the burden of sanctity enveloping the monster, and as with a thump and a great explosion of dust the thick old mats and carpets and things fell, he had experienced a kind of hideous relief. But could he do it again?

Her dresses and stockings and hats and shoes mercifully disappeared together with Claudina when the latter, soon after Hedron's arrest, was bullied by police agents into leaving. The agencies he called, in an attempt to find a trained nurse to replace her, could not help him; but a couple of days after Claudina had gone, the bell rang and there, on the landing, was a very young girl with a suitcase offering her services. "I answer," she amusingly said, "to the name of Mariette"; she had been employed as maid and model in the household of the well-known artist who had lived in apartment 30, right above Krug; but now he was obliged to depart with his wife and two other painters for a much less comfortable prison camp in a remote province. Mariette brought down a second suitcase and quietly moved into the room near the nursery. She had good references from the Department of Public Health, graceful legs and a pale, delicately shaped, not particularly pretty, but attractively childish face with parched-looking lips, always parted, and strange lustreless dark eyes; the pupil almost merged in tint with the iris, which was placed somewhat higher than is usual and was obliquely shaded by sooty lashes. No paint or powder touched her singularly bloodless, evenly translucid cheeks. She wore her hair long. Krug had a confused feeling that he had seen her before, probably on the stairs. Cinderella, the little slattern, moving and dusting in a dream, always ivory pale and unspeakably tired after last night's ball. On the whole, there was something rather irritating about her, and her wavy brown hair had a strong chestnutty smell; but David liked her, so she might do after all.

# 11

On his birthday, Krug was informed by telephone that the Head of the State desired to grant him an interview, and hardly had the fuming philosopher laid down the receiver than the door flew open and—very much like one of those stage valets that march in stiffly half a second before their fictitious master (insulted and perhaps beaten up by them between acts) claps his hands—a dapper, heel-clicking aide-de-camp saluted from the threshold. By the time that the palace motor car, a huge black limousine, which made one think of first-class funerals in alabaster cities, arrived at its destination, Krug's annoyance had given way to a kind of grim curiosity. Though otherwise fully dressed, he was wearing bedroom slippers, and the two gigantic janitors (whom Paduk had inherited together with the abject caryatids supporting the balconies) stared at his absent-minded feet as he shuffled up the marble steps. From then on a multitude of uniformed rascals kept silently seething around him, causing him to follow this or that course by means of a bodiless elastic pressure rather than by definite gestures or words. He was steered into a waiting room where, instead of the usual magazines, one was offered various games of skill (such as for instance, glass gadgets within which little bright hopelessly mobile balls had to be coaxed into the orbits of eyeless clowns). Presently two masked men came in and searched him thoroughly. Then one of them retired behind the screen while the other produced a small vial marked $H_2SO_4$, which he proceeded to conceal under Krug's left armpit. Having had Krug assume a "natural position," he called his companion, who approached with an eager smile and immediately found the object: upon which he was accused of having peeped through the *kwazinka* [a slit between the folding parts of a screen]. A rapidly mounting squabble was stopped by the arrival of the *zemberl* [chamberlain]. This prim old personage noticed at once that Krug was inadequately shod; there followed a feverish search through the oppressive vastness of the palace. A small collection of footgear began accumulating around Krug—a number of seedy-looking pumps, a girl's tiny slipper trimmed with moth-eaten squirrel fur, some bloodstained arctics, brown shoes, black shoes and even a pair of half boots with screwed on skates. Only the last fitted Krug and some more time elapsed before adequate hands and instruments were found to deprive the soles of their rusty but gracefully curved supplements.

Then the *zemberl* ushered Krug into the presence of the *ministr dvortza*, a von Embit of German extraction. Embit at once pronounced himself a humble admirer of Krug's genius. His mind had been formed by "*Mirokonzepsia*," he said. Moreover, a cousin of his had been a student of Professor Krug's—the famous physician—was he any relation? He wasn't. The *ministr* kept up his social patter for a few minutes (he had a queer way of emitting a quick little snort before saying something) and then took

Krug by the arm and they walked down a long passage with doors on one side and a stretch of pale-green and spinach-green tapestry on the other, displaying what seemed to be an endless hunt through a subtropical forest. The visitor was made to inspect various rooms, i.e. his guide would softly open a door and in a reverent whisper direct his attention to this or that interesting item. The first room to be shown contained a contour map of the State, made of bronze with towns and villages represented by precious and semiprecious stones of various colours. In the next, a young typist was poring over the contents of some documents, and so absorbed was she in deciphering them, and so noiselessly had the *ministr* entered, that she emitted a wild shriek when he snorted behind her back. Then a classroom was visited: a score of brown-skinned Armenian and Sicilian lads were diligently writing at rosewood desks while their *eunig*, a fat old man with dyed hair and bloodshot eyes, sat in front of them painting his fingernails and yawning with closed mouth. Of special interest was a perfectly empty room, in which some extinct furniture had left squares of honey-yellow colour on the brown floor: von Embit lingered there and bade Krug linger, and mutely pointed at a vacuum cleaner, and lingered on, eyes moving this way and that as if flitting over the sacred treasures of an ancient chapel.

But something even more curious than that was kept *pour la bonne bouche. Notamment, une grande pièce bien claire* with chairs and tables of a clean-cut laboratory type and what looked like an especially large and elaborate radio set. From this machine came a steady thumping sound not unlike that of an African drum, and three doctors in white were engaged in checking the number of beats per minute. In their turn, two violent-looking members of Paduk's bodyguard controlled the doctors by keeping count separately. A pretty nurse was reading *Flung Roses* in a corner, and Paduk's private physician, an enormous baby-faced man in a dusty-looking frockcoat, was fast asleep behind a projection screen. Thump-ah, thump-ah, thump-ah, went the machine, and every now and then there was an additional systole, causing a slight break in the rhythm.

The owner of the heart to the amplified beatings of which the experts were listening, was in his study some fifty feet away. His guardian soldiers, all leather and cartridges, carefully examined Krug's and von Embit's papers. The latter gentleman had forgotten to provide himself with a photostat of his birth certificate and so could not pass, much to his good-natured discomfiture. Krug went in alone.

Paduk, clothed from carbuncle to bunion in field grey, stood with his hands behind his back and his back to the reader. He stood, thus oriented and clothed, before a bleak French window. Ragged clouds rode the white sky and the windowpane rattled slightly. The room, alas, had been formerly a ballroom. A good deal of stucco ornamentation enlivened the walls. The few chairs that floated about in the mirrory wilderness were gilt. So was the radiator. One corner of the room was cut off by a great writing desk.

"Here I am," said Krug.

Paduk wheeled around and without looking at his visitor marched to the desk. There he sank in a leathern armchair. Krug, whose left shoe had begun to hurt, sought a seat and not finding one in the vicinity of the table, looked back at the gilt chairs. His host, however, saw to that: there was a click, and a replica of Paduk's *klubzessel* [armchair] Jack-in-the-boxed from a trap near the desk.

Physically the Toad had hardly changed except that every particle of his visible organism had been expanded and roughened. On the top of his bumpy, bluish, shaven head a patch of hair was neatly brushed and parted. His blotched complexion was worse than ever, and one wondered what tremendous will power a man must possess to refrain from squeezing out the blackheads that clogged the coarse pores on and near the wings of his fattish nose. His upper lip was disfigured by a scar. A bit of porous plaster adhered to the side of his chin, and a still larger bit, with a soiled corner turned back and a pad of cotton awry, could be seen in the fold of his neck just above the stiff collar of his semi-military coat. In a word, he was a little too repulsive to be credible, and so let us ring the bell (held by a bronze eagle) and have him beautified by a mortician. Now the skin is thoroughly cleansed and has assumed a smooth marchpane colour. A glossy wig with auburn and blond tresses artistically intermixed covers his head. Pink paint has dealt with the unseemly scar. Indeed, it would be an admirable face, were we able to close his eyes for him. But no matter what pressure we exert upon the lids, they snap open again. I never noticed his eyes, or else his eyes have changed.

They were those of a fish in a neglected aquarium, muddy meaningless eyes, and moreover the poor man was in a state of morbid embarrassment at being in the same room with big heavy Adam Krug.

"You wanted to see me. What is your trouble? What is your truth? People always want to see me and talk of their troubles and truths. I am tired, the world is tired, we are both tired. The trouble of the world is mine. I tell them to tell me their troubles. What do you want?"

This little speech was delivered in a slow flat toneless

mumble. And having delivered it Paduk bent his head and stared at his hands. What remained of his fingernails looked like thin strings sunk deep in the yellowish flesh.

"Well," said Krug, "if you put it like this, *dragotzennyĭ* [my precious], I think I want a drink."

The telephone emitted a discreet tinkle. Paduk attended to it. His cheek twitched as he listened. Then he handed the receiver to Krug who comfortably clasped it and said "Yes."

"Professor," said the telephone, "this is merely a suggestion. The chief of the State is not generally addressed as '*dragotzennyĭ*.' "

"I see," said Krug, stretching out one leg. "By the way, will you please send up some brandy? Wait a bit——"

He looked interrogatively at Paduk who had made a somewhat ecclesiastical and Gallic gesture of lassitude and disgust, raising both hands and letting them sink again.

"One brandy and a glass of milk," said Krug and hung up.

"More than twenty-five years, Mugakrad," said Paduk after a silence. "You have remained what you were, but the world spins on. Gumakrad, poor little Gumradka."

"And then," said Krug, "the two proceeded to speak of old times, to remember the names of teachers and their idiosyncrasies—curiously the same throughout the ages, and what can be funnier than a habitual oddity? Come, *dragotzennyĭ*, come sir, I know all that, and really we have more important things to discuss than snowballs and ink blots."

"You might regret it," said Paduk.

Krug drummed for a while on his side of the desk. Then he fingered a long paper knife of ivory.

The telephone rang again. Paduk listened.

"You are not supposed to touch knives here," he said to

Krug as, with a sigh, he replaced the receiver. "Why did you want to see me?"

"*I* did not. You did."

"Well—why did I? Do you know that, mad Adam?"

"Because," said Krug, "I am the only person who can stand on the other end of the seesaw and make your end rise."

Knuckles briskly rapped on the door and the *zemberl* marched in with a tinkling tray. He deftly served the two friends and presented a letter to Krug. Krug took a sip and read the note. "Professor," it said, "this is still not the right manner. You should bear in mind that notwithstanding the narrow and fragile bridge of school memories uniting the two sides, these are separated in depth by an abyss of power and dignity which even a great philosopher (and that is what *you* are—yes, sir!) cannot hope to measure. You must not indulge in this atrocious familiarity. One has to warn you again. One beseeches you. Hoping that the shoes are not too uncomfortable, one remains a well-wisher."

"And that's that," said Krug.

Paduk moistened his lips in the pasteurized milk and spoke in a huskier voice.

"Now let me tell you. They come and say to me: Why is this good and intelligent man idle? Why is he not in the service of the State? And I answer: I don't know. And they are puzzled also."

"Who are they?" asked Krug dryly.

"Friends, friends of the law, friends of the lawmaker. And the village fraternities. And the city clubs. And the great lodges. Why is it so, why is he not with us? I only echo their query."

"The hell you do," said Krug.

The door opened slightly and a fat grey parrot with a

note in its beak walked in. It waddled towards the desk on clumsy hoary legs and its claws made the kind of sound that unmanicured dogs make on varnished floors. Paduk jumped out of his chair, walked rapidly towards the old bird and kicked it like a football out of the room. Then he shut the door with a bang. The telephone was ringing its heart out on the desk. He disconnected the current and clapped the whole thing into a drawer.

"And now the answer," he said.

"Which you owe me," said Krug. "First of all I wish to know why you had those four friends of mine arrested. Was it to make a vacuum around me? To leave me shivering in a void?"

"The State is your only true friend."

"I see."

Grey light from long windows. The dreary wail of a tugboat.

"A nice picture we make—you as a kind of *Erlkönig* and myself as the male baby clinging to the matter-of-fact rider and peering into the magic mists. Pah!"

"All we want of you is that little part where the handle is."

"There is none," cried Krug and hit his side of the table with his fist.

"I beseech you to be careful. The walls are full of camouflaged holes, each one with a rifle which is trained upon you. Please, do not gesticulate. They are jumpy today. It's the weather. This grey menstratum."

"If," said Krug, "you cannot leave me and my friends in peace, then let them and me go abroad. It would save you a world of trouble."

"What is it exactly you have against my government?"

"I am not in the least interested in your government.

What I resent is your attempt to make me interested in it. Leave me alone."

" 'Alone' is the vilest word in the language. Nobody is alone. When a cell in an organism says 'leave me alone,' the result is cancer."

"In what prison or prisons are they kept?"

"I beg your pardon?"

"Where is Ember, for instance?"

"You want to know too much. These are dull technical matters of no real interest to your type of mind. And now——"

No, it did not go on quite like that. In the first place Paduk was silent during most of the interview. What he did say amounted to a few curt platitudes. To be sure, he did do some drumming on the desk (they all drum) and Krug retaliated with some of his own drumming but otherwise neither showed nervousness. Photographed from above, they would have come out in Chinese perspective, doll-like, a little limp but possibly with a hard wooden core under their plausible clothes—one slumped at his desk in a shaft of grey light, the other seated sideways to the desk, legs crossed, the toe of the upper foot moving up and down—and the secret spectator (some anthropomorphic deity, for example) surely would be amused by the shape of human heads seen from above. Paduk curtly asked Krug whether his (Krug's) apartment were warm enough (nobody, of course, could have expected a revolution *without* a shortage of coal), and Krug said yes, it was. And did he have any trouble in getting milk and radishes? Well, yes, a little. He made a note of Krug's answer on a calendar slip. He had learned with sorrow of Krug's bereavement. Was Professor Martin Krug a relative of his? Were there any relatives on his late wife's side? Krug supplied him with the necessary data. Paduk leaned back in his chair and tapped his nose with the rubber end of his six-faceted pencil. As his thoughts took a different course, he changed the position of the pencil: he now held it by the end, horizontally, rolling it slightly between the finger and thumb of either hand, seemingly interested in the disappearance and reappearance of Eberhard Faber No. 2⅜. It is not a difficult part but still the actor must be careful not to overdo what Graaf somewhere calls "villainous deliberation." Krug in the meantime sipped his brandy and tenderly nursed the glass. Suddenly Paduk plunged towards his desk; a drawer shot out, a beribboned typescript was produced. This he handed to Krug.

"I must put on my spectacles," said Krug.

He held them before his face and looked through them at a distant window. The left glass showed a dim spiral nebula in the middle not unlike the imprint of a ghostly thumb. While he breathed upon it and rubbed it away with his handkerchief, Paduk explained matters. Krug was to be nominated college president in place of Azureus. His salary would be three times that of his predecessor which had been five thousand kruns. Moreover, he would be provided with a motorcar, a bicycle, and a padograph. At the public opening of the University he would kindly deliver a speech. His works would be republished in new editions, revised in the light of political events. There might be bonuses, sabbatical years, lottery tickets, a cow—lots of things.

"And this, I presume, is the speech," said Krug cozily. Paduk remarked that in order to save Krug the trouble of composing it, the speech had been prepared by an expert.

"We hope you will like it as well as we do."

"So this," repeated Krug, "is the speech."

"Yes," said Paduk. "Now take your time. Read it carefully. Oh, by the way, there was one word to be changed. I wonder if that has been done. Will you please——"

He stretched his hand to take the typescript from Krug, and in doing so knocked down the tumbler of milk with his elbow. What was left of the milk made a kidney-shaped white puddle on the desk.

"Yes," said Paduk, handing the typescript back, "it has been changed."

He busied himself with removing various things from the desk (a bronze eagle, a pencil, a picture post card of Gainsborough's "Blue Boy," and a framed reproduction of Aldobrandini's "Wedding," of the half-naked wreathed, adorable minion whom the groom is obliged to renounce for the sake of a lumpy, muffled-up bride), and then messily dabbed at the milk with a piece of blotting paper. Krug read *sotto voce:*

" 'Ladies and gentlemen! Citizens, soldiers, wives and mothers! Brothers and sisters! The revolution has brought to the fore problems [*zadachi*] of unusual difficulty, of colossal importance, of world-wide scope [*mirovovo mashtaba*]. Our leader has resorted to most resolute revolutionary measures calculated to arouse the unbounded heroism of the oppressed and exploited masses. In the shortest [*kratchaïshiï*] time [*srok*] the State has created central organs for providing the country with all the most important products which are to be distributed at fixed prices in a playful manner. Sorry—*planful* manner. Wives, soldiers and mothers! The hydra of the reaction may still raise its head . . . !'

"This won't do, the creature has more heads than one, has it not?"

"Make a note of it," said Paduk through his teeth. "Make a note in the margin and for goodness' sake go on."

" 'As our old proverb has it, "the ugliest wives are the

truest," but surely this cannot apply to the "ugly rumours" which our enemies are spreading. It is rumoured for instance that the cream of our intelligentsia is opposed to the present regime.'

"Wouldn't 'whipped cream' be fitter? I mean, pursuing the metaphor——"

"Make a note, make a note, these details do not matter."

" 'Untrue! A mere phrase, an untruth. Those who rage, storm, fulminate, gnash their teeth, pour a ceaseless stream [*potok*] of abusive words upon us do not accuse us of anything directly, they only "insinuate." This insinuation is stupid. Far from opposing the regime, we professors, writers, philosophers, and so forth, support it with all possible learning and enthusiasm.

" 'No, gentlemen; no, traitors, your most "categorical" words, declarations and notes will not diminish these facts. You may gloss over the fact that our foremost professors and thinkers support the regime, but you cannot dismiss the fact that they do support it. We are happy and proud to march with the masses. Blind matter regains the use of its eyes and knocks off the rosy spectacles which used to adorn the long nose of so-called Thought. Whatever I have thought and written in the past, one thing is clear to me now: no matter to whom they belong, two pairs of eyes looking at a boot see the same boot since it is identically reflected in both; and further, that the larynx is the seat of thought so that the working of the mind is a kind of gargling.'

"Well, well, this last sentence seems to be a garbled passage from one of my works. A passage turned inside out by somebody who did not understand the gist of my remarks. I was criticizing that old——"

"Please, go on. Please."

" 'In other words, the new Education, the new University which I am happy and proud to direct will inaugurate the era of Dynamic Living. In result, a great and beautiful simplification will replace the evil refinements of a degenerate past. We shall teach and learn, first of all, that the dream of Plato has come true in the hands of the Head of our State....'

"This is sheer drivel. I refuse to go on. Take it away."

He pushed the typescript towards Paduk, who sat with closed eyes.

"Do not make any hasty decisions, mad Adam. Go home. Think it over. Nay, do not speak. They cannot hold their fire much longer. Prithee, go."

Which, of course, terminated the interview. Thus? Or perhaps in some other way? Did Krug really glance at the prepared speech? And if he did, was it really as silly as all that? He did; it was. The seedy tyrant or the president of the State, or the dictator, or whoever he was—the man Paduk in a word, the Toad in another—did hand my favourite character a mysterious batch of neatly typed pages. The actor playing the recipient should be taught not to look at his hand while he takes the papers *very slowly* (keeping those lateral lower-jaw muscles in movement, please) but to stare straight at the giver: in short, look at the giver first, *then* lower your eyes to the gift. But both were clumsy and cross men, and the experts in the cardiarium exchanged solemn nods at a certain point (when the milk was upset), and they, too, were not acting. Tentatively scheduled to take place in three months' time, the opening of the new University was to be a most ceremonious and widely publicized affair, with a host of reporters from foreign countries, ignorant overpaid correspondents, with noiseless little typewriters in their laps, and photographers with souls as cheap as dried figs. And the one great thinker in the country would appear in scarlet robes (click) beside the chief and symbol of the State (click, click, click, click, click, click) and proclaim in a thundering voice that the State was bigger and wiser than any mortal could be.

# 12

THINKING of that farcical interview, he wondered how long it would be till the next attempt. He still believed that so long as he kept lying low nothing harmful could happen. Oddly enough, at the end of the month his usual cheque arrived although for the time being the University had ceased to exist, at least on the outside. Behind the scenes there was an endless sequence of sessions, a turmoil of administrative activity, a regrouping of forces, but he declined either to attend these meetings or to receive the various delegations and special messengers that Azureus and Alexander kept sending to his house. He argued that, when the Council of Elders had exhausted its power of seduction, he would be left alone since the Government, while not daring to arrest him and being reluctant to grant him the luxury of exile, would still keep hoping with forlorn obstinacy that finally he might relent. The drab colour the future took matched well the grey world of his widowhood, and had there been no friends to worry about and no child to hold against his cheek and heart, he might have devoted the twilight to some quiet research: for example he had always wished to know more about the Aurignacian Age and those portraits of singular beings (perhaps Neanderthal half-men—direct ancestors of Paduk and his likes—used by Aurignacians as slaves) that a Spanish nobleman and his little daughter had discovered in the painted cave of Altamira. Or he might take up some dim problem of Victorian telepathy (the cases reported by clergymen, nervous ladies, retired colonels who had seen service in India) such as the remarkable dream a Mrs. Storie had of her brother's death. And in our turn we shall follow the brother as he walks along the railway line on a very dark night: having gone sixteen miles, he felt a little tired (as who would not); he sat down to take off his boots and dozed off to the chirp of the crickets, and then a train lumbered by. Seventy-six sheep trucks (in a curious "count-sheep-sleep" parody) passed without touching him, but then some projection came in contact with the back of his head killing him instantly. And we might also probe the "*illusions hypnagogiques*" (only illusion?) of dear Miss Bidder who once had a nightmare from which a most distinct demon survived after she woke so that she sat up to inspect its hand which was clutching the bedrail but it faded into the ornaments over the mantelpiece. Silly, but I can't help it, he thought as he got out of his armchair and crossed the room to rearrange the leering folds of his brown dressing gown which, as it sprawled across the divan, showed at one end a very distinct medieval face.

He looked up various odds and ends he had stored at odd moments for an essay which he had never written and would never write because by now he had forgotten its leading idea, its secret combination. There was for instance the papyrus a person called Rhind bought from some Arabs (who said they had found it among the ruins of small buildings near Ramesseum); it began with the promise to disclose "all the secrets, all the mysteries" but (like Miss Bidder's demon) turned out to be merely a schoolbook with blank spaces which some unknown Egyptian farmer in the seventeenth century B.C. had used for his clumsy calculations. A newspaper clipping mentioned that the State Entomologist had retired to become Adviser on Shade Trees, and one wondered whether this was not some dainty oriental euphemism for death. On the next slip of paper he had transcribed passages from a famous American poem

*A curious sight—these bashful bears,*
*These timid warrior whalemen*

*And now the time of tide has come;*
*The ship casts off her cables*

*It is not shown on any map;*
*True places never are*

*This lovely light, it lights not me;*
*All loveliness is anguish—*

and, of course, that bit about the delicious death of an Ohio honey hunter (for my humour's sake I shall preserve the style in which I once narrated it at Thula to a lounging circle of my Russian friends).

Truganini, the last Tasmanian, died in 1877, but the last Kruganini could not remember how this was linked up with the fact that the edible Galilean fishes in the first century A.D. would be principally chromids and barbels although in Raphael's representation of the miraculous draught we find among nondescript piscine forms of the young painter's fancy two specimens which obviously belong to the skate family, never found in fresh water. Speaking of Roman *venationes* (shows with wild beasts) of the same epoch, we note that the stage, on which ridiculously picturesque rocks (the later ornaments of "romantic" landscapes) and an indifferent forest were represented, was made to rise out of the crypts below the urine-soaked arena with Orpheus on it among real lions and bears with gilded claws; but this Orpheus was acted by a criminal and the scene ended with a bear killing him, while Titus or Nero, or Paduk, looked on with that complete pleasure which "art" shot through with "human interest" is said to produce.

The nearest star is Alpha Centauri. The Sun is about 93 millions of miles away. Our solar system emerged from a spiral nebula. De Sitter, a man of leisure, has estimated the circumference of the "finite though boundless" universe at about one hundred million light-years and its mass at about a quintillion quadrillions of grams. We can easily imagine people in 3000 A.D. sneering at our naïve nonsense and replacing it by some nonsense of their own.

"Civil war is destroying Rome which none could ruin, not even the wild beast Germany with its blue-eyed youth." How I envy Cruquius who had actually seen the Blandinian MSS of Horace (destroyed in 1556 when the Benedictine abbey of St. Peter at Blankenbergh near Ghent was sacked by the mob). Oh, what was it like travelling along the Appian Way in that large four-wheeled coach for long journeys known as the *rhēda?* Same Painted Ladies fanning their wings on the same thistleheads.

Lives that I envy: longevity, peaceful times, peaceful country, quiet fame, quiet satisfaction: Ivar Aasen, Norwegian philologist, 1813–1896, who invented a language. Down here we have too much of *homo civis* and too little of *sapiens.*

Dr. Livingstone mentions that on one occasion, after talking with a Bushman for some time about the Deity, he found that the savage thought he was speaking of Sakomi, a local chief. The ant lives in a universe of shaped odours, of chemical configurations.

Old Zoroastrian motif of the rising sun, origin of Persian ogee design. The blood-and-gold horrors of Mexican sacrifices as told by Catholic priests or the eighteen thousand Formosan boys under nine whose little hearts were burned out upon an altar at the command of the spurious prophet Psalmanazar—the whole thing being a European forgery of the pale-green eighteenth century.

He tossed the notes back into the drawer of his desk. They were dead and unusable. Leaning his elbow on the desk and swaying slightly in his armchair, he slowly scratched his scalp through his coarse hair (as coarse as that of Balzac, he had a note of that too somewhere). A dismal feeling grew upon him: he was empty, he would never write another book, he was too old to bend and rebuild the world which had crashed when she died.

He yawned and wondered what individual vertebrate had yawned first and whether one might suppose that this dull spasm was the first sign of exhaustion on the part of the whole subdivision in its evolutional aspect. Perhaps, if I had a new fountain pen instead of this wreck, or a fresh bouquet of, say, twenty beautifully sharpened pencils in a slim vase, and a ream of ivory smooth paper instead of these, let me see, thirteen, fourteen more or less frumpled sheets (with a two-eyed dolichocephalic profile drawn by David upon the top one) I might start writing the unknown thing I want to write; unknown, except for a vague shoe-shaped outline, the infusorial quiver of which I feel in my restless bones, a feeling of *shchekotiki* (as we used to say in our childhood) half-tingle, half-tickle, when you are trying to remember something or understand something or find something, and probably your bladder is full, and your nerves are on edge, but the combination is on the whole not unpleasant (if not protracted) and produces a minor orgasm or "*petit éternuement intérieur*" when at last you find the picture-puzzle piece which exactly fits the gap.

As he completed his yawn, he reflected that his body was much too big and healthy for him: had he been all shrivelled up and flaccid and pestered by petty diseases, he might have been more at peace with himself. Baron Munchausen's horse-decorpitation story. But the individual atom is free: it pulsates as it wants, in low or high gear; it decides itself when to absorb and when to radiate energy. There is something to be said for the method employed by male characters in old novels: it is indeed soothing to press one's brow to the deliciously cold windowpane. So he stood, poor percipient. The morning was grey with patches of thawing snow.

David would have to be fetched from the kindergarten in a few minutes (if his watch was right). The slow languid sounds and half-hearted thumps coming from the next room meant that Mariette was engaged in expressing her vague notions of order. He heard the sloppy tread of her old bed slippers trimmed with dirty fur. She had an irritating way of performing her household duties with nothing on to conceal her miserably young body save a dim nightgown, the frayed hem of which hardly reached to her knees. *Femineum lucet per bombycina corpus.* Lovely ankles: she had won a prize for dancing, she said. A lie, I guess, like most of her utterances: though, on second thoughts, she did have in her room a Spanish fan and a pair of castanets. For no special reason (or was he looking for something? No) he had been led to peep into her room in passing while she was out with David. It smelt strongly of her hair and of *Sanglot* (a cheap musky perfume);

flimsy soiled odds and ends lay on the floor and the bed-table was occupied by a brownish-pink rose in a glass and a large X-ray picture of her lungs and vertebrae. She had proved such an execrable cook that he was forced to have at least one square meal a day brought for all three from a good restaurant round the corner, while relying on eggs and gruels and various preserves to provide breakfasts and suppers.

Having glanced at his watch again (and even listened to it) he decided to take his restlessness out for a walk. He found Cinderella in David's bedroom: she had interrupted her labours to pick up one of David's animal books and was now engrossed in it, half-sitting, half-lying athwart the bed, with one leg stretched far out, the bare ankle resting on the back of a chair, the slipper off, the toes moving.

"I shall fetch David myself," he said, averting his eyes from the brownish-pink shadows she showed.

"What?" (The queer child did not trouble to change her attitude—merely stopped twitching her toes and lifted her lustreless eyes.)

He repeated the sentence.

"Oh, all right," she said, her eyes back on the book.

"And do, please, dress," Krug added before leaving the room.

Ought to get somebody else, he thought, as he walked down the street; somebody totally different, an elderly person, completely clothed. It was, he had understood, merely a matter of habit, the result of having constantly posed naked for the black-bearded artist in apartment 30. In fact, during summer, none of them, she said, wore anything at all indoors—neither he, nor she, nor the artist's wife (who, according to sundry oils exhibited before the revolution had a grand body with numerous navels, some frowning, others looking surprised).

The kindergarten was a bright little institution run by one of his former students, a woman called Clara Zerkalsky and her brother Miron. The main enjoyment of the eight little children in their care was provided by an intricate set of padded tunnels, just high enough to let one crawl through on all fours, but there were also brilliantly painted cardboard bricks and mechanical trains and picture books and a live shaggy dog called Basso. The place had been found by Olga the year before and David was getting a little too big for it though he still loved to crawl through the tunnels. In order to avoid exchanging salutations with the other parents, Krug stopped at the gate beyond which was the little garden (now mostly consisting of puddles) with benches for visitors. David was the first to run out of the gaily coloured wooden house.

"Why didn't Mariette come?"

"Instead of me? Put on your cap."

"You and she could have come together."

"Didn't you have any rubbers?"

"Uh-uh."

"Then give me your hand. And if you walk into a puddle but once . . ."

"And if I do it by chance [*nechaianno*]?"

"I shall see to that. Come, *raduga moia* [my rainbow], give me your hand and let us be moving."

"Billy brought a bone today. Gee whizz—some bone. I want to bring one, too."

"Is it the dark Billy or the little fellow with the glasses?"

"The glasses. He said my mother was dead. Look, look, a woman chimney sweep."

(These had recently appeared owing to some obscure shift or rift or sift or drift in the economics of the State—and much to the delight of the children.) Krug was silent. David went on talking.

"*That* was your fault, not mine. My left shoe is full of water, Daddy!"

"Yes."

"My left shoe is full of water."

"Yes. I'm sorry. Let's walk a little faster. What did you answer?"

"When?"

"When Billy said that stupid thing about your mother."

"Nothing. What should I have said?"

"But you knew it *was* a stupid remark?"

"I guess so."

"Because even *if* she were dead she would not be dead for you or me."

"Yes, but she isn't, is she?

"Not in our sense. A bone is nothing to you or me but it means a lot to Basso."

"Daddy, he *growled* over it. He just lay there and growled with his paw on it. Miss Zee said we must not touch him or talk to him while he had it."

"*Raduga moia!*"

They were now in Peregolm Lane. A bearded man whom Krug knew to be a spy and who always appeared punctually at noon was at his post before Krug's home. Sometimes he hawked apples, once he had come disguised as a postman. On very cold days he would try standing in the window of a tailor, mimicking a dummy, and Krug had amused himself by outstaring the poor chap. Today he was inspecting the house fronts and jotting down something on a pad.

"Counting the raindrops, inspector?"

The man looked away; moved; and in moving stubbed his toe against the curb. Krug smiled.

"Yesterday," said David, "as we were going by, that man winked at Mariette."

Krug smiled again.

"You know what, Daddy? I think she talks to him on the telephone. She talks on the telephone every time you go out."

Krug laughed. That queer little girl, he imagined, enjoyed the love-making of quite a number of swains. She had two afternoons off, probably full of fauns and footballers and matadors. Is this getting to be an obsession? Who is she—a servant? an adopted child? Or what? Nothing. I know perfectly well, thought Krug, as he stopped laughing, that she merely goes to the pictures with a stumpy girl friend—so she says—and I have no reason to disbelieve her; and if I really did think she was what she certainly is, I should have fired her instantly: because of the germs she might bring into the nursery. Just as Olga would have done.

Sometime during the last month the elevator had been removed bodily. Men had come, sealed the door of the unfortunate Baron's tiny house and carried it into a van, intact. The bird inside was too terrified to flutter. Or had he been a spy, too?

"It's all right. Don't ring. I have the key."

"Mariette!" shouted David.

"I suppose she is out shopping," said Krug and made his way to the bathroom.

She was standing in the tub, sinuously soaping her back or at least such parts of her narrow, variously dimpled, glistening back which she could reach by throwing her arm across her shoulder. Her hair was up, with a kerchief or something twisted around it. The mirror reflected a brown armpit and a poppling pale nipple. "Ready in a sec," she sang out.

Krug slammed the door with a great show of disgust. He stalked to the nursery and helped David to change his shoes. She was still in the bathroom when the man from the Angliskii Club brought a meat pie, a rice pudding, and her adolescent buttocks. When the waiter had gone, she emerged, shaking her hair, and ran into her room where she slipped into a black frock and a minute later ran out again and started to lay the table. By the time dinner was over, the newspaper had come and the afternoon mail. What news could there be?

# 13

THE GOVERNMENT had taken to sending him a good deal of printed matter advertising its achievements and aims. Together with the telephone bill and his dentist's Christmas greeting he would find in his mailbox some mimeographed circular running thus:

Dear Citizen, according to Article 521 of our Constitution the following four freedoms are to be enjoyed by the nation: 1. freedom of speech, 2. freedom of the press, 3. freedom of meetings, and 4. freedom of processions. These freedoms are guaranteed by placing at the disposal of the people efficient printing machines, adequate supplies of paper, well-aerated halls and broad streets. What should one understand by the first two freedoms? For a citizen of our State a newspaper is a collective organizer whose business is to prepare its readers for the accomplishment of various assignments allotted to them. Whereas in other countries newspapers are purely business ventures, firms that sell their printed wares to the public (and therefore do their best to attract the public by means of lurid headlines and naughty stories), the main object of *our* press is to supply such information as would give every citizen a clear perception of the knotty problems presented by civic and international affairs, consequently, they guide the activities and the emotions of their readers in the necessary direction.

In other countries we observe an enormous number of competing organs. Each newspaper tugs its own way and this baffling diversity of tendencies produces complete confusion in the mind of the man in the street; in our truly democratic country a homogeneous press is responsible before the nation for the correctness of the political education which it provides. The articles in our newspapers are not the outcome of this or that individual fancy but a mature carefully prepared message to the reader who, in turn, receives it with the same seriousness and intentness of thought.

Another important feature of our press is the voluntary collaboration of local correspondents—letters, suggestions, discussions, criticism, and so on. Thus we observe that our citizens have free access to the papers, a state of affairs which is unknown anywhere else. True, in other countries there is a lot of talk about "freedom" but in reality a lack of funds does not allow one the use of the printed word. A millionaire and a working man clearly do not enjoy equal opportunities.

Our press is the public property of our nation. Therefore it is not run on a commercial basis. Even the advertisements in a capitalistic newspaper can influence its political trend: this of course would be quite impossible here.

Our newspapers are published by governmental and public organizations and are absolutely independent of individuals, private and commercial interests. Independence, in its turn. is synonymous with freedom. This is obvious.

Our newspapers are completely and absolutely independent of all such influences as do not coincide with the interests of the People to whom they belong and whom they serve to the exclusion of all other masters. Thus our country enjoys the use of free speech not in theory but in real practice. Obvious again.

The constitutions of other countries also mention various "freedoms." In reality, however, these "freedoms" are extremely restricted. A shortage of paper limits the freedom of the press; unheated halls do not encourage free gatherings; and under the pretext of regulating traffic the police break up demonstrations and processions.

Generally the newspapers of other countries are in the service of capitalists who either have their own organs or acquire columns in other papers. Recently, for instance, a journalist called Ballplayer was sold by one businessman to another for several thousand dollars.

On the other hand, when half a million American textile workers went on strike, the papers wrote about kings and queens, movies and theatres. The most popular photograph which appeared in *all* capitalist newspapers of that period was a picture of two rare butterflies glittering *vsemi tzvetami radugi* [with all the hues of the rainbow]. But not a word about the strike of the textile workers!

As our Leader has said: "The workers know that 'freedom of speech' in the so-called 'democratic' countries is an empty sound." In our own country there cannot be any contradiction between reality and the rights granted to the citizens by Paduk's Constitution for we have sufficient supplies of paper, plenty of good printing presses, spacious and warm public halls, and splendid avenues and parks.

We welcome queries and suggestions. Photographs and detailed booklets mailed free on application.

(I will keep it, thought Krug, I shall have it treated by some special process which will make it endure far into the future to the eternal delight of free humorists. O yes, I will keep it.)

As for news, there was practically none in the *Ekwilist* or the *Evening Bell* or any of the other government-controlled dailies. The editorials, however, were superb:

We believe that the only true Art is the Art of Discipline. All other arts in our Perfect City are but submissive variations of the supreme Trumpet-call. We love the corporate body we belong to better than ourselves and still better do we love the Ruler who symbolizes that body in terms of our times. We are for perfect Co-operation blending and balancing the three orders of the State: the productive, the executive, and the contemplative one. We are for an absolute community of interests among fellow citizens. We are for the virile harmony between lover and beloved.

(As Krug read this he experienced a faint "Lacedaemonian" sensation: whips and rods; music; and strange nocturnal terrors. He knew slightly the author of the article —a shabby old man who under the pen name of "Pankrat Tzikutin" had edited a pogromystic magazine years ago.)

Another serious article—it was curious how austere newspapers had become.

"A person who has never belonged to a Masonic Lodge or to a fraternity, club, union, or the like, is an abnormal and dangerous person. Of course, some organizations used to be pretty bad and are forbidden today, but nevertheless it is better for a man to have belonged to a politically incorrect organization than not to have belonged to any organization at all. As a model that every citizen ought to sincerely admire and follow we should like to mention a neighbour of ours who confesses that nothing in the world, not even the most thrilling detective story, not even his young wife's plump charms, not even the day-dreams every young man has of becoming an executive some day can vie with the weekly pleasure of foregathering with his likes and singing community songs in an atmosphere of good cheer and, let us add, good business."

Lately the elections to the Council of Elders were taking up a good deal of space. A list of candidates, thirty in number, drawn by a special commission under Paduk's management, was circulated throughout the country; of these the voters had to select eleven. The same commission nominated "*backer-grupps*," that is, certain clusters of names received the support of special agents, called "*megaphonshchiki*" [megaphone-armed "backers"] that boosted the civic virtues of their candidates at street corners, thus creating the illusion of a hectic election fight. The whole business was extremely confused and it did not matter in the least who won, who lost, but nevertheless the newspapers worked themselves into a state of mad agitation, giving every day, and then every hour, by means of special editions, the results of the struggle in this or that district. An interesting feature was that at the most exciting moments teams of agricultural or industrial workers, like insects driven to copulation by some unusual atmospheric condition, would suddenly issue challenges to other such teams declaring their desire to arrange "production matches" in honour of the elections. Therefore the net result of these "elections" was not any particular change in the composition of the Council, but a tremendously enthusiastic albeit somewhat exhausting "zoom-curve" in the manufacture of reaping machines, cream caramels (in bright wrappers with pictures of naked girls soaping their shoulder blades), *kolbendeckelschrauben* [piston-follower-bolts], *nietwippen* [lever-dollies], *blechtafel* [sheet iron], *krakhmalchiki* [starched collars for men and boys], *glockenmetall* [bronzo da campane], *geschützbronze* [bronzo da cannoni], *blasebalgen* [vozdukhoduvnye mekha] and other useful gadgets.

Detailed accounts of various meetings of factory people or collective kitchen gardeners, snappy articles, devoted to the problems of bookkeeping, denunciations, news of the activities of innumerable professional unions and the clipped accents of poems printed *en escalier* (incidentally tripling the per line honorarium) dedicated to Paduk, completely replaced the comfortable murders, marriages, and boxing matches of happier and more flippant times. It was as if one side of the globe had been struck with paralysis while the other smiled an incredulous—and slightly foolish—smile.

# 14

He had never indulged in the search for the True Substance, the One, the Absolute, the Diamond suspended from the Christmas Tree of the Cosmos. He had always felt the faint ridicule of a finite mind peering at the iridescence of the invisible through the prison bars of integers. And even if the Thing could be caught, why should he, or anybody else for that matter, wish the phenomenon to lose its curls, its mask, its mirror, and become the bald noumenon?

On the other hand, if (as some of the wiser neo-mathematicians thought) the physical world could be said to consist of measure groups (tangles of stresses, sunset swarms of electric midgets) moving like *mouches volantes* on a shadowy background that lay outside the scope of physics, then, surely, the meek restriction of one's interest to measuring the measurable smacked of the most humiliating futility. Take yourself away, you, with your ruler and scales! For without your rules, in an unscheduled event other than the paper chase of science, barefooted Matter *does* overtake Light.

We shall imagine then a prism or prison where rainbows are but octaves of ethereal vibrations and where cosmogonists with transparent heads keep walking into each other and passing through each other's vibrating voids while, all around, various frames of reference pulsate with Fitz-Gerald contractions. Then we give a good shake to the telescopoid kaleidoscope (for what is your cosmos but an instrument containing small bits of coloured glass which, by an arrangement of mirrors, appear in a variety of symmetrical forms when rotated—mark: when rotated) and throw the damned thing away.

How many of us have begun building anew—or thought they were building anew! Then they surveyed their construction. And lo: Heraclitus the Weeping Willow was shimmering by the door and Parmenides the Smoke was coming out of the chimney and Pythagoras (already inside) was drawing the shadows of the window frames on the bright polished floor where the flies played (I settle and you buzz by; then I buzz up and you settle; then jerk-jerk-jerk; then we both buzz up).

Long summer days. Olga playing the piano. Music, order.

The trouble with Krug, thought Krug, was that for long summer years and with enormous success he had delicately taken apart the systems of others and had acquired thereby a reputation for an impish sense of humour and delightful common sense whereas in fact he was a big sad hog of a man and the "common-sense" affair had turned out to be the gradual digging of a pit to accommodate pure smiling madness.

He was constantly being called one of the most eminent philosophers of his time but he knew that nobody could really define what special features his philosophy had, or what "eminent" meant or what "his time" exactly was, or who were the other worthies. When writers in foreign countries were called his disciples he never could find in their writings anything remotely akin to the style or temper of thought which, without his sanction, critics had assigned to him, so that he finally began regarding himself (robust rude Krug) as an illusion or rather as a shareholder in an illusion which was highly appreciated by a great number of cultured people (with a generous sprinkling of semi-cultured ones). It was much the same thing as is liable to happen in novels when the author and his yes-characters assert that the hero is a "great artist" or a "great poet" without, however, bringing any proofs (reproductions of his paintings, samples of his poetry); indeed, taking care *not* to bring such proofs since any sample would be sure to fall short of the reader's expectations and fancy. Krug, while wondering who had puffed him up, who had projected him on to the screen of fame, could not help feeling that in some odd way he did deserve it, that he really was bigger and brighter than most of the men around him; but he also knew that what people saw in him, without realizing it perhaps, was not an admirable expansion of positive matter but a kind of inaudible frozen explosion (as if the reel had been stopped at the point where the bomb bursts) with some debris gracefully poised in mid-air.

When this type of mind, so good at "creative destruction," says to itself as any poor misled philosopher (oh, that cramped uncomfortable "I," that chess-Mephisto concealed in the *cogito!*) might say: "Now I have cleared the ground, now I will build, and the gods of ancient philosophy shall not intrude"—the result generally is a cold little heap of truisms fished out of the artificial lake into which they had been especially put for the purpose. What Krug hoped to fish out was something belonging not only to an undescribed species or genus or family or order, but something representing a brand-new class.

Now let us have this quite clear. What is more important to solve: the "outer" problem (space, time, matter, the unknown without) or the "inner" one (life, thought, love, the unknown within) or again their point of contact (death)? For we agree, do we not, that problems *as* problems do exist even if the world be something made of nothing within nothing made of something. Or is "outer" and "inner" an illusion too, so that a great mountain may be said to stand a thousand dreams high and hope and terror can be as easily charted as the capes and bays they helped to name?

Answer! Oh, that exquisite sight: a wary logician picking his way among the thorn bushes and pitfalls of thought, marking a tree or a cliff (this I have passed, this Nile is settled), looking back ("in other words") and cautiously testing some quaggy ground (now let us proceed——); having his carload of tourists stop at the base of a metaphor or Simple Example (let us suppose that an elevator——); pressing on, surmounting all difficulties and finally arriving in triumph at the very first tree he had marked!

And then, thought Krug, on top of everything, I am a slave of images. We speak of one thing being like some other thing when what we are really craving to do is to describe something that is like nothing on earth. Certain mind pictures have become so adulterated by the concept of "time" that we have come to believe in the actual existence of a permanently moving bright fissure (the point of perception) between our retrospective eternity which we cannot recall and the prospective one which we cannot know. We are not really able to measure time because no gold second is kept in a case in Paris but, quite frankly, do you not imagine a length of several hours more exactly than a length of several miles?

And now, ladies and gentlemen, we come to the problem of death. It may be said with as fair an amount of truth as is practically available that to seek perfect knowledge is the attempt of a point in space and time to identify itself with every other point: death is either the instantaneous gaining of perfect knowledge (similar say to the instantaneous disintegration of stone and ivy composing the circular dungeon where formerly the prisoner had to content himself with only two small apertures optically fusing into one; whilst now, with the disappearance of all walls, he can survey the entire circular landscape), or absolute nothingness, *nichto.*

And this, snorted Krug, is what you call a brand-new class of thinking! Have some more fish.

Who could have believed that his powerful brain would become so disorganized? In the old days whenever he took up a book, the underscored passages, his lightning notes in the margin used to come together almost automatically, and a new essay, a new chapter was ready—but now he was almost incapable of lifting the heavy pencil from the dusty thick carpet where it had fallen from his limp hand.

# 15

ON THE FOURTH, he searched through some old papers and found a reprint of a Henry Doyle Lecture which he had delivered before the Philosophical Society of Washington. He reread a passage he had polemically quoted in regard to the idea of substance: "When a body is sweet and white all over, the motions of whiteness and sweetness are repeated in various places and intermixed. . . ." [*Da mi basia mille.*]

On the fifth, he went on foot to the Ministry of Justice and demanded an interview in connection with the arrest of his friends but it gradually transpired that the place had been turned into a hotel and that the man whom he had taken for a high official was merely the headwaiter.

On the eighth, as he was showing David how to touch a pellet of bread with the tips of two crossed fingers so as to produce a kind of mirror effect in terms of contact (the feel of a second pellet), Mariette laid her bare forearm and elbow upon his shoulder and watched with interest, fidgeting all the time, tickling his temple with her brown hair and scratching her thigh with a knitting needle.

On the tenth, a student called Phokus attempted to see him but was not admitted, partly because he never allowed any scholastic matters to bother him outside his (for the moment nonexistent) office, but mainly because there were reasons to think that this Phokus might be a Government spy.

On the night of the twelfth, he dreamt that he was surreptitiously enjoying Mariette while she sat, wincing a little, in his lap during the rehearsal of a play in which she was supposed to be his daughter.

On the night of the thirteenth, he was drunk.

On the fifteenth, an unknown voice on the telephone informed him that Blanche Hedron, his friend's sister, had been smuggled abroad and was now safe in Budafok, a place situated apparently somewhere in Central Europe.

On the seventeenth, he received a curious letter:

"Rich Sir, an agent of mine abroad has been informed by two of your friends, Messrs Berenz and Marbel, that you are seeking to purchase a reproduction of Turok's masterpiece "Escape." If you care to visit my shop ("Brikabrak," Dimmerlamp Street 14) around five in the afternoon Monday, Tuesday or Friday, I shall be glad to discuss the possibility of your——" a large blot eclipsed the end of the sentence. The letter was signed "Peter Quist, Antiques."

After a prolonged study of a map of the city, he discovered the street in its north-western corner. He laid down his magnifying glass and removed his spectacles. Making those little sticky sounds he was wont to make at such times, he put his spectacles on again, and took up the glass and tried to discover whether any of the bus routes (marked in red) would bring him there. Yes, it could be done. In a casual flash, for no reason at all, he recollected a way Olga had of lifting her left eyebrow when she looked at herself in the mirror.

Do all people have that? A face, a phrase, a landscape,

an air bubble from the past suddenly floating up as if released by the head warden's child from a cell in the brain while the mind is at work on some totally different matter? Something of the sort also occurs just before falling asleep when what you think you are thinking is not at all what you think. Or two parallel passenger trains of thought, one overtaking the other.

Outside, the roughish edges of the air had a touch of spring about them although the year had only begun.

An amusing new law demanded that everyone boarding a motor bus not only show his or her passport, but also give the conductor a signed and numbered photograph. The process of checking whether the likeness, signature and number corresponded to those of the passport was a lengthy one. It had been further decreed that in case a passenger did not have the exact fare (17⅓ cents per mile), whatever surplus he paid would be refunded to him at a remote post office, provided he took his place in the queue there not more than thirty-three hours after leaving the bus. The writing and stamping of receipts by a harassed conductor resulted in some more delay; and since, in accordance with the same decree, the bus stopped only at those points at which not fewer than three passengers wished to alight, a good deal of confusion was added to the delay. In spite of these measures buses were singularly crowded these days.

Nevertheless, Krug managed to reach his destination: together with two youths whom he had bribed (ten kruns each) for helping to make up the necessary trio, he landed precisely where he had decided to land. His two companions (who frankly confessed that they were making a living of it) immediately boarded a moving trolley car (where the regulations were still more complicated).

It had grown dark while he had been travelling and the

crooked little street lived up to its name. He felt excited, insecure, apprehensive. He saw the possibility of escaping from Padukgrad into a foreign country as a kind of return into his own past because his own country had been a free country in the past. Granted that space and time were one, escape and return became interchangeable. The peculiar character of the past (bliss unvalued at the time, her fiery hair, her voice reading of small humanized animals to her child) looked as if it could be replaced or at least mimicked by the character of a country where his child could be brought up in security, liberty, peace (a long long beach dotted with bodies, a sunny honey and her satin Latin—advertisement of some American stuff somewhere seen, somehow remembered). My God, he thought, *que j'ai été veule*, this ought to have been done months ago, the poor dear man was right. The street seemed to be full of bookshops and dim little pubs. Here we are. Pictures of birds and flowers, old books, a polka-dotted china cat. He went in.

The owner of the shop, Peter Quist, was a middle-aged man with a brown face, a flat nose, a clipped black moustache and wavy black hair. He was simply but neatly attired in a blue-and-white striped washable summer suit. As Krug entered he was saying goodbye to an old lady who had an old-fashioned feathery grey boa round her neck. She glanced at Krug keenly before lowering her *voilette* and swept out.

"Know who that was?" asked Quist.

Krug shook his head.

"Ever met the late President's widow?"

"Yes," said Krug, "I have."

"And what about his sister—ever met her?"

"I do not think so."

"Well, that was his sister," said Quist negligently. Krug

blew his nose and while wiping it cast a look at the contents of the shop: mainly books. A heap of *Librairie Hachette* volumes (Molière and the like), vile paper, disintegrating covers, were rotting in a corner. A beautiful plate from some early nineteenth-century insect book showed an ocellated hawk moth and its shagreen caterpillar which clung to a twig and arched its neck. A large discoloured photograph (1894) representing a dozen or so bewhiskered men in tights with artificial limbs (some had as many as two arms and one leg) and a brightly coloured picture of a Mississippi flatboat graced one of the panels.

"Well," said Quist, "I am certainly glad to meet you."

Shake hands.

"It was Turok who gave me your address," said the genial antiquarian as he and Krug settled down in two armchairs in the depth of the shop. "Before we come to any arrangement I want to tell you quite frankly: all my life I have been smuggling—dope, diamonds, old masters. . . . And now—people. I do it solely to meet the expenses of my private urges and orgies, but I do it well."

"Yes," said Krug, "yes, I see. I tried to locate Turok some time ago but he was away on business."

"Well, he got your eloquent letter just before he was arrested."

"Yes," said Krug, "yes. So he has been arrested. That I did not know."

"I am in touch with the whole group," explained Quist with a slight bow.

"Tell me," said Krug, "have you any news of my friends—the Maximovs, Ember, Hedron?"

"None, though I can easily imagine how distasteful they must find the prison regime. Allow me to embrace you, Professor."

He leaned forward and gave Krug an old-fashioned kiss

on the left shoulder. Tears came to Krug's eyes. Quist coughed self-consciously and continued:

"However, let us not forget that I am a hard businessman and therefore above these... unnecessary emotions. True, I want to save you, but I also want money for it. You would have to pay me two thousand kruns."

"It is not much," said Krug.

"Anyway," said Quist dryly, "it is sufficient to pay the brave men who take my shivering clients across the border."

He got up, fetched a box of Turkish cigarettes, offered one to Krug (who refused), lit up, carefully arranged the burning match in a pink and violet sea shell for ashtray so that it would go on burning. Its end squirmed, blackened.

"You will excuse me," he said, "for having yielded to a movement of affection and exaltation. See this scar?"

He showed the back of his hand.

"This," he said, "I received in a duel, in Hungary, four years ago. We used cavalry sabres. In spite of my several wounds, I managed to kill my opponent. He was a great man, a brilliant brain, a gentle heart, but he had had the misfortune of jokingly referring to my young sister as '*cette petite Phryné qui se croit Ophélie.*' You see, the romantic little thing had attempted to drown herself in his swimming pool."

He smoked in silence.

"And there is no way to get them out of there?" asked Krug.

"Out of where? Oh, I see. No. My organization is of a different type. We call it *fruntgenz* [frontier geese] in our professional jargon, not *turmbrokhen* [prison breakers]. So you are willing to pay me what I ask? *Bene.* Would you still be willing if I asked as much money as you have in the world?"

"Certainly," said Krug. "Any of the foreign universities would repay me."

Quist laughed and became rather coyly engaged in fishing a bit of cotton out of a little bottle containing some tablets.

"You know what?" he said with a simper. "If I were an *agent provocateur*, which of course I am not, I would make at this point the following mental observation: Madamka (supposing this to be your nickname in the spying department) is eager to leave the country, no matter what it would cost him."

"And by golly you would be right," said Krug.

"You will also have to make a special present to me," continued Quist. "Namely, your library, your manuscripts, every scrap of writing. You would have to be as naked as an earthworm when you left this country."

"Splendid," said Krug. "I shall save the contents of my waste basket for you."

"Well," said Quist, "if so, then, this is about all."

"When could you arrange it?" asked Krug.

"Arrange what?"

"My flight."

"Oh that. Well—Are you in a hurry?"

"Yes. In a tremendous hurry. I want to get my child out of here."

"Child?"

"Yes, a boy of eight."

"Yes. Of course, you have a child."

There was a curious pause. A dull red slowly suffused Quist's face. He looked down. With soft claws he plucked at his mouth and cheeks. What fools they had been! Now promotion was his.

"My clients," said Quist, "have to do about twenty miles on foot, through blueberry woods and cranberry bogs. The rest of the time they lie at the bottom of trucks, and every jolt tells. The food is scant and crude. The satisfaction of natural needs has to be denied one's self for ten hours at a stretch or more. Your physique is good, you will stand it. Of course, taking your child with you is quite out of the question."

"Oh, I think he would be as quiet as a mouse," said Krug. "And I could carry him as long as I can carry myself."

"One day," murmured Quist, "you were not able to carry him a couple of miles to the railway station."

"I beg your pardon?"

"I said: some day you will not be able to carry him as far as it is from here to the station. That however, is not the essential point. Do you visualize the dangers?"

"Vaguely. But I could never leave my child behind."

There was another pause. Quist twisted a bit of cotton round the head of a match and probed the inner recesses of his left ear. He inspected with satisfaction the gold he obtained.

"Well," he said, "I shall see what can be done. We must keep in touch of course."

"Could we not fix an appointment?" suggested Krug, rising from his chair and looking for his hat. "I mean you might want some money in advance. Yes, I can see it. It is under the table. Thanks."

"You are welcome," said Quist. "What about some day next week? Would Tuesday do? Around five in the afternoon?"

"That would be perfect."

"Would you care to meet me on Neptune Bridge? Say, near the twentieth lamp-post?"

"Gladly."

"At your service. I confess our little talk has clarified

the whole situation to a most marvellous degree. It is a pity you cannot stay longer."

"I shudder," said Krug, "to think of the long journey home. It will take me hours to get back."

"Oh, but I can show you a shorter way," said Quist. "Wait a minute. A very short and pleasant cut."

He went to the foot of a winding staircase and looking up called:

"Mac!"

There was no answer. He waited, with his face now turned upwards, now half turned to Krug—not really looking at Krug: blinking, listening.

"Mac!"

Again there was no reply, and after a while Quist decided to go upstairs and fetch what he wanted himself.

Krug examined some poor things on a shelf: an old rusty bicycle bell, a brown tennis racket, an ivory penholder with a tiny peephole of crystal. He peeped, closing one eye; he saw a cinnabar sunset and a black bridge. *Gruss aus Padukbad.*

Quist came down the steps humming and skipping, with a bundle of keys in his hand. Of these he selected the brightest and unlocked a secret door under the stairs. Silently he pointed down a long passage. There were obsolete posters and elbowed water pipes on its dimly lit walls.

"Why, thank you very much," said Krug.

But Quist had already closed the door after him. Krug walked down the passage, his overcoat unbuttoned, his hands thrust into his trouser pockets. His shadow accompanied him like a Negro porter carrying too many bags.

Presently he came to another door consisting of rough boards roughly knocked together. He pushed it and stepped into his own back yard. Next morning he went down to inspect this exit from an ingressive angle. But now it was cunningly camouflaged, merging partly with some planks that were propped against the wall of the yard and partly with the door of a proletarian privy. On some bricks nearby the mournful detective assigned to his house and an organ-grinder of sorts sat playing *chemin de fer;* a soiled nine of spades lay on the ashstrewn ground at their feet, and, with a pang of impatient desire, he visualized a railway platform and glanced at a playing card and bits of orange peel enlivening the coal dust between the rails under a Pullman car which was still waiting for him in a blend of summer and smoke but a minute later would be gliding out of the station, away, away, into the fair mist of the incredible Carolinas. And following it along the darkling swamps, and hanging faithfully in the evening aether, and slipping through the telegraph wires, as chaste as a wove-paper watermark, as smoothly moving as the transparent tangle of cells that floats athwart an overworked eye, the lemon-pale double of the lamp that shone above the passenger would mysteriously travel across the turquoise landscape in the window.

# 16

THREE CHAIRS placed one behind the other.

Same idea

"The what?"

"The cowcatcher."

A Chinese checker board resting against the legs of the first chair represented the cowcatcher. The last chair was the observation car.

"I see. And now the engine driver must go to bed."

"Hurry up, daddy. Get on. The train is moving!"

"Look here, my darling——"

"Oh, *please*. Sit down just for a minute."

"No, my darling—I told you."

"But it's just one minute. Oh, daddy! Mariette does not want to, you don't want to. Nobody wants to travel with me on my supertrain."

"Not now. It is really time to——"

To be going to bed, to be going to school,—bedtime, dinnertime, tubtime, never just "time"; time to get up, time to go out, time to go home, time to put out all the lights, time to die.

And what agony, thought Krug the thinker, to love so

madly a little creature, formed in some mysterious fashion (even more mysterious to us than it had been to the very first thinkers in their pale olive groves) by the fusion of two mysteries, or rather two sets of a trillion of mysteries each; formed by a fusion which is, at the same time, a matter of choice and a matter of chance and a matter of pure enchantment; thus formed and then permitted to accumulate trillions of its own mysteries; the whole suffused with consciousness, which is the only real thing in the world and the greatest mystery of all.

He saw David a year or two older, sitting on a vividly labelled trunk at the customs house on the pier.

He saw him riding a bicycle in between brilliant forsythia shrubs and thin naked birch trees down a path with a "no bicycles" sign. He saw him on the edge of a swimming pool, lying on his stomach, in wet black shorts, one shoulder blade sharply raised, one hand stretched shaking out iridescent water that clogged a toy destroyer. He saw him in one of those fabulous corner stores that have face creams on one side and ice creams on the other, perched there at the bar and craning towards the syrup pumps. He saw him throwing a ball with a special flip of the wrist, unknown in the old country. He saw him as a youth crossing a technicoloured campus. He saw him wearing the curious garb (jockeylike except for the shoes and stockings) used by players in the American ball game. He saw him learning to fly. He saw him, aged two, sitting on his chamber pot, jerking, crooning, moving by jerks on his scraping chamber pot right across the nursery floor. He saw him as a man of forty.

On the eve of the day fixed by Quist he found himself on the bridge: he was out reconnoitring, since it had occurred to him that as a meeting place it might be unsafe because of the soldiers; but the soldiers had gone long ago, the bridge was deserted, Quist could come whenever he liked. Krug had only one glove, and he had forgotten his glasses, so could not reread the careful note Quist had given him with all the passwords and addresses and a sketch map and the key to the code of Krug's whole life. It mattered little however. The sky immediately overhead was quilted with a livid and billowy expanse of thick cloud; very large, greyish, semitransparent, irregularly shaped snowflakes slowly and vertically descended; and when they touched the dark water of the Kur, they floated upon it instead of melting at once, and this was strange. Further on, beyond the edge of the cloud, a sudden nakedness of heaven and river smiled at the bridge-bound observer, and a mother-of-pearl radiance touched up the curves of the remote mountains, from which the river, and the smiling sadness, and the first evening lights in the windows of riverside buildings were variously derived. Watching the snowflakes upon the dark and beautiful water, Krug argued that either the flakes were real, and the water was not real water, or else the latter was real, whereas the flakes were made of some special insoluble stuff. In order to settle the question, he let his mateless glove fall from the bridge; but nothing abnormal happened: the glove simply pierced the corrugated surface of the water with its extended index, dived and was gone.

On the south bank (from which he had come) he could see, further upstream, Paduk's pink palace and the bronze dome of the Cathedral, and the leafless trees of a public garden. On the other side of the river there were rows of old tenement houses beyond which (unseen but throbbingly present) stood the hospital where she had died. As he brooded thus, sitting sideways on a stone bench and looking at the river, a tugboat dragging a barge appeared in the distance and at the same time one of the last snowflakes (the cloud overhead seemed to be dissolving in the now generously flushed sky) grazed his underlip: it was a regular soft wet flake, he reflected, but perhaps those that had been descending upon the water itself had been different ones. The tug steadily approached. As it was about to plunge under the bridge, the great black funnel, doubly encircled with crimson, was pulled back, back and down by two men clutching at its rope and grinning with sheer exertion; one of them was a Chinese as were most of the river people and washermen of the town. On the barge behind, half a dozen brightly coloured shirts were drying and some potted geraniums could be seen aft, and a very fat Olga in the yellow blouse he disliked, arms akimbo, looked up at Krug as the barge in its turn was smoothly engulfed by the arch of the bridge.

He awoke (asprawl in his leather armchair) and immediately understood that something extraordinary had happened. It had nothing to do with the dream or the quite unprovoked and rather ridiculous physical discomfort he felt (a local congestion) or anything that he recalled in connection with the appearance of his room (untidy and dusty in an untidy and dusty light) or the time of the day (a quarter past eight P.M.; he had fallen asleep after an early supper). What had happened was that again he knew he could write.

He went to the bathroom, took a cold shower, like the good little boy scout he was, and tingling with mental eagerness and feeling comfortable and clean in pyjamas and dressing gown, let his fountain pen suck in its fill, but then remembered that it was David's tucking-in hour, and decided to get it over with, so as not to be interrupted by nursery calls. In the passage three chairs still stood one behind the other. David was lying in bed and with rapid back and forth movements of his lead pencil was evenly shading a portion of a sheet of paper placed on the fibroid fine-grained cover of a big book. This produced a not unpleasant sound, both shuffling and silky with a kind of rising buzzing vibration underlying the scrabble. The punctate texture of the cover gradually appeared as a grey grating on the paper and then, with magical precision and quite independent of the (accidentally oblique) direction of the pencil strokes, the impressed word ATLAS came out in tall narrow white letters. One wondered if by shading one's life in like fashion——

The pencil cracked. David tried to straighten the loose tip in its pine socket and use the pencil in such a way as to have the longer projection of the wood act as a prop, but the lead broke off for good.

"And anyway," said Krug, who was impatient to get back to his own writing, "it is time to put out the lights."

"First the travel story," said David

For several nights already Krug had been evolving a serial which dealt with the adventures awaiting David on his way to a distant country (we had stopped at the point where we crouched at the bottom of a sleigh, holding our breaths, very very quiet under sheepskin blankets and empty potato sacks).

"No, not tonight," said Krug. "It is much too late and I am busy."

"It is *not* too late," cried David sitting up suddenly, with blazing eyes, and striking the atlas with his fist.

Krug removed the book and bent over David to kiss him good night. David abruptly turned away to the wall.

"Just as you like," said Krug, "but you'd better say good night [*pokoĭnoĭ nochi*] because I'm not going to come again."

David drew the bedclothes over his head, sulking. With a little cough Krug unbent and put out the lamp.

"I am not going to sleep," said David in a muffled voice.

"That's up to you," said Krug, trying to imitate Olga's smooth pedagogic tones.

A pause in the dark.

"*Pokoĭnoĭ nochi, dushka* [*animula*]," said Krug from the threshold. Silence. He told himself with a certain degree of irritation that he would have to come back in ten minutes and go through the whole act in detail. This was, as often happened, only the first rough draft of the good night ritual. But then, of course, sleep might settle the matter. He closed the door and as he turned the bend of the passage bumped into Mariette. "Look where you are going, child," he said sharply, and hit his knee against one of the chairs left by David.

In this preliminary report on infinite consciousness a certain scumbling of the essential outline is unavoidable. We have to discuss sight without being able to see. The knowledge we may acquire in the course of such a discussion will necessarily stand in the same relation to the truth as the black peacock spot produced intraoptically by pressure on the palpebra does in regard to a garden path brindled with genuine sunlight.

Ah yes, the glair of the matter instead of its yolk, the reader will say with a sigh; *connu, mon vieux!* The same old sapless sophistry, the same old dust-coated alembics—and thought speeds along like a witch on her besom! But you are wrong, you captious fool.

Ignore my invective (a question of impetus) and consider the following point: can we work ourself into a state of abject panic by trying to imagine the infinite number of years, the infinite folds of dark velvet (stuff their dryness into your mouth), in a word the infinite past, which extends on the minus side of the day of our birth? We cannot. Why? For the simple reason that we have already gone through eternity, have already non-existed once and have discovered that this *néant* holds no terrors whatever. What we are now trying (unsuccessfully) to do is to fill the abyss we have safely crossed with terrors borrowed from the abyss in front, which abyss is borrowed itself from the infinite past. Thus we live in a stocking which is in the process of being turned inside out, without our ever knowing for sure to what phase of the process our moment of consciousness corresponds.

Once launched he went on writing with a somewhat pathetic (if viewed from the side) gusto. He *was* wounded, something *had* cracked but, for the time being, a rush of second-rate inspiration and somewhat precious imagery kept him going nicely. After an hour or so of this sort of thing he stopped and reread the four and a half pages he had written. The way was now clear. Incidentally in one compact sentence he had referred to several religions (not forgetting "that wonderful Jewish sect whose dream of the gentle young rabbi dying on the Roman *crux* had spread over all Northern lands"), and had dismissed them together with ghosts and kobolds. The pale starry heaven of untrammelled philosophy lay before him, but he thought he would like a drink. With his bared fountain pen still in his hand he trudged to the dining-room. She again.

"Is he asleep?" he asked in a kind of atonic grunt without turning his head, while bending for the brandy in the lower part of the sideboard.

"Should be," she replied.

He uncorked the bottle and poured some of its contents into a green glass goblet.

"Thank you," she said.

He could not help glancing at her. She sat at the table

mending a stocking. Her bare neck and legs looked uncommonly pale in contrast to her black frock and black slippers.

She glanced up from her work, her head cocked, soft wrinkles on her forehead.

"Well?" she said.

"No liquor for you," he answered. "Root beer if you like. I think there is some in the icebox."

"You nasty man," she said, lowering her untidy eyelashes and crossing her legs anew. "You horrible man. I feel pretty tonight."

"Pretty what?" he asked slamming the door of the sideboard.

"Just pretty. Pretty all over."

"Good night," he said. "Don't sit up too late."

"May I sit in your room while you are writing?"

"Certainly not."

He turned to go but she called him back:

"Your pen's on the sideboard."

Moaning, he came back with his goblet and took the pen.

"When I'm alone," she said, "I sit and do like this, like a cricket. Listen, please."

"Listen to what?"

"Don't you hear?"

She sat with parted lips, slightly moving her tightly crossed thighs, producing a tiny sound, soft, labiate, with an alternate crepitation as if she were rubbing the palms of her hands which, however, lay idle.

"Chirruping like a poor cricket," she said.

"I happen to be partly deaf," remarked Krug and trudged back to his room.

He reflected he ought to have gone to see whether David was asleep. Oh, he should be, because otherwise he would have heard his father's footsteps and called. Krug did not care to pass again by the open door of the dining-room and so told himself that David was at least half asleep and likely to be disturbed by an intrusion, however well-meant. It is not quite clear why he indulged in all this ascetic self-restraint business when he might have ridden himself so deliciously of his quite natural tension and discomfort with the assistance of that keen *puella* (for whose lively little abdomen younger Romans than he would have paid the Syrian slavers 20,000 dinarii or more). Perhaps he was held back by certain subtle supermatrimonial scruples or by the dismal sadness of the whole thing. Unfortunately his urge to write had suddenly petered out and he did not know what to do with himself. He was not sleepy having slept after dinner. The brandy only added to the nuisance. He was a big heavy man of the hairy sort with a somewhat Beethovenlike face. He had lost his wife in November. He had taught philosophy. He was exceedingly virile. His name was Adam Krug.

He reread what he had written, crossed out the witch on her besom and started to pace the room with his hands in the pockets of his robe. Gregoire peered from under the armchair. The radiator purled. The street was silent behind thick dark-blue curtains. Little by little his thoughts resumed their mysterious course. The nutcracker cracking one hollow second after another, came to a full meaty one again. An indistinct sound like the echo of some remote ovation met the appearance of a new eidolon.

A fingernail scraped, tapped.

"What is it? What do you want?"

No answer. Smooth silence. Then an audible dimple. Then silence again.

He opened the door. She was standing there in her nightgown. A slow blink concealed and revealed again the queer stare of her dark opaque eyes. She had a pillow under her arm and an alarm clock in her hand. She sighed deeply.

"Please, let me come in," she said, the somewhat lemurian features of her small white face puckering up entreatingly. "I am terrified, I simply can't be alone. I feel something dreadful is about to happen. May I sleep here? Please!"

She crossed the room on tiptoe and with infinite care put the round-faced clock down on the night table. Penetrating her flimsy garment, the light of the lamp brought out her body in peachblow silhouette.

"Is it O.K.?" she whispered. "I shall make myself very small."

Krug turned away, and as he was standing near a bookcase, pressed down and released again a torn edge of calf's leather on the back of an old Latin poet. *Brevis lux. Da mi basia mille.* He pounded in slow motion the book with his fist.

When he looked at her again she had crammed the pillow under her nightgown in front and was shaking with mute laughter. She patted her false pregnancy. But Krug did not laugh.

Knitting her brow and letting the pillow and some peach petals drop to the floor between her ankles.

"Don't you like me at *all?*" she said [*inquit*].

If, he thought, my heart could be heard, as Paduk's heart is, then its thunderous thumping would awaken the dead. But let the dead sleep.

Going on with her act, she flung herself on the bedded sofa and lay there prone, her rich brown hair and the edge of a flushed ear in the full blaze of the lamp. Her pale young legs invited an old man's groping hand.

He sat down near her; morosely, with clenched teeth, he accepted the banal invitation, but no sooner had he touched her, than she got up and, lifting and twisting her thin white chestnutty-smelling bare arms, yawned.

"I guess I'll go back now," she said.

Krug said nothing, Krug sat there, sullen and heavy, bursting with vine-ripe desire, poor thing.

She sighed, put her knee against the bedding and, baring her shoulder, investigated the marks that some playmate's teeth had left near a small, very dark birthmark on the diaphanous skin.

"Do you want me to go?" she asked.

He shook his head.

"Shall we make love if I stay?"

His hands compressed her frail hips as if he were taking her down from a tree.

"You know too little or much too much," he said. "If too little, then run along, lock yourself up, never come near me because this is going to be a bestial explosion, and you might get badly hurt. I warn you. I am nearly three times your age and a great big sad hog of a man. And I don't love you."

She looked down at the agony of his senses. Tittered.

"Oh, you don't?"

*Mea puella, puella mea.* My hot, vulgar, heavenly delicate little *puella.* This is the translucent amphora which I slowly set down by the handles. This is the pink moth clinging——

A deafening din (the door bell, loud knocking) interrupted these anthological preambulations.

"Oh, please, please," she muttered wriggling up to him, "let's go on, we have just enough time to do it before they break the door, please."

He pushed her away violently and snatched up his dressing gown from the floor.

"It's your last cha-ance," she sang out with that special

rising note which produces as it were a faint interrogatory ripple, the liquid reflection of a question mark.

Catching up and hastily interlacing the ends of the brown cord of his somewhat monastic robe, he swung down the passage followed by Mariette and, a hunchback again, unlocked the impatient door.

Young woman with pistol in gloved hand; two raw youths of S.B. (Schoolboy Brigade): repulsive patches of unshaven skin and pustules, plaid wool shirts, worn loose and flapping.

"Hi, Linda," said Mariette.

"Hi, Mariechen," said the woman. She had an Ekwilist soldier's greatcoat carelessly hanging from her shoulders and a crumpled military cap was rakishly poised on her neatly waved honey-coloured hair. Krug recognized her at once.

"My fiancé is waiting outside in a car," she explained to Mariette after giving her a smiling kiss. "The Professor can go as he is. He will get some nice sterilized regulation togs at the place we are taking him to."

"Is it my turn at last?" asked Krug.

"How are you, Mariechen? We shall go to a party after we drop the Professor. Is that O.K.?"

"That's fine," said Mariette, and then asked, lowering her voice: "Can I play with the nice boys?"

"Come, come, honey, you deserve better. Fact is, I have a big surprise for you. You, kids, get busy. The nursery is down there."

"No, you don't," said Krug blocking the way.

"Let them pass, Professor, they are doing their duty. And they will not steal a pin."

"Step aside, Doc, we are doing our duty."

There was a businesslike knuckle-rap on the half-closed hall door, and when Linda, who stood with her back to it and against whose spine it gently butted, flung it wide open, a tall, broad-shouldered man in a smart semipolice uniform walked in with a heavyweight wrestler's rotund step. He had bushy black eyebrows, a square heavy jaw and the whitest of white teeth.

"Mac," said Linda, "this here is my little sister. Escaped from a boarding school on fire. Mariette, this is my fiancé's best friend. I hope you two will like each other."

"I sure hope we do," said hefty Mac in a deep mellow voice. Dental display, extended palm the size of a steak for five.

"I sure am glad to meet a friend of Hustav," said Mariette demurely.

Mac and Linda exchanged a twinkling smile.

"I'm afraid we have not made this too clear, honey. The fiancé in question is not Hustav. Definitely not Hustav. Poor Hustav is by now an abstraction."

("You shall not pass," rumbled Krug, holding the two youths at bay.)

"What happened?" asked Mariette.

"Well, they had to wring his neck. He was a *schlapp* [a failure], you see."

"A *schlapp* who during his short life made many a fine arrest," remarked Mac with the generosity and broadmindedness so characteristic of him.

"This here belonged to him," said Linda in confidential tones, showing the pistol to her sister.

"The flashlight too?"

"No, that's Mac's."

"My!" said Mariette reverently touching the huge leathery thing.

One of the youths, propelled by Krug, collided with the umbrella stand.

"Now, now, will you please stop this unseemly scuffle,"

said Mac pulling Krug back (poor Krug executed a cake-walk). The two youths at once made for the nursery.

"They will frighten him," muttered and gasped Krug trying to free himself from Mac's hold. "Let me go at once. Mariette, do me a favour": he frantically signalled to her to run, to run to the nursery and see that my child, my child, my child——

Mariette looked at her sister and giggled. With wonderful professional precision and *savoir-faire*, Mac suddenly dealt Krug a cutting backhand blow with the edge of his pig-iron paw: the blow caught Krug neatly on the inside of the right arm and instantly paralysed it. Mac proceeded to treat Krug's left arm in like fashion. Krug, bent double holding his dead arms in his dead arms, sank down on one of the three chairs that stood (by now askew and meaningless) in the passage.

"Mac's awfully good at this sort of thing," remarked Linda.

"Yes, isn't he?" said Mariette.

The sisters had not seen each other for some time and kept smiling and blinking sweetly and touching each other with limp girlish gestures.

"That's a nice brooch," said the younger.

"Three fifty," said Linda, a fold adding itself to her chin.

"Shall I go and put on my black lace panties and the Spanish dress?" asked Mariette.

"Oh, I think you look just cute in this rumpled nighty. Doesn't she, Mac?"

"Sure," said Mac.

"And you won't catch cold because there is a mink coat in the car."

Owing to the door of the nursery suddenly opening (before slamming again) David's voice was heard for a moment: oddly enough, the child, instead of whimpering and crying for help, seemed to be trying to reason with his impossible visitors. Perhaps he had not been asleep after all. The sound of that dutiful and bland little voice was worse than the most anguished moaning.

Krug moved his fingers—the numbness was gradually passing away. As calmly as possible. As calmly as possible, he again appealed to Mariette.

"Does anybody know what he wants of me?" asked Mariette.

"Look," said Mac to Adam, "either you do what you're told or you don't. And if you don't, it's going to hurt like hell, see? Get up!"

"All right," said Krug. "I will get up. What next?"

"*Marsh vniz* [Go downstairs]!"

And then David began to scream. Linda made a tchk-tchk sound ("now those dumb kids have done it") and Mac looked at her for directions. Krug lurched towards the nursery. Simultaneously David in pale-blue, the little mite, ran out but was immediately caught. "I want my daddy," he cried off stage. Humming, Mariette in the bathroom with the door open was making up her lips. Krug managed to reach his child. One of the hoodlums had pinned David to the bed. The other was trying to catch David's rapidly kicking feet.

"Leave him alone, *merzavtzy!*" [a term of monstrous abuse] cried Krug.

"They want him to be quiet, that's all," said Mac, who again had taken control of the situation.

"David, my love," said Krug, "it's all right, they won't hurt you."

The child, still held by the grinning youths, caught Krug by a fold of his dressing gown.

This little hand must be unclenched.

"It's all right, leave it to me, gentlemen. Don't touch him. My darling——"

Mac, who had had enough of it, briskly kicked Krug in the shins and bundled him out.

They have torn my little one in two.

"Look here, you brute," he said, half on his knees, clinging to the wardrobe in the passage (Mac was holding him by the front of his dressing gown and pulling), "I cannot leave my child to be tortured. Let him come with me wherever you are taking me."

A toilet was flushed. The two sisters joined the men and looked on with bored amusement.

"My dear man," said Linda, "we quite understand that it is your child, or at least your late wife's child, and not a little owl of porcelain or something, but our duty is to take you away and the rest does not concern us."

"Please, let us be moving," pleaded Mariette, "it's getting frightfully late."

"Allow me to telephone to Schamm," (one of the members of the Council of Elders) said Krug. "Just that. One telephone call."

"Oh, *do* let us go," repeated Mariette.

"The question is," said Mac, "will you go quietly, under your own power, or shall I have to maim you and then roll you down the steps as we do with logs in Lagodan?"

"Yes," said Krug suddenly making up his mind. "Yes. Logs. Yes. Let us go. Let us get there quickly. After all, the solution is simple!"

"Put out the lights, Mariette," said Linda, "or we shall be accused of stealing this man's electricity."

"I shall be back in ten minutes," shouted Krug in the direction of the nursery, using the full force of his lungs.

"Aw, for Christ's sake," muttered Mac, pushing him towards the door.

"Mac," said Linda, "I'm afraid she might catch cold on the stairs. I think, you'd better carry her down. Look, why doesn't he go first, then me, then you. Come on, pick her up."

"I don't weigh much, you know," said Mariette, raising her elbows towards Mac. Blushing furiously, the young policeman cupped a perspiring paw under the girl's grateful thighs, put another around her ribs and lightly lifted her heavenwards. One of her slippers fell off.

"It's O.K.," she said quickly, "I can put my foot into your pocket. There. Lin will carry my slipper."

"Say, you sure don't weigh much," said Mac.

"Now hold me tight," she said. "Hold me tight. And give me that flashlight, it's hurting me."

The little procession made its way downstairs. The place was still and dark. Krug walked in front, with a circle of light playing upon his bent bare head and brown dressing gown—looking for all the world like a participant in some mysterious religious ceremony painted by a master of chiaroscuro, or copied from such a painting, or recopied from that or some other copy. Linda followed, her pistol pointing at his back, her prettily arched feet daintily negotiating the steps. Then came Mac carrying Mariette. Exaggerated parts of the banisters and sometimes the shadow of Linda's hair and cap slipped across Krug's back and along the ghostly wall, as the electric torch, fingered by sly Mariette, moved spasmodically. Her very thin wrist had a funny little bony knob on the outside. Now let us figure it out, let us look at it squarely. They have found the handle. On the night of the twenty-first, Adam Krug was arrested. This was unexpected since he had not thought they would find the handle. In fact, he had hardly known there was any handle at all. Let us proceed logically. They will not harm the child. On the contrary, it is their most valued asset. Let us not imagine things, let us stick to pure reason.

"Oh, Mac, this is divine... I wish there were a billion steps!"

He may go to sleep. Let us pray he does. Olga once said that a billion was a million with a bad cold. Shin hurts. Anything, anything, anything, anything, anything. Your boots, *dragotzennyĭ*, have a taste of candied plums. And look, my lips bleed from your spurs.

"I can't see a thing," said Linda. "Quit fooling with that flashlight, Mariechen."

"Hold it straight, kiddo," grumbled Mac, breathing somewhat heavily, his great raw paw steadily melting; despite the lightness of his auburn burden; because of her burning rose.

Keep telling yourself that whatever they do they will not harm him. Their horrible stink and bitten nails—the smell and dirt of high-school boys. They may start breaking his playthings. Toss to each other, toss and catch, handy-dandy, one of his pet marbles, the opal one, unique, sacred, which even I dared not touch. He in the middle, trying to stop them, trying to catch it, trying to save it from them. Or, for instance, twisting his arm, or some filthy adolescent joke, or—no, this is all wrong, hold on, I must not imagine things. They will let him sleep. They will merely ransack the flat and have a good meal in the kitchen. And as soon as I reach Schamm or the Toad himself and say what I shall say——

A blustering wind took charge of our four friends as they came out of the house. An elegant car was waiting for them. At the wheel sat Linda's fiancé, a handsome blond man with white eyelashes and——

"Oh, but we do know each other. Yes, indeed. As a matter of fact, I have had the honour of being the Professor's chauffeur once before. And so this is the little sister. Glad to meet you, Mariechen."

"Get in, you fat numbskull," said Mac—and Krug heavily settled down next to the driver.

"Here's your slipper and here's your fur," said Linda, as she handed the promised coat to Mac who took it and started to help Mariette into it.

"No—just round my shoulders," said the debutante.

She shook her smooth brown hair; then, with a special disengaging gesture (the back of her hand rapidly passing along the nape of her delicate neck), she lightly swished it up so that it would not catch under the collar of the coat.

"There is room for three," she sang out sweetly in her best golden-oriole manner from the depths of the car, and sidling up to her sister, patted the free space on the outer side.

But Mac unfolded one of the front seats so as to be right behind his prisoner; resting both elbows on the partition and chewing the mint-flavoured cud, he told Krug to behave.

"All aboard?" queried Dr. Alexander.

At this moment the nursery window (last one on the left, fourth floor) flew open and one of the youths leant out, bawling something in a questioning tone. Because of the gusty wind, nothing could be made out of the jumble of words that came forth.

"What?" cried Linda, her nose impatiently puckered.

"Uglowowgloowoo?" called the youth from the window.

"Okay," said Mac to no one in particular. "Okay," he grumbled. "We hear you."

"Okay!" cried Linda upwards, making a megaphone of her hands.

The second youth loomed in violent motion within the

trapezoid of light. He was cuffing David who had climbed upon a table in a futile attempt to reach the window. The bright-haired pale-blue little figure disappeared. Krug, bellowing and plunging, was half out of the car, with Mac hanging on to him, tackling him round the waist. The car was moving. The struggle was useless. A procession of small coloured animals raced along an oblique strip of wallpaper. Krug sank back in his seat.

"I wonder what he was asking," remarked Linda. "Are you quite sure it's all right, Mac? I mean——"

"Well, they have their instructions, haven't they?"

"I guess so."

"All six of you," said Krug gasping, "all six will be tortured and shot if my child gets hurt."

"Now, now, these are ugly words," said Mac, and none too gently rapped him with the loose joints of four fingers behind the ear.

It was Dr. Alexander who relieved the somewhat strained situation (for there is no doubt that for a moment everybody felt something had gone wrong):

"Well," he said with a sophisticated semi-smile, "ugly rumours and plain facts are not always as true as ugly brides and plain wives invariably are."

Mac spluttered with laughter—right into Krug's neck.

"I must say, your new steady has a regular sense of humour," whispered Mariette to her sister.

"He is a college man," said big-eyed Linda, nodding in awe and protruding her lower lip. "He knows simply everything. It gives me the creeps. You should see him with a fuse or a monkey wrench."

The two girls settled down to some cozy chatting as girls in back seats are prone to do.

"Tell me some more about Hustav," asked Mariette. "How was he strangled?"

"Well, it was like this. They came by the back door while I was making breakfast and said they had instructions to get rid of him. I said aha but I don't want any mess on the floor and I don't want any shooting. He had bolted into a clothes closet. You could hear him shivering there and clothes falling down upon him and hangers jingling at every shiver. It was just too gruesome. I said, I don't want to see you guys doing it and I don't want to spend all day cleaning up. So they took him to the bathroom and started to work on him there. Of course, my morning was ruined. I had to be at my dentist's at ten, and there they were in the bathroom making simply hideous noises—especially Hustav. They must have been at it for at least twenty minutes. He had an Adam's apple as hard as a heel, they said—and of course I was late."

"As usual," commented Dr. Alexander.

The girls laughed. Mac turned to the younger of the two and stopped chewing to ask:

"Sure you not cold, Cin?"

His baritone voice was loaded with love. The teenager blushed and furtively pressed his hand. She said she was warm, oh, very warm. Feel for yourself. She blushed because he had employed a secret diminutive which none knew, which he had somehow divined. Intuition is the sesame of love.

"All right, all right, caramel eyes," said the shy young giant disengaging his hand. "Remember, I'm on duty."

And Krug felt again the man's drugstore breath.

# 17

THE CAR came to a stop at the north gate of the prison. Dr. Alexander, mellowly manipulating the plump rubber of the horn (white hand, white lover, pyriform breast of black concubine), honked.

A slow iron yawn was induced and the car crawled into yard No. 1. There a swarm of guards, some wearing gas masks (which in profile bore a striking resemblance to greatly magnified ant heads), clambered upon the footboards and other accessible parts of the car; two or three even grunted their way up to the roof. Numerous hands, several of which were heavily gloved, tugged at torpid recurved Krug (still in the larval stage) and pulled him out. Guards A and B took charge of him; the rest zigzagged away, darting this way and that, in search of new victims. With a smile and a semi-salute Dr. Alexander said to guard A: "I'll be seeing you," then backed and proceeded to energetically unravel the wheel. Unravelled, the car turned, jerked forward: Dr. Alexander repeated his semi-salute, while Mac, after wagging a great big forefinger at Krug, squeezed his haunches into the place Mariette had made for him next to herself. Presently the car was heard uttering festive honks as it sped away, down to a private musk-scented apartment. O joyous, red-hot, impatient youth!

Krug was led through several yards to the main building. In yards Nos. 3 and 4 outlines of condemned men for target practice had been chalked on a brick wall. An old Russian legend says that the first thing a *rastrelianyĭ* [person executed by the firing squad] sees on entering the "other world" (no interruption please, this is premature, take your hands away) is not a gathering of ordinary "shades" or "spirits" or repulsive dear repulsive unutterably dear unutterably repulsive dear ones in antiquated clothes, as you might think, but a kind of silent slow ballet, a welcoming group of these chalked outlines moving wavily like transparent Infusoria; but away with those bleak superstitions.

They entered the building and Krug found himself in a curiously empty room. It was perfectly round, with a well-scrubbed cement floor. So suddenly did his guards disappear that, had he been a character in fiction, he might well have wondered whether the strange doings and so on had not been some evil vision, and so forth. He had a throbbing headache: one of those headaches that seem to transcend on one side the limits of one's head, like the colours in cheap comics, and do not quite fill the head space on the other; and the dull throbs were saying: one, one, one, never reaching two, never. Of the four doors at the cardinal points of the circular room, only one, one, one was unlocked. Krug pushed it open.

"Yes?" said a pale-faced man, still looking down at the seesaw blotter with which he was dabbing whatever he had just written.

"I demand immediate action," said Krug.

The official looked at him with tired watery eyes.

"My name is Konkordii Filadelfovich Kolokololiteishchikov," he said, "but they call me Kol. Take a seat."

"I——" began Krug anew.

Kol, shaking his head, hurriedly selected the necessary forms:

"Wait a minute. First of all we must have all the answers. Your name is——?"

"Adam Krug. Will you please have my child brought here at once, at once——"

"A little patience," said Kol dipping his pen. "I admit the procedure is tiresome but the sooner we get it over with the better. All right. K,r,u,g. Age?"

"Will this nonsense be necessary if I tell you straightaway that I have changed my mind?"

"It is necessary under all circumstances. Sex—male. Eyebrows—shaggy. Father's name——"

"Same as mine, curse you."

"Now, don't curse me. I am as tired as you are. Religion?"

"None."

" 'None' is no answer. The law requires every male to declare his religious affiliation. Catholic? Vitalist? Protestant?"

"There is no answer."

"My dear sir, you have been baptized, at least?"

"I do not know what you are talking about."

"Well, this is most—Look here, I must put down *something*."

"How many questions more? Have you got to fill all this?" (pointing with a madly trembling finger at the page).

"I am afraid so."

"In that case I refuse to continue. Here I am with a

declaration of the utmost importance to make—and you take up my time with nonsense."

"Nonsense is a harsh word."

"Look here, I will sign anything if my son——"

"One child?"

"One. A boy of eight."

"A tender age. Pretty hard upon you, sir, I admit. I mean—I am a father myself and all that. However I can assure you that your boy is perfectly safe."

"He is not!" cried Krug. "You delegated two ruffians——"

"I did not delegate anybody. You are in the presence of an underpaid *chinovnik*. As a matter of fact, I deplore everything that has happened in Russian literature."

"Anyway, whoever is responsible must choose: either I remain silent for ever, or else I speak, sign, swear—anything the Government wants. But I will do all this, and more, only if my child is brought here, to this room, at once."

Kol pondered. The whole thing was very irregular.

"The whole thing is very irregular," he said at length, "but I guess you are right. You see, the general procedure is something like this: first the questionnaire must be filled, then you go to your cell. There you have a heart-to-heart talk with a fellow prisoner who really is one of our agents. Then, around two in the morning, you are roused from a fitful sleep and I start to question you again. It was thought by competent people that you would break down between six-forty and seven-fifteen. Our meteorologist predicted a particularly cheerless dawn. Dr. Alexander, a colleague of yours, agreed to translate into everyday language your cryptic utterances, for no one could have predicted this bluntness, this . . . I suppose, I may also add that a child's voice would have been relayed to you emitting moans of artificial pain. I had been rehearsing it with my own little children—they will be bitterly disappointed. Do you really mean to say that you are ready to pledge allegiance to the State and all that, if——"

"You had better hurry. The nightmare may get out of control."

"Why, of course, I shall have things fixed immediately. Your attitude is most satisfactory. Our great prison has made a man of you. It is a real treat. I shall be congratulated for having broken you so quickly. Excuse me."

He got up (a small slender State employee with a large pale head and black serrated jaws), plucked aside the folds of a velvet *portière*, and then the captive remained alone with his dull "one-one-one." A filing cabinet concealed the entrance Krug had used some minutes before. What looked like a curtained window turned out to be a curtained mirror. He rearranged the collar of his dressing gown.

Four years elapsed. Then disjointed parts of a century. Odds and ends of torn time. Say, twenty-two years in all. The oak tree before the old church had lost all its birds; alone, gnarled Krug had not changed.

Preceded by a slight hunching or bunching or both of the curtain and then by his own visible hand, Konkordiĭ Filadelfovich returned. He looked pleased.

"Your boy will be brought here in a jiffy," he said brightly. "Everybody is very much relieved. Been in the care of a trained nurse. She says, the kid behaved pretty badly. A problem child, I suppose? By the way, I am asked to ask you: would you like to write your own speech and submit it in advance or will you use the material prepared?"

"The material. I am terribly thirsty."

"We shall have some refreshments presently. Now, there

is another question. Here are a few papers to be signed. We could start right now."

"Not before I see my child."

"You are going to be a very busy man, *sudar*, [sir], I warn you. There is sure to be a journalist or two hanging around already. Oh, the worries we have gone through! We thought, the University would never open again. I suppose, tomorrow there will be student demonstrations, processions, public thanksgiving. Do you know d'Abrikossov, the film producer? Well, he said he had known all along you would suddenly realize the greatness of the State and all that. He said it was like *la grâce* in religion. A revelation. He said it was very difficult to explain things to anybody who had not experienced this sudden dazzling shock of truth. Personally, I am very happy to have had the privilege of witnessing your beautiful conversion. Still sulking? Come, let us erase those wrinkles. Hark! Music!"

He had apparently pressed a button or turned a knob for some trumpety-strumpety sounds issued from somewhere, and the good fellow added in a reverent whisper:

"Music in your honour."

The band was drowned, however, by a shrill telephone peal. Capital news, evidently, for Kol replaced the receiver with a triumphant flourish and motioned Krug towards the curtained door. After you.

He was a man of the world; Krug was not, and pressed forward like a boorish boar.

Unnumbered scene (belonging to one of the last acts, anyway): the spacious waiting room of a fashionable prison. Cute little model of guillotine (with stiff top-hatted doll in attendance) under glass bell on mantelpiece. Oil pictures dealing darkly with various religious subjects. A collection of magazines on a low table (the *Geographical Magazine*, *Stolitza i Usad'ba*, *Die Woche*, *The Tatler*,

*L'Illustration*). One or two bookcases with the usual books (*Little Women*, volume III of the *History of Nottingham* and so on). A bunch of keys on a chair (mislaid there by one of the wardens). A table with refreshments: a plate of herring sandwiches and a pail of water surrounded with several mugs coming from various German kurorts. (Krug's mug had a view of Bad Kissingen.)

A door at the back swung open; several press photographers and reporters formed a living gallery for the passage of two burly men leading in a thin frightened boy of twelve or thirteen. His head was newly bandaged (nobody was to blame, they said, he had slipped on a highly polished floor and hit his forehead against a model of Stevenson's engine in the Children's Museum). He wore a schoolboy's black uniform, with belt. His elbow flew up to shield his face as one of the men made a sudden gesture meant to curb the eagerness of the press people.

"This is not my child," said Krug.

"Your dad is always joking, always joking," said Kol to the boy kindly.

"I want my own child. This is somebody else's child."

"What's that?" asked Kol sharply. "Not your child? Nonsense, man. Use your eyes."

One of the burly men (a policeman in plain clothes) produced a document which he handed to Kol. The document said clearly: Arvid Krug, son of Professor Martin Krug, former Vice-President of the Academy of Medicine.

"The bandage perhaps changes him a little," said Kol hastily, a note of desperation creeping into his patter. "And then, of course, little boys grow so fast——"

The guards were knocking down the apparatus of the photographers and pushing the reporters out of the room. "Hold the boy," said a brutal voice.

The newcomer, a person called Crystalsen (red face,

blue eyes, tall starched collar) who was, as it soon transpired, Second Secretary of the Council of Elders, came up close to Kol and asked poor Kol while holding him by the knot of his necktie whether Kol did not think he was sort of responsible for this idiotic misunderstanding. Kol was still hoping against hope——

"Are you *quite* sure," he kept asking Krug, "are you quite sure this little fellow is not your son? Philosophers are absentminded, you know. The light in this room is not very grand——"

Krug closed his eyes and said through clenched teeth:

"I want my own child."

Kol turned to Crystalsen, spread out his hands and produced a helpless, hopeless bursting sound with his lips (ppwt). Meanwhile, the unwanted boy was led away.

"We apologize," said Kol to Krug. "Such mistakes are bound to occur when there are so many arrests."

"Or not enough," interrupted Crystalsen crisply.

"He means," said Kol to Krug, "that those who made this mistake will be dearly punished."

Crystalsen, *même jeu:*

"Or pay for it severely."

"Exactly. Of course, matters will be straightened out without delay. There are four hundred telephones in this building. Your little lost child will be found at once. I understand now why my wife had that terrible dream last night. Ah, Crystalsen, *was ver a trum* [what a dream]!"

The two officials, the smaller one talking volubly and pawing at his tie, the other maintaining a grim silence, his Polar Sea eyes looking straight ahead, left the room.

Krug waited again.

At 11:24 P.M. a policeman (now in uniform) stole in, looking for Crystalsen. He wanted to know what was to be done with the wrong boy. He spoke in a hoarse whisper. When told by Krug that they had gone that way, he repointed to the door delicately, interrogatively, then tiptoed across the room, his Adam's apple moving diffidently. Was centuries long in closing, quite noiselessly, the door.

At 11:43, the same man, but now wild-eyed and dishevelled, was led back through the waiting room by two Special Guards, to be shot later as a minor scapegoat, together with the other "burly man" (*vide* unnumbered scene) and poor Konkordiĭ.

At 12 punctually Krug was still waiting.

Little by little, however, various sounds, coming from the neighbouring offices, increased in volume and agitation. Several times clerks crossed the room at a breathless run and once a telephone operator (a Miss Lovedale) who had been disgracefully manhandled, was carried to the prison hospital on a stretcher by two kind-hearted stone-faced colleagues.

At 1:08 A.M. rumours of Krug's arrest reached the little group of anti-Ekwilist conspirators of which the student Phokus was leader.

At 2:17, a bearded man who said he was an electrotechnician came to inspect the heat radiator, but was told by a suspicious warden that no electricity was involved in their heating system and would he please come another day.

The windows had turned a ghostly blue when Crystalsen at last reappeared. He was glad to inform Krug that the child had been located. "You will be reunited in a few minutes," he said, adding that a new torture room completely modernized was right at the moment being prepared to receive those who had blundered. He wanted to know whether he had been correctly informed regarding Adam Krug's sudden conversion. Krug answered—yes, he was ready to broadcast to some of the richer foreign states his firm conviction that Ekwilism was all right, if, and only if, his child were returned to him safe and sound. Crystalsen led him to a police car, and on the way started to explain things.

It was quite clear that something had gone dreadfully wrong; the child had been taken to a kind of—well, Institute for Abnormal Children—instead of the best State Rest House, as had been arranged. You are hurting my wrist, sir. Unfortunately, the director of the Institute had understood, as who would not, that the child delivered to him was one of the so-called "Orphans," now and then used to serve as a "release-instrument" for the benefit of the most interesting inmates with a so-called "criminal" record (rape, murder, wanton destruction of State property, etc.). The theory—and we are not here to discuss its worth, and you shall pay for my cuff if you tear it—was that if once a week the really difficult patients could enjoy the possibility of venting in full their repressed yearnings (the exaggerated urge to hurt, destroy, etc.) upon some little human creature of no value to the community, then, by degrees, the evil in them would be allowed to escape, would be, so to say, "effundated," and eventually they would become good citizens. The experiment might be criticized, of course, but that was not the point (Crystalsen carefully wiped the blood from his mouth and offered his none too clean handkerchief to Krug—to wipe Krug's knuckles; Krug refused; they entered the car; several soldiers joined them). Well, the enclosure where the "release games" took place was so situated that the director from his window and the other doctors and research workers, male and female (Doktor Amalia von Wytwyl, for instance, one of the most fascinating personalities you have ever met, an aristocrat, you would enjoy meeting her under happier circumstances, sure you would) from other *gemütlich* points of vantage, could watch the proceedings and take notes. A nurse led the "orphan" down the marble steps. The enclosure was a beautiful expanse of turf, and the whole place, especially in summer, looked extremely attractive, reminding one of some of those open-air theatres that were so dear to the Greeks. The "orphan" or "little person" was left alone and allowed to roam all over the enclosure. One of the photographs showed him lying disconsolately on his stomach and uprooting a bit of turf with listless fingers (the nurse reappeared on the garden steps and clapped her hands to make him stop. He stopped). After a while the patients or "inmates" (eight all told) were let into the enclosure. At first, they kept at a distance, eyeing the "little person." It was interesting to observe how the "gang" spirit gradually asserted itself. They had been rough lawless unorganized individuals, but now something was binding them, the community spirit (positive) was conquering the individual whims (negative); for the first time in their lives they were *organized;* Doktor von Wytwyl used to say that this was a wonderful moment: one felt that, as she quaintly put it, "something was really happening," or in technical language: the "ego," he goes "ouf" (out) and the pure "egg" (common extract of egos) "remains." And then the fun began. One of the patients (a "representative" or "potential leader"), a heavy handsome boy of seventeen went up to the "little person" and sat down beside him on the turf and said "open your mouth." The "little person" did what he was told and with unerring precision the youth spat a pebble into the child's open mouth. (This was a wee bit against the rules, because generally speaking, all missiles, instruments, arms and so forth were forbidden.) Sometimes the "squeezing game" started at once after the "spitting game" but in other cases the development from harmless pinching and poking or mild sexual investigations to limb tearing, bone breaking, deoculation, etc. took a considerable time. Deaths were of course unavoidable, but quite often the "little person" was afterwards patched up and gamely made to return to the fray. Next Sunday, dear, you will play with the big boys again. A patched up "little person" provided an especially satisfactory "release."

Now we take all this, press it into a small ball, and fit it into the centre of Krug's brain where it gently expands.

The drive was a long one. Somewhere, in a rough mountain region four or five thousand feet above sea level they stopped: the soldiers wanted their *frishtik* [early luncheon] and were not loath to make a quiet picnic of it in that wild and picturesque place. The car stood inert, very slightly leaning on one side among dark rocks and patches of dead white snow. They took out their bread and cucumbers and regimental thermos bottles and moodily munched as they sat hunched up on the footboard or on the withered tousled coarse grass beside the highway. The Royal Gorge, one of nature's wonders, cut by sand-laden waters of the turbulent Sakra river through eons of time, offered scenes of splendour and glory. We try very hard at Bridal Veil Ranch to understand and appreciate the attitude of mind in which many of our guests arrive from their city homes and businesses, and this is the reason we endeavour to have our guests do just exactly as they wish in the way of fun, exercise, and rest.

Krug was allowed to get out of the car for a minute. Crystalsen, who had no eye for beauty, remained inside eating an apple and skimming through a long private letter he had received the day before and had not had the time to peruse (even these men of steel have their domestic troubles). Krug stood with his back to the soldiers in front of a rock. This went on for such a long time that at last one of the soldiers remarked with a laugh:

"*Podi galonishcha dva vysvistal za-noch* [I fancy he must have drunk a couple of gallons during the night]."

Here she had her accident. Krug came back and slowly, painfully penetrated into the car where he joined Crystalsen who was still reading.

"Good morning," mumbled the latter withdrawing his foot. Presently he lifted his head, hastily crammed the letter into his pocket and called out to the soldiers.

Highway 76 brought them down into another part of the plain and very soon they saw the smoking chimneys of the little factory town in the neighbourhood of which the famous experimental station was situated. Its director was a Dr. Hammecke: short, sturdy, with a bushy yellowish-white moustache, protruding eyes and stumpy legs. He, his assistants and the nurses were in a state of excitement bordering on ordinary panic. Crystalsen said he did not know yet whether they were to be destroyed or not; he expected, he said, to get destructions (a spoonerism for "instructions") by telephone (he looked at his watch) soon. They all were horribly obsequious, toadying to Krug, offering him a shower bath, the assistance of a pretty *masseuse*, a mouth organ requisitioned from an inmate, a glass of beer, brandy, breakfast, the morning paper, a shave, a game of cards, a suit of clothes, anything. They were obviously playing for time. Finally Krug was ushered into a projection hall. He was told that he would be led to his child in a minute (the child was still asleep, they said), and in the meantime would not he like to see a movie picture taken but a few hours ago? It showed, they said, how healthy and happy the child was.

He sat down. He accepted the flask of brandy which

one of the shivering smiling nurses was thrusting into his face (so scared was she that she first attempted to feed him as she would an infant). Dr. Hammecke, his false teeth rattling in his head like dice, gave the order to start the performance. A young Chinese brought David's fur-trimmed little overcoat (yes, I recognize it, it is his) and turned it this way and that (newly cleaned, no more holes, see) with the flickering gestures of a conjuror to show there was no deceit: the child had been really found. Finally, with a twittering cry he turned out of one of the pockets a little toy car (yes, we bought it together) and a child's silver ring with most of the enamel gone (yes). Then he bowed and retired. Crystalsen, who sat next to Krug in the first row, looked gloomy and suspicious; his arms were crossed. "A trick, a damned trick," he kept muttering.

The lights went out and a square shimmer of light jumped on to the screen. But the whirr of the machine was again broken off (the engineer being affected by the general nervousness). In the dark Dr. Hammecke leant towards Krug and spoke in a thick stream of apprehensiveness and halitosis.

"We are happy to have you with us. We hope you will enjoy the picture. In the interest of silence. Put in a good word. We did our best."

The whirring noise was resumed, an inscription appeared upside down, again the engine stopped.

A nurse giggled.

"Science, please!" said the doctor.

Crystalsen, who had had enough of it, quickly left his place; the unfortunate Hammecke tried to restrain him, but was shaken off by the gruff official.

A trembling legend appeared on the screen: Test 656.

This melted into a subtle subtitle: "A Night Lawn Party." Armed nurses were shown unlocking doors. Blinking, the inmates trooped out. "Frau Doktor von Wytwyl, Leader of the Experiment (No Whistling, Please!)" said the next inscription. In spite of the dreadful predicament he was in, even Dr. Hammecke could not restrain an appreciative ha-ha. The woman Wytwyl, a statuesque blonde, holding a whip in one hand and a chronometer on the other, swept haughtily across the screen. "Watch Those Curves": a curving line on a blackboard was shown and a pointer in a rubber-gloved hand pointed out the climactic points and other points of interest in the yarovization of the ego.

"The Patients Are Grouped at the Rosebush Entrance of the Enclosure. They Are Searched for Concealed Weapons." One of the doctors drew out of the sleeve of the fattest boy a lumberman's saw. "Bad Luck, Fatso!" A collection of labelled implements was shown on a tray: the aforeseen saw, a piece of lead pipe, a mouth organ, a bit of rope, one of those penknives with twenty-four blades and things, a peashooter, a sixshooter, awls, augers, gramophone needles an old-fashioned battle-axe. "Lying in Wait." They lay in wait. "The Little Person Appears."

Down the floodlit marble steps leading into the garden he came. A nurse in white accompanied him, then stopped and bade him descend alone. David had his warmest overcoat on, but his legs were bare and he wore his bedroom slippers. The whole thing lasted a moment: he turned his face up to the nurse, his eyelashes beat, his hair caught a gleam of lambent light; then he looked around, met Krug's eyes, showed no sign of recognition and uncertainly went down the few steps that remained. His face became larger, dimmer, and vanished as it met mine. The nurse remained on the steps, a faint not untender smile playing on her dark lips. "What a Treat," said the legend, "For a Little Person to be Out Walking in the Middle of the Night," and then "Uh-Uh. Who's that?"

Loudly Dr. Hammecke coughed and the whirr of the machine stopped. The light went on again.

I want to wake up. Where is he? I shall die if I do not wake up.

He declined the refreshments, refused to sign the distinguished visitors' book, walked through the people barring his way as if they were cobwebs. Dr. Hammecke, rolling his eyes, panting, pressing his hand to his diseased heart, motioned the head nurse to lead Krug to the infirmary.

There is little to add. In the passage Crystalsen with a big cigar in his mouth was engaged in jotting down the whole story in a little book which he pressed to the yellow wall on the level of his forehead. He jerked his thumb towards door A-1. Krug entered. Frau Doktor von Wytwyl née Bachofen (the third, eldest, sister) was gently, almost dreamily, shaking a thermometer as she looked down at the bed near which she stood in the far corner of the room. Then she turned to Krug and advanced towards him.

"Brace yourself," she said quietly. "There has been an accident. We have done our best——"

Krug pushed her aside with such force that she crashed into a white weighing machine and broke the thermometer she was holding.

"Oops," she said.

The murdered child had a crimson and gold turban around its head; its face was skilfully painted and powdered: a mauve blanket, exquisitely smooth, came up to its chin. What looked like a fluffy piebald toy dog was prettily placed at the foot of the bed. Before rushing out of the ward, Krug knocked this thing off the blanket, whereupon the creature, coming to life, gave a snarl of pain and its jaws snapped, narrowly missing his hand.

Krug was caught by a friendly soldier.

"*Yablochko, kuda-zh ty tak kotishsa* [little apple, whither are you rolling]?" asked the soldier and added:

"*A po zhabram, milaĭ, khochesh* [want me to hit you, friend]?"

*Tut pocherk zhizni stanovitsa kraĭne nerazborchivym* [here the long hand of life becomes extremely illegible]. *Ochevidtzy, sredi kotorykh byl i evo vnutrenniĭ sogliadataĭ* [witnesses among whom was his own something or other ("inner spy?" "private detective?" The sense is not at all clear)] *potom govorili* [afterwards said] *shto evo prishlos' sviazat'* [that he had to be tied]. *Mezhdu tem* [among the themes? (Perhaps: among the subjects of his dreamlike state)] *Kristalsen, nevozmutimo dymia sigaroĭ* [Crystalsen calmly smoking his cigar], *sobral ves' shtat v aktovom zale* [called a meeting of the whole staff in the assembly hall] and informed them [*i soobshchil im*] that he had just received a telephone message according to which they would all be court-martialled for doing to death the only son of Professor Krug, celebrated philosopher, President of the University, Vice-President of the Academy of Medicine. Weak-hearted Hammecke slid from his chair and went on sliding, tobogganing down sinuous slopes, and after a smooth swoon-run finally came to rest like a derelict sleigh on the virgin snows of anonymous death. The woman Wytwyl, without losing her poise, swallowed a pill of poison. After trying and burying the rest of the staff and setting fire to the building where the buzzing patients were locked up, the soldiers carried Krug to the car.

They drove back to the capital across the wild mountains. Beyond Lagodan Pass the valleys were already brimming with dusk. Night took over among the great fir trees near the famous Falls. Olga was at the wheel, Krug, a non-driver, sat beside her, his gloved hands folded in his lap; behind sat Ember and an American professor of philosophy, a gaunt hollow-cheeked, white-haired man who had come all the way from his remote country to discuss with Krug the illusion of substance. Gorged with landscapes and rich local food (wrongly accented *piróshki*, wrongly spelled *schtschi* and an unpronounceable meat course followed by a hot crisscross-crusted cherry pie) the gentle scholar had fallen asleep. Ember was trying to recall the American name for a similar kind of fir tree in the Rocky Mountains. Two things happened together: Ember said "Douglas" and a dazzled doe plunged into the blaze of our lights.

# 18

THIS OUGHT never to have happened. We are terribly sorry. Your child will be given the most scrumptious burial a white man's child could dream up; but still we quite understand, that for those who remain this is ——" (two words indistinct). "We are more than sorry. Indeed, it can be safely asserted that never in the history of this great country has a group, a government, or a ruler been as sorry as we are today."

(Krug had been brought to a spacious room resplendent with megapod murals, in the Ministry of Justice. A picture of the building itself as it had been planned but not actually built yet—in consequence of fires Justice and Education shared the Hotel Astoria—showed a white skyscraper mounting like an albino cathedral into a morpho-blue sky. The voice belonging to one of the Elders who were holding an extraordinary session in the Palace two blocks away poured forth from a handsome walnut cabinet. Crystalsen and several clerks were whispering together in another part of the hall.)

"We feel, however," continued the walnut voice, "that nothing has changed in the relationship, the bond, the agreement which you, Adam Krug, so solemnly defined just before the personal tragedy occurred. Individual lives are insecure; but we guarantee the immortality of the State. Citizens die so that the city may live. We cannot believe that any personal bereavement can come between you and our Ruler. On the other hand, there is practically no limit to the amends we are ready to make. In the first place our foremost Funeral Home has agreed to deliver a bronze casket with garnet and turquoise incrustations. Therein your little Arvid will lie clasping his favourite toy, a box of tin soldiers, which at this very moment several experts at the Ministry of War are minutely checking in regard to the correctness of uniforms and weapons. In the second place, the six main culprits will be executed by an inexperienced headsman in your presence. This is a sensational offer."

(Krug had been shown these persons in their death cells a few minutes before. The two dark pimply youths attended by a Catholic priest were putting on a brave show, due mainly to lack of imagination. Mariette sat with closed eyes, in a rigid faint, bleeding gently. Of the other three the less said the better.)

"You will certainly appreciate," said the walnut and fudge voice, "the effort we make to atone for the worst blunder that could have been committed under the circumstances. We are ready to condone many things, including murder, but there is one crime that can never, never be forgiven; and that is carelessness in the performance of one's official duty. We also feel that having made the handsome amends just stated, we are through with the whole miserable business and do not have to refer to it any more. You will be pleased to hear that we are ready to discuss with you the various details of your new appointment."

Crystalsen came over to where Krug sat (still in his

dressing gown, his bristly cheek propped on his abrased knuckles) and spread out several documents on the lion-clawed table whose edge supported Krug's elbow. With his red and blue pencil the blue-eyed, red-faced official made little crosses here and there on the papers, showing Krug where to sign.

In silence, Krug took the papers and slowly crushed and tore them with his big hairy hands. One of the clerks, a thin nervous young man who knew how much thought and labour the printing of the documents (on precious edelweiss paper!) had demanded, clutched at his brow and uttered a shriek of pure pain. Krug, without leaving his seat, caught the young man by his coat and with the same ponderous crushing slow gestures began to strangle his victim, but was made to desist.

Crystalsen, who alone had retained a most perfect calm, notified the microphone in the following terms:

"The sounds you have just heard, gentlemen, are the sounds made by Adam Krug in tearing the papers he had promised to sign last night. He has also attempted to choke one of my assistants."

Silence ensued. Crystalsen sat down and began cleaning his nails with a steel shoe-buttoner contained, together with twenty-three other instruments, in a fat pocketknife which he had filched somewhere during the day. The clerks on their hands and knees were collecting and smoothing out what remained of the documents.

Apparently there took place a consultation among the Elders. Then the voice said:

"We are ready to go even further. We offer to let you, Adam Krug, slaughter the culprits yourself. This is a very special offer and not likely to be renewed."

"Well?" asked Crystalsen without looking up.

"Go and——" (three words indistinct) said Krug.

There was another pause. ("The man is crazy . . . utterly crazy," whispered one effeminate clerk to another. "To turn down such an offer! Incredible! Never heard of such a thing." "Me neither." "Wonder where the boss got that knife.")

The Elders reached a certain decision but before making it known the more conscientious among them thought they would like to have the disc run again. They heard Krug's silence as he surveyed the prisoners. They heard one of the youths' wrist watch and a sad little gurgle inside the supperless priest. They heard a drop of blood fall upon the floor. They heard forty satisfied soldiers in the neighbouring guardhouse compare carnal notes. They heard Krug being led to the radio room. They heard the voice of one of them saying how sorry they all were and how ready to make amends: a beautiful tomb for the victim of carelessness, a terrible doom for the careless. They heard Crystalsen sorting out papers and Krug tearing them. They heard the cry of the impressionable young clerk, the sounds of a struggle, then Crystalsen's crisp tones. They heard Crystalsen's firm fingernails getting at one twenty-fourth of the tight penknife. They heard themselves voicing their generous offer and Krug's vulgar reply. They heard Crystalsen closing the knife with a click and the clerks whispering. They heard themselves hearing all this.

The walnut cabinet moistened its lips:

"Let him be led to his bed," it said.

No sooner said than done. He was given a roomy cell in the prison; so roomy and pleasant, in fact, that the director had used it more than once to lodge some poor relatives of his wife when they came to town. On a second straw mattress right on the floor a man lay with his face to the wall, every inch of his body shivering. A huge curly brown wig sprawled all over his head. His clothes were those of an old-fashioned vagabond. His must have been a dark crime indeed. As soon as the door was closed and Krug had heavily sunk on to his own patch of straw and sackcloth, the tremor of his fellow prisoner ceased to be visible but at once became audible as a reedy quaking ably disguised voice:

"Do not seek to find who I am. My face will be turned to the wall. To the wall my face will be turned. Turned to the wall for ever and ever my face will be. Madman, you. Proud and black is your soul as the damp macadam at night. Woe! Woe! Question thy crime. 'Twill show the depth of thy guilt. Dark are the clouds, denser they grow. The Hunter comes riding his terrible steed. Ho-yo-to-ho! Ho-yo-to-ho!"

(Shall I tell him to stop? thought Krug. What's the use? Hell is full of these mummers.)

"Ho-yo-to-ho! Now listen, friend. Listen, Gurdamak. We are going to make you a last offer. Four friends you had, four staunch friends and true. Deep in a dungeon they languish and moan. Listen, Drug, listen Kamerad. I am ready to give them and some twenty other *liberalishki* their freedom, if you agree to what you had practically agreed to yesterday. Such a small thing! The lives of twenty-four men are in your hands. If you say 'no,' they will be destroyed, if it is 'aye,' they live. Think, what marvellous power! You sign your name and twenty-two men and two women flock out into the sunlight. It is your last chance. Madamka, say yes!"

"Go to hell, you filthy Toad," said Krug wearily.

The man uttered a cry of rage, and snatching a bronze cowbell from under his mattress shook it furiously. Masked guards with Japanese lanterns and lances invaded the cell and reverently helped him to his feet. Covering his face with the hideous locks of his red-brown wig he passed by Krug's elbow. His jack boots smelled of dung and glistened with innumerable teardrops. The darkness swept back into place. One could hear the prison governor's creaking spine and his voice telling the Toad what a dandy actor he was, what a swell performance, what a treat. The echoing steps retreated. Silence. Now, at last, you may think.

But swoon or slumber, he lost consciousness before he could properly grapple with his grief. All he felt was a slow sinking, a concentration of darkness and tenderness, a gradual growth of sweet warmth. His head and Olga's head, cheek to cheek, two heads held together by a pair of small experimenting hands which stretched up from a dim bed, were (or was—for the two heads formed one) going down, down, down towards a third point, towards a silently laughing face. There was a soft chuckle just as his and her lips reached the child's cool brow and hot cheek, but the descent did not stop there and Krug continued to sink into the heart-rending softness, into the black dazzling depths of a belated but—never mind—eternal caress.

In the middle of the night something in a dream shook him out of his sleep into what was really a prison cell with bars of light (and a separate pale gleam like the footprint of some phosphorescent islander) breaking the darkness. At first, as sometimes happens, his surroundings did not match any form of reality. Although of humble origin (a vigilant arc light outside, a livid corner of the prison yard, an oblique ray coming through some chink or bullet hole in the bolted and padlocked shutters) the luminous pattern he saw assumed a strange, perhaps fatal significance, the key to which was half-hidden by a flap of dark consciousness on the glimmering floor of a half-remembered nightmare. It would seem that some promise had been broken, some design thwarted, some opportunity missed—or so grossly exploited as to leave an afterglow of sin and shame. The pattern of light was somehow the result of a kind of stealthy, abstractly vindictive, groping, tampering movement that had been going on in a dream, or behind a dream, in a tangle of immemorial and by now formless and aimless machinations. Imagine a sign that warns you of an explosion in such cryptic or childish language that you wonder whether everything—the sign, the frozen explosion under the window sill and your quivering soul—has not been reproduced artificially, there and then, by special arrangement with the mind behind the mirror.

It was at that moment, just after Krug had fallen through the bottom of a confused dream and sat up on the straw with a gasp—and just before his reality, his remembered hideous misfortune could pounce upon him—it was then that I felt a pang of pity for Adam and slid towards him along an inclined beam of pale light—causing instantaneous madness, but at least saving him from the senseless agony of his logical fate.

With a smile of infinite relief on his tear-stained face, Krug lay back on the straw. In the limpid darkness he lay, amazed and happy, and listened to the usual nocturnal sounds peculiar to great prisons: the occasional akh-kha, kha-akha yawn of a guard, the laborious mumble of sleepless elderly prisoners studying their English grammar books (My aunt has a visa. Uncle Saul wants to see Uncle Samuel. The child is bold.), the heartbeats of younger men noiselessly digging an underground passage to freedom and recapture, the pattering sound made by the excrementa of bats, the cautious crackling of a page which had been viciously crumpled and thrown into the wastebasket and was making a pitiful effort to uncrumple itself and live just a little longer.

When at dawn four elegant officers (three Counts and a Georgian Prince) came to take him to a crucial meeting with friends, he refused to move and lay smiling at them and playfully trying to chuck them under their chins by means of his bare toes. He could not be made to put on any clothes and after a hurried consultation the four young guardsmen, swearing in old-fashioned French, carried him as he was, i.e. dressed only in (white) pyjamas, to the very same car that had once been so smoothly driven by the late Dr. Alexander.

He was given a programme of the confrontation ceremony and led through a kind of tunnel into a central yard.

As he contemplated the shape of the yard, the jutting roof of yonder porch, the gaping arch of the tunnel-like entrance through which he had come, it dawned upon him with a kind of frivolous precision difficult to express, that this was the yard of his school; but the building itself had been altered, its windows had grown in length and through them one could see a flock of hired waiters from the Astoria laying a table for a fairy tale feast.

He stood in his white pyjamas, bareheaded, barefooted, blinking, looking this way and that. He saw a number of unexpected people: near the dingy wall separating the yard from the workshop of a surly old neighbour who never threw back one's ball, there stood a stiff and silent little group of guards and bemedalled officials, and among them stood Paduk, one heel scraping the wall, his arms folded. In another, dimmer part of the yard several shabbily clothed men and two women "represented the hostages," as the programme given to Krug said. His sister-in-law sat in a swing, her feet trying to catch the ground, and her blond-bearded husband was in the act of plucking at one of the ropes when she snarled at him for causing the swing to wobble, and slithered off with an ungraceful movement, and waved to Krug. Somewhat apart stood Hedron and Ember and Rufel and a man he could not quite place, and Maximov, and Maximov's wife. Everybody wanted to talk to the smiling philosopher (for it was not known that his son had died and that he himself was insane) but the soldiers had their orders and allowed the petitioners to approach only in pairs.

One of the Elders, a person called Schamm, bent his plumed head towards Paduk and half-pointing with a nervously diffident finger, taking back, as it were, every jerky poke he made with it and using some other finger to repeat the gesture, explained the goings on in a low voice. Paduk nodded and stared at nothing, and nodded again.

Professor Rufel, a high-strung, angular, extremely hirsute little man with hollow cheeks and yellow teeth came up to Krug together with——

"Goodness, Schimpffer!" exclaimed Krug. "Fancy meeting you here after all these years—let me see——."

"A quarter of a century," said Schimpffer in a deep voice.

"Well, well, this certainly is like old times," Krug went on with a laugh. "And what with the Toad there——"

A gust of wind overturned an empty sonorous ash can; a small vortex of dust raced across the yard.

"I have been elected as spokesman," said Rufel. "You know the situation. I shall not dwell upon details because time is short. We want you to know that we do not wish your plight to influence you in any way. We want to live very much, very much indeed, but we shall not bear you any grudge whatsoever——" He cleared his throat. Ember, still far away, was bobbing and straining, like Punch, trying to get a glimpse of Krug over the shoulders and heads.

"No grudge, none at all," Rufel continued rapidly. "In fact, we shall quite understand if you decline to yield—*Vy ponimaete o chom rech? Daĭte zhe mne znak, shto vy ponimaete*—[Do you understand what it is all about? Make me a sign that you understand]."

"It's all right, go on," said Krug. "I was just trying to remember. You were arrested—let me see—just before the cat left the room. I suppose——" (Krug waved to Ember whose big nose and red ears kept appearing here and there between soldiers and shoulders). "Yes, I think I remember now."

"We have asked Professor Rufel to be our spokesman," said Schimpffer.

"Yes, I see. A wonderful orator. I have heard you, Rufel, in your prime, on a lofty platform, among flowers and flags. Why is it that bright colours——"

"My friend," said Rufel, "time is short. Please, let me continue. We are no heroes. Death is hideous. There are two women among us sharing our fate. Our miserable flesh would throb with exquisite joy, if you consented to save our lives by selling your soul. But we do not ask you to sell your soul. We merely——"

Krug, interrupting him with a gesture, made a dreadful grimace. The crowd waited in breathless suspense. Krug rent the silence with a tremendous sneeze.

"You silly people," he said, wiping his nose with his hand, "what on earth are you afraid of? What does it all matter? Ridiculous! Same as those infantile pleasures—Olga and the boy taking part in some silly theatricals, she getting drowned, he losing his life or something in a railway accident. What on earth does it matter?"

"Well, if it does not matter," said Rufel, breathing hard, "then, damn it, tell them you are ready to do your best, and stick to it, and we shall not be shot."

"You see, it's a horrible situation," said Schimpffer, who had been a brave banal red-haired boy, but now had a pale puffy face with freckles showing through his sparse hair. "We have been told that unless you accepted the Government's terms this is our last day. I have a big factory of sport articles in Ast-Lagoda. I was arrested in the middle of the night and clapped into prison. I am a law-abiding citizen and do not understand in the least why anybody should turn down a governmental offer, but I know that you are an exceptional person and may have exceptional reasons, and believe me I should hate to make you do anything dishonourable or foolish."

"Krug, do you hear what we are saying?" asked Rufel abruptly, and as Krug continued to look at them with a benevolent and somewhat loose-lipped smile, they realized with a shock that they were addressing a madman.

"*Khoroshen'koe polozhen'itze* [a pretty business]," remarked Rufel to dumbfounded Schimpffer.

A coloured photograph taken a moment or two later showed the following: on the right (facing the exit) near the grey wall, Paduk was seated with thighs parted, in a chair which had just been fetched for him from the house. He wore the green and brown mottled uniform of one of his favourite regiments. His face was a dead pink blob under a waterproof cap (which his father had once invented). He sported bottle-shaped brown leggings. Schamm, a gorgeous person in a brass breastplate and wide-brimmed white-feathered hat of black velvet, was leaning toward him, saying something to the sulky little dictator. Three other Elders stood near by, wrapped in black cloaks, like cypresses or conspirators. Several handsome young men in operatic uniforms, armed with brown and green mottled automatic pistols, formed a protective semicircle around this group. On the wall behind Paduk and just above his head, an inscription in chalk, an obscene word scrawled by some schoolboy, had been allowed to remain; this gross negligence quite spoiled the right-hand part of the picture. On the left, in the middle of the yard, hatless, his coarse dark greying locks moving in the wind, clothed in ample white pyjamas with a silken girdle, and barefooted like a saint of old, loomed Krug. Guards were pointing rifles at Rufel and Schimpffer who were remonstrating with them. Olga's sister, her face twitching, her eyes trying to look unconcerned, was telling her inefficient husband to go a few steps forward and occupy a more favourable position so that he and she might get to Krug next. In the background, a nurse was giving Maximov an injection: the old man had collapsed, and his kneeling wife was wrapping his feet in her black shawl (they both had been cruelly treated in prison). Hedron, or rather an extremely gifted impersonator (for Hedron himself had committed suicide a few days before), was smoking a Dunhill pipe. Ember, shivering (the outline was blurred) despite the astrakhan coat he wore, had taken advantage of the altercation between the first pair and the guards and was almost at Krug's elbow. You can move again.

Rufel gesticulated. Ember caught Krug by the arm and Krug turned quickly to his friend.

"Wait a minute," said Krug. "Don't start complaining until I settle this misunderstanding. Because, you see, this *confrontation* is a complete misunderstanding. I had a dream last night, yes, a dream. . . . Oh, never mind, call it a dream or call it a haloed hallucination—one of those oblique beams across a hermit's cell—look at my bare feet—cold as marble, of course, but—Where was I? Listen, you are not as stupid as the others, are you? You know as well as I do that there is nothing to fear?"

"My dear Adam," said Ember, "let us not go into such details as fear. I am ready to die.... But there is one thing that I refuse to endure any longer, *c'est la tragédie des cabinets*, it is killing me. As you know, I have a most queasy stomach, and they lead me into an enseamed draught, an inferno of filth, once a day for a minute. *C'est atroce*. I prefer to be shot straightaway."

As Rufel and Schimpffer still kept struggling and telling the guards that they had not finished talking to Krug, one of the soldiers appealed to the Elders, and Schamm walked over and softly spoke.

"This will never do," he said in very careful accents (by sheer will power he had cured himself of an explosive stammer in his youth). "The programme must be carried out without all this chatter and confusion. Let us have done with it. Tell them" (he turned to Krug) "that you have been elected Minister of Education and Justice and in this capacity are giving them back their lives."

"Your breastplate is fantastically beautiful," murmured Krug and with a rapid movement of all ten fingers drummed upon the convex metal.

"The days when we pup-played in this very yard are gone," said Schamm severely.

Krug reached for Schamm's headgear and deftly transferred it to his own locks.

It was a sissy sealskin bonnet. The boy, with a stutter of rage, tried to retrieve it. Adam Krug threw it to Pinkie Schimpffer who, in turn, threw it up a snow-fringed amassment of stacked birch logs where it stuck. Schamm ran back into the schoolhouse to complain. The Toad, homeward bound, stealthily walked along the low wall towards the exit. Adam Krug slung his book satchel across his shoulder and remarked to Schimpffer that it was funny—did Schimpffer also get sometimes that feeling of a "repeated sequence," as if all this had already happened before: fur cap, I threw it to you, you threw it up, logs, snow on logs, cap got stuck, the Toad came out . . .? Being of a practical turn of mind, Schimpffer suggested they better give the Toad a good fright. The two boys watched him from behind the logs. The Toad stopped near the wall, apparently waiting for Mamsch. With a tremendous huzza, Krug led the attack.

"For God's sake, stop him," cried Rufel, "he has gone mad. We are not responsible for his actions. Stop him!"

In a burst of vigorous speed, Krug was running towards the wall, where Paduk, his features dissolving in the water of fear, had slipped from his chair and was trying to vanish. The yard seethed in wild commotion. Krug dodged the embrace of a guard. Then the left side of his head seemed to burst into flames (that first bullet took off part of his ear), but he stumbled on cheerfully:

"Come on, Schrimp, come on," he roared without looking back, "let us trim him, let us get at his guts, come on!"

He saw the Toad crouching at the foot of the wall, shaking, dissolving, speeding up his shrill incantations, protecting his dimming face with his transparent arm, and Krug ran towards him, and just a fraction of an instant before another and better bullet hit him, he shouted again: You, you—and the wall vanished, like a rapidly withdrawn slide, and I stretched myself and got up from among the chaos of written and rewritten pages, to investigate the sudden twang that something had made in striking the wire netting of my window.

As I had thought, a big moth was clinging with furry feet to the netting, on the night's side; its marbled wings kept vibrating, its eyes glowed like two miniature coals.

I had just time to make out its streamlined brownish-pink body and a twinned spot of colour; and then it let go and swung back into the warm damp darkness.

Well, that was all. The various parts of my comparative paradise—the bedside lamp, the sleeping tablets, the glass of milk—looked with perfect submission into my eyes. I knew that the immortality I had conferred on the poor fellow was a slippery sophism, a play upon words. But the very last lap of his life had been happy and it had been proven to him that death was but a question of style. Some tower clock which I could never exactly locate, which, in fact, I never heard in the daytime, struck twice, then hesitated and was left behind by the smooth fast silence that continued to stream through the veins of my aching temples; a question of rhythm.

Across the lane, two windows only were still alive. In one, the shadow of an arm was combing invisible hair; or perhaps it was a movement of branches; the other was crossed by the slanting black trunk of a poplar. The shredded ray of a streetlamp brought out a bright green section of wet boxhedge. I could also distinguish the glint of a special puddle (the one Krug had somehow perceived through the layer of his own life), an oblong puddle invariably acquiring the same form after every shower because of the constant spatulate shape of a depression in the ground. Possibly something of the kind may be said to occur in regard to the imprint we leave in the intimate texture of space. Twang. A good night for mothing.